THE RED HERRING

R.G. Link

Black Rose Writing | Texas

ISBN: 978-1-68433-475-9
PUBLISHED BY BLACK ROSE WRITING
www.blackrosewriting.com

Printed in the United States of America
Suggested Retail Price (SRP) $18.95

The Red Herring is printed in Chaparral Pro

*As a planet-friendly publisher, Black Rose Writing does its best to eliminate unnecessary waste to reduce paper usage and energy costs, while never compromising the reading experience. As a result, the final word count vs. page count may not meet common expectations.

Photographer of Author Photo: https://www.ninaashotz.ca/
Cover Art: Anna Cram/Canva Designs
Editor: Anna Cram

Normally I am not attracted to novels that are based on a hard-nosed, male, macho, cursing- a-blue streak, private investigator. At first glance, this is what I thought I was getting. I was so wrong.

The author does a fabulous job at revealing, like a slow burn, the complexities, demons and fascinating back story of the central character, PI, Will Miller. The title, *The Red Herring*, is well suited to the story, as time and time again, the reader thinks one thing is happening, but really something else is occurring, underneath.

At first, the reader thinks the story is about a cheating spouse, but then it's about a runaway teenage girl, but then another, more tragic story unfolds. The author's ability to draw the reader in with a fast paced, unputdownable, plot, keeps one entranced. But it is not just a galloping plot that keeps one reading and reading. One is also drawn in by the slow reveal about the protagonist's character. He too seems like a red herring, as at first, he seems one thing, but is something else. He is full of his own demons, that are revealed in conversations with a psychologist, and the hauntings of his own memories of war and a difficult family life. Threaded throughout the story, which I did not expect, were issues of the horrors of war, father and son relationships, abuse, addictions, recovery, and a frail and uncertain, reconciliation.

At various points in the story, I was drawn in, not just because of the plot and strong character development, but the lyricism of the words and visceral descriptions of locations. The author's description of the pharmacy and the cabin are so well done, that I felt I was in the scene, as if I was an invisible participant in the story. Phrases like "the look etched on her face" and "the quiet still of the night, before the shelling began" have a kind of poetry to them. The sly way certain single words are repeated and then strategically placed on the page, give the story a lyrical feel. Sometimes I felt a kind of clickety clacketing to the words. There is a rhythm and beat to the story, that I have not noticed in other novels. Walter Mosely, a well-known mystery novelist once said, "If you don't have poetry in your story, your writing will be dull." This novel is definitely not dull and worth a read. Watch out for the red herrings, and pause long enough to hear the poetry.

— Kathie Cram. author of *If the Sky Could Dream*

ACKNOWLEDGEMENTS

The author extends thanks and appreciation to the following:

Mom and Dad: thank you for all of your love and endless support. Alicia and Melissa: for the same. Brody: for not only being a brother-in-law, but a good friend as well. Isaac and Riley, it's a blessing and a gift to watch you both grow up. Love and gratitude to the rest of the family who are too numerous to be named here.

Colton: best friend through thick and thin for over two decades. Thanks for everything.

Friends from the library: Marla, Emory, Pam, and Vivian. Great mothers, wonderful colleagues, and good people. Also, thanks to Alyssa and everyone else at the library whose names couldn't possibly all fit here.

Aurora: wise beyond your years, it's a gift to be your friend.

Special thanks to the editor:

Anna: friend, loving mother, fearless editor and collaborator. This book would not have been finished were it not for your endless encouragement, feedback, and tireless work. Thank you for seeing something in me and the book that I was oblivious to. I look forward to our future works.

Lastly, thanks are humbly extended to Black Rose Writing.

Thank you for taking a chance on me.

THE RED HERRING

"People who try hard to do the right thing always seem mad."
~Stephen King, *The Stand*

"Really, detective work is simple, it's just not very easy."
~Philip Kerr, *Field Gray*

"and you will know the truth, and the truth will make you free."
~John 8:32 NRSV

BEFORE

The client is sitting across from him; his insecurity and anxiety overwhelming the office like a noxious gas. This is the kind of shit that grates on his nerves. He knows that he should be more understanding, show some empathy. The pathetic man was suspicious; certain that his wife was cheating on him, so the (alleged) cuckold had hired a PI.

The very acronym made him nauseous. *PI*. It conjured various images in people's minds. It varied from the classic notion of a film noir character – the suave Humphrey Bogart type, to the more honest and realistic: greasy shysters trying to con people out of their money. Will was not certain which category he fell into.

The client, Herman, hired him a week ago. It was a simple job. The type of chore that sounds exciting to people who have read too much Raymond Chandler or Dashiell Hammett, but it was in actuality mind-numbingly boring. It mostly involved sitting on your ass, watching and waiting. The emphasis was, is, and will always be on the *waiting*.

Waiting for the wife outside a salon. Waiting for the wife outside a restaurant that he could never afford while her and her friends slung back mimosas. Waiting for her outside of the department store while she spent her husband's money.

Waiting.

Waiting.

Waiting.

Waiting.

Waiting.

Fucking waiting and wasting away.

That's what most people didn't understand. The job sounds exciting and glamorous, but it was dull, greasy, and boring. The bread and butter of being a private investigator was, is, and will always be following a cheating spouse. This means sitting in a car for hours on end. Drinking an endless amount of caffeine to stay awake (and pissing in the empty cups). Waiting for the *money shot*.

The money shot is proof of a transgression – infidelity. More importantly, it means that he gets to go home. He doesn't like to leave his house if he doesn't have to.

After days of following the spouse, he got lucky. He followed her to a house in an exclusive (a euphemism for exorbitantly expensive) neighborhood. An older man, probably in his late forties, greeted her at the door. Will gave it five minutes, then grabbed his camera and carefully approached the house.

Exiting the car, he quietly pressed the car door closed. He walked to the house, crossing by the cars parked in the driveway. Looking for windows without the blinds drawn, he made his way to the backyard.

The gate was locked. Sighing inwardly, he placed his camera on the ledge and hefted himself over to the other side. Slowly lowering himself to the ground, he swiftly approached a bay window. The blinds were open. He crouched below the window, careful to remain out of sight.

He could hear music. The prick was actually playing Marvin Gaye. What. A. Dick. He had nothing against the music of Marvin Gaye. What he loathed was the fact that the douchebag was playing it because it was part of his hook-up playbook.

He saw the man saunter into the living room like he was the cock of the walk. Smiling, the douche took a seat on the couch. Moments later, the woman entered the frame. Sitting on his lap, she began to grind against the man's crotch. He began to take pictures, conscious of the time factor. He couldn't be certain that one of the two wouldn't see him.

He clenched his jaw. He didn't have the money shot, not yet. He knew that the client could remain comfortably shrouded in his denial of the affair unless he saw her face in the act. As if the women could read his mind and was anxious to accommodate his wishes, she abruptly stood up, turned, and began to slowly drop her dress.

Mindful to avoid her gaze, he quickly snapped off a few shots, then ducked back below the window. He promptly reviewed the captured images. *Money shot*. He had snagged a picture of the unfaithful spouse half naked – her face clearly recognizable, at least to her husband.

He slowly raised his head above the window. The two lovers were oblivious to their voyeur's gaze. The man had his eyes closed in ecstasy as the woman was on her knees, sucking on his dick. He took this opportune moment to vacate the premises.

Making his way back to the car, he silently congratulated himself on a job well done. He planned on contacting the client in the morning.

• • •

He called Herman at nine am. It was his belief that maintaining usual business hours illustrated his level of professionalism. He didn't want clients to think that he was sitting on his ass, not earning his money. Herman had paid him the retainer, but the work he had put in on the job had exceeded that. He wasn't worried about the money. Herman (despite his wimpy name) was actually a vicious and well-paid defense attorney.

Shockingly, Herman answered on the first ring, as if he were anxiously awaiting this call. Later, he would remember this for the troubling factor that it was.

"Herman, are you able to stop by the office today?"

"Do you have pictures? Is the bitch cheating?" Herman grumbled into the phone.

As a rule, he didn't give clients bad news over the phone. It was better to do it face to face, for two reasons. Firstly, he felt it was unprofessional. Doctors didn't give patients bad news over the phone and neither did he. Secondly, he needed the client to be anxiously anticipating the outcome of the investigation. Preferably, the client would be so devastated by the evidence that they wouldn't look too carefully at the bill.

"I'd rather discuss the matter in person at my office," he answered, pleased with his professional tone.

"I fucking knew it! That little whore!" Herman spat.

"Herman, just relax. Take a few deep breaths, maybe have a stiff drink. Then, once you've settled down, come to my office," he sternly retorted.

"I'll be there in an hour."

Herman hung up.

He wasn't worried. Herman was just a prick. Just some defense attorney that was used to being in control – he probably treated his clients the same way. All bark and no bite. When he got to the office, he would have ditched the tough guy persona.

•   •   •

Herman was late. Forty-five minutes late. He began to wonder if he should try calling him. The prospect of sitting on his ass at the office all day was an unwelcome prospect.

Herman stalked in without knocking. *Prick.*

"Herman, take a seat," he said, motioning to the chair in front of his desk.

Upon seeing Herman, he was disconcerted. The man who had a reputation as a bull dog in the courtroom, and had been a genuine prick over the phone, seemed oddly calm. Something wasn't right.

"What is that? You don't seem like a fisherman," Herman remarked, gesturing at the wall.

He didn't bother to look at it. Will knew what he was referring to.

The red herring. It was a gag. He had found it at a garage sale. It seemed fitting for the office. He thought it was funny.

"It's a red herring," he answered curtly, wanting to get this over with.

"So, you're a fisherman." It wasn't a question, more of a statement.

"No. It's a joke. You know, like in mysteries, there's always a red herring."

"Explain, Mr. Miller. I work for a living, don't have time to read," Herman lashed out.

Fucking prick.

"The red herring. It refers to something like a clue that's supposed to distract the reader. It keeps the reader interested and engaged," he said, gritting his teeth.

"I bet you thought that was clever," Herman growled.

"Look, how about we just get this over with? I know how busy you are," Will stated with a hint of malice.

Herman's cheeks began to flush. He wasn't used to being talked to like that, most likely. This fact filled him with an overwhelming sense of satisfaction.

"So, you've got pictures? For what I'm paying you, you had better have some pictures. Give me the fucking pictures," Herman responded in kind.

He was gritting his teeth so hard that his jaw began to throb. He opened the desk drawer. He had printed out the pictures earlier, having deposited them inside a manila folder. He gently slid the folder across the desk.

Herman ripped open the folder. It was at this point that an odd transformation seemed to take place. He seemed resigned. As if having his suspicions confirmed had seemingly deflated him. His prestige, wealth, position, none of it protected him from the inalienable facts. Perhaps this is what heartbreak looked like. If that was possible for a prick like Herman.

"That should help smooth things along. If your wife tries to contest the divorce," he offered.

"We're not getting divorced," Herman mumbled.

This was fucked. Cuckolded husbands like Herman did not take shit lying down. Men who were not intimidating physically (like Herman), always resorted to the legal realm to flex their muscles.

"Well, you've got what you wanted. We'll settle up and have you on your way."

"What I wanted?" Herman queried quietly.

Will saw where this was going. "I apologize," he offered diplomatically, "I misspoke, I mean that you have the pictures that you asked for."

"We're not getting divorced," Herman reiterated.

"Okay. It's your business."

"I handled it."

"I'm sorry?" he asked, his adrenaline beginning to pump through his veins.

At this point, Herman pulled out the gun that he had been concealing within his suit jacket. Herman, blank-faced, pointed the gun at him. This was not the first time that a weapon had been pointed at him. What was concerning was that his hand was devoid of tremors. He was pointing it at him as if he was committed to killing him. Guys like Herman typically avoided violence.

"Herman, put the gun down," he calmly stated.

"You know what you are?" his client quietly asked.

Trapped sitting behind his desk, there was very little that he could do in this situation. Herman blocked the only available exit. This wasn't the movies. There was no John Woo type bullshit that could get him out of this. Forget about trying to grab the gun. That was bullshit dreamed up in Hollywood. If he went for the gun, he would either end up getting shot by Herman, or shoot himself in the ensuing tussle. It took a minimal amount of pressure to squeeze a trigger. It took a fraction of a second for a bullet to fire. The only available option was dialogue – negotiation.

"You're a leech," Herman answered for him. "You subsist on the misery of others. No, you're worse; you're a fucking cancer."

Despite the enormity of the situation, he could not help but reflect on the fact that lawyers also made their bread and butter off of suffering and conflict. *The pot calling the kettle black.*

"Just take off, Herman. You've done nothing yet. Just leave, there's no need to involve the police. Take off. We're done here."

"I handled it," Herman repeated like a mantra.

Will knew it was coming. Herman made eye contact with him.

He pulled the trigger.

He'd been shot before. Years ago. That was different. That was war.

The impact drove him from the chair onto the floor. He felt the blood pooling under his body. He limply dragged his body towards the wall to prop himself against it. The principles of his training came back to him. He ripped open his shirt to look at the wound, finding it in his gut, slightly above his hip. He gasped as he fingered the exit wound. Hastily, he put pressure on the mess of the blood, trying to staunch the flow.

He began to feel calm. He was clearly going into shock. He slid down the wall, landing flat on his back, staring at the ceiling. Herman entered his field of vision. *Fuck.*

Herman examined the human wreckage like Will was some sort of science experiment. Dispassionately. As if he were disinterested and unmoved by the dying before him. As for Will, he became oddly euphoric as he waited for his executioner to finish what he had started.

Herman raised the gun once again, but not at Will. Instead, he planted it firmly under his jaw, the gun pressed against his neck, and swiftly pulled the trigger. The body that used to be Herman collasped onto him. Darkness overtook him.

When he regained consciousness in the hospital, Will would reflect on his shallow and callous character. Was it simply shock? Or had he lost what remained of his humanity? As the corpse that had formerly been Herman landed onto him, his last conscious thought had been, *Fuck, I didn't even get paid.*

•   •   •

"How are you holding up?"

"I'm completely healed. One hundred percent."

"I meant emotionally."

"Fine."

"It's normal for a victim of trauma to experience mental health issues such as depression and anxiety, even PTSD following a violent attack."

"I served in Afghanistan. I'm fine. He was just some prick who lost his shit."

"Did you ever consult with a psychologist to talk about your experiences during the war?"

"Didn't need to. I was fine...I am fine."

"I see. Do you feel that you are in any way responsible for what happened?"

"No."

"None whatsoever?"

"No."

"According to what you said earlier, your client seemed to think you bore some level of guilt."

"He snapped. That's all. Called me a leech and a cancer. That I made my living off of the misery of others."

"Do you feel that's true?"

"No more so than any lawyer, doctor, or police officer, or even dare I say, psychologist?"

"So, you accept that on some level this is an accurate assessment?"

"I'd say it's somewhat accurate."

"Does that bother you?"

"No. If I hadn't taken the job, it would have been somebody else."

"Are you in a relationship?"

"No. Work has shown me that the majority of relationships are built on lies, deceit. At the very least, even honest and open relationships are doomed to fail."

"Does that aspect of your job bother you?"

"No. It's an integral part of the job. The job requires me to act as a witness."

"A witness? Witness to what?"

"Human nature. I witness the shitty things that people do to one another. And in turn, I provide the truth. You know, as in 'the truth shall set you free.'"

"You really believe that?"

"Isn't that what you do here? Get people to be honest and open about their problems? Help them move forward?"

"Yes. To a certain extent. Have you been completely honest with me?"

"Damn. I walked right into that one."

"I need to ask again: do you feel responsible for what happened that day?"

"Honestly?"

"Yes, please."

"I don't feel anything about it. He just lost it. He shot me and then killed himself. I survived. Life goes on."

"You misunderstand me. I mean, do you feel responsible for what happened to his wife?"

"You mean, do I think it's my fault that he killed his wife?"

"Yes."

"It's like I said earlier; if I didn't take the job, he would've gone to someone else."

AFTER

He didn't like to leave the apartment.

The aversion to the outside world had been a part of his psyche since he returned home from the war. It wasn't agoraphobia. The reluctance to engage with the life outside had more to do with his distaste for people. In Afghanistan he had seen the cruelty and violence that humanity could inflict upon one another, and as a civilian his job had served to illustrate the morally bankrupt nature of humanity. It wasn't just that society was a moral vacuum.

He hated crowds. The density of bodies in close proximity; the overwhelming stench of cologne, perfume, sweat, stale cigarette smoke, and the overwhelming odor of toxic breath. He was certain that the lowest circle of hell was reserved for mouth breathers and those narcissistic bastards speaking on their cell phones on speaker phone in public spaces. There is nothing that he could do to assuage this situation; you cannot control people's behavior, only your own.

He had put in place certain guidelines to moderate the tension or conflict in his daily life. He didn't leave the confines of his home without being fully caffeinated. Nor would he go into a public space without his earbuds embedded, the music fully blasting – drowning out the noise of the world. Most importantly, avoid eye contact with others at all costs, then establish and maintain body language that signaled he was not a person that should be approached with questions or conversation.

He needed coffee. This desire presented a conundrum. What was the more powerful force? The vehement distaste for prolonged interaction with the unwashed masses? Or the addiction to caffeine?

Fuck.

Fuck.

Fuck.

Fuck.

Fuck.

Determined to make this as quick and painless as possible, he placed the earbuds in his ears, selected the artist Motorhead and raised the volume. Collecting his wallet, phone, and keys, he took a deep breath and exited the apartment.

Despite his attempts to combat the intrusiveness of the outside world, the cacophony of the soundtrack of society continued to desperately invade his mind and soul.

Fuck.

Fuck.

Fuck.

Fuck.

Fuck.

Fuck.

Making his way to the nearest grocery store, he resolutely remained focused on the task at hand. *Get coffee, go home. Get coffee, go home.* Silently cursing himself for forgetting to pick up coffee the last time he was out, he continued on, trudging his way through the forsaken wasteland of the city.

What. Fresh. Hell. Is. This?

Despite the early hour, he had somehow managed to come across a duo who were unmistakably Mormons (the matching shirts, ties and name tags were a giveaway) propagating their nonsense that masqueraded as the "good news." *Fuck me, they've started invading the shopping centres of the country. Was it not their mandate to only go door-to-door?*

Despite his regulations forsaking eye contact, the pale and pudgy one on the left managed to catch his eye. The pale and pudgy apostle immediately smiled and approached him. *The fucking balls on this bastard. You picked the wrong guy, you magical underwear-wearing bastard.*

"Good morning, sir. Do you have a moment to talk about God?" the pale and pudgy bastard happily queried.

"Are you Mormons?" Will pleasantly asked.

"Yes, we are," Pale and Pudgy responded, gratified that he had some measure of notoriety.

"Wonderful. I was wondering if I could actually ask you a couple of questions about Mormonism?" he asked, continuing on with his nice-guy charade.

"Absolutely, we'd love to," replied the skinny, bland Mormon on the left.

"Does it make you feel like a dumbass, knowing that you've wasted your life dedicating your time and money to a religion that was founded by a known con man?" Will spat out, gritting his teeth and finally dropping his pretense.

"I don't know what you mean," Pale and Pudgy shockingly replied.

"Joseph Smith. That is the founder of your religion, right? He was a known con man, with a record."

"Sir, I can see that we're bothering you, my apologies," Skinny Bland Mormon interjected.

"Oh, no. No, no, no. I still have some questions: doesn't it bother you that despite the prohibition of liquor in Mormonism, Joseph Smith both owned and operated a bar? In addition, when he got bored with his wife and wanted a younger woman, he claimed that God spoke to him and told him that men were meant to be polygamous. Now, isn't that convenient?! I've heard men make some fairly outrageous arguments to get pussy, but the excuse that "God wants me to" is by far the ballsiest. Your religion is truly a sham. But you're both still young; you have time to get out and start a new life."

The duo had begun to waver. They abruptly turned around and quickly proceeded in the opposite direction.

"But you haven't spoken to me about God yet," Will called after them.

Once the duo had gained enough distance, he resumed his trip to the store. His rage and adrenaline having subsided, he began to feel at peace. Once in the store, he quickly found the coffee, paid, and returned home.

While the coffee brewed, he sat in his favorite chair reading from one of the many books that lined his shelves. Having returned home, he allowed himself to relax.

His cell phone began to ring. *Fuck. Fuck. Fuck. Fuck.*

Ignoring the loathsome sound, he let the call go unanswered. Taking a deep breath, he resumed his reading.

The phone began to ring again. *Fuck. Fuck. Fuck. Fuck.*

He swiped the "Ignore" icon. Gritting his teeth, he forced himself to once again take a deep breath. Finding his spot on the page, he resumed reading.

Once again, the phone began to ring, violating the silence and sanctitude of his peaceful abode. He realized that the person on the other end of the phone was going to continue to call until he answered. There were no other options. He despairingly answered the phone.

"Yes," he said wearily.

"Hello. Is this William Miller of Miller Investigations?" asked the female voice

He hesitated before answering in the affirmative.

"I need your help; my daughter is missing."

Fuck. Fuck. Fuck. Fuck. Fuck.

• • •

"Is there much work for a private investigator in a city this size?"

"Not really. It's typically small-fry. And I'm very…selective with my clientele."

"You mentioned earlier that you have a friend at a law firm that periodically gives you assignments. Tell me more about him."

"Thomas. We served together. He's some hotshot lawyer; already made partner at his firm."

"Are you close?"

"Define close."

"Is he a reliable part of your support network? Can you go to him for help? Is he there for you when you need someone to talk to?"

"We have a drink together every now and again."

"I see. So, you see him outside of the work atmosphere?"

"Sometimes. We're both busy and introverted."

"Right. If you don't mind me asking, as you previously mentioned, there isn't much work available. How do you supplement your income?"

"You're asking if I engage in illegal activity?"

"No. Not at all. I'm just trying to gain a comfortable understanding of who you are."

"My father owned an apartment complex. He left it to me when he died."

"Were you close?"

"No. I only met the man a handful of times in my life."

"But he left you something substantial. Don't you think that shows that he cared for you on some level, even if he wasn't able to show it?"

"It was guilt that drove him to it. He left my mother shortly after I was born. He didn't want to see me. He made it quite clear that he wanted nothing to do with me. When he was diagnosed with terminal cancer, it was the guilt of what a shitty father he was that seemed to eat away at him more than the cancer did. He left me the building so I would forgive him."

"Did you forgive him?"

"No. The building isn't that nice."

•   •   •

Mrs. Haynesworth arrived promptly at ten am for her appointment.

Scrutinizing her through the security camera, she looked exhausted and forlorn; as if an overwhelming weight were pressing down upon her. However, she seemed to bear this pain with a dignified air. She was strong. That much was obvious.

Her strength was all too evident in her knock. She had knocked three times on the door. The knocks sounded like gongs amidst the emptiness and silence of the office.

Taking a deep breath, he raised himself slowly from his chair and made his way to the door. *Let's get this shit over with.* He was going to politely (but firmly) decline her request for assistance. He had promised himself he would never get involved with family affairs. It was one thing to aid/assist in the ruination of a marriage that was already in the process of imploding. But a unified family suffering loss was something that made his sphincter clench in discomfort.

"Good morning, Mrs. Haynesworth," he greeted her as pleasantly as possible.

"Morning. Please, call me Laura," she offered humbly.

"Okay. I'm Will."

She took the seat across from his. It quickly flashed through his mind that she was sitting in the same chair as Herman. The phantom pain emanating from his scar began to throb violently. He closed his eyes tightly; the pain would pass momentarily.

"Will, I'm going to cut to the chase: I need your help."

"Yes, I understand that. You mentioned it on the phone," he said, bracing himself for the inevitable conflict.

"Look, it was quite clear to me when we spoke over the phone that you were reluctant to help me," she stated forcefully.

"Yeah, I don't want to waste your time, and I can tell that you're upset, but I don't do this sort of thing. I would've told you that over the phone, but you weren't exactly letting me get a word in edge-wise," he rebutted as politely as he could manage. And he was still trying to regain his total composure from the coffee incident.

"Yes, well, I know that it's a lot easier to refuse someone over the phone," she countered with a mild smile.

"Yes. Yes, it is."

If he spent much more time with her, he would start to like her. This didn't mean that he was going to take the job, though.

"Laura, missing kids are a job for the police. I cannot get involved in an ongoing case; I would lose my license," he offered, hoping it would quell the debate.

"The police won't help!" she desperately cried out.

"I beg your pardon?"

"My daughter, Natalie, she's sixteen," she said, choking back tears.

Fuck. Fuck. Fuck. Fuck. Fuck. Fuck. Fuck.

"Which, according to the law, makes her an adult; she can make her own choices. The cops won't do anything to help bring her home," he said with defeat.

"Yes. She told me that she doesn't want to come home. She won't tell me where she is. She claims to be staying with friends," she said, breaking down in tears.

Fuck. Fuck. Fuck. Fuck. Fuck. Fuck. Fuck.

"When was the last time that you spoke with her?" he asked, resigned to his fate.

"A week...about a week. It was last Thursday."

Five days ago.

"What did she say? Did she ask for money?"

"I didn't get to speak with her. I was coming home from the store; she had snuck into the house. She was exiting the door as I pulled into the driveway. I called her name, begged her to come back. She looked at me, then ran away," she answered, looking down at her feet.

"Was anything missing?"

"Money," she responded quietly.

"How much money?"

"Three hundred dollars," she responded.

Drug money.

"Does your daughter take drugs?" he asked abruptly.

Laura looked taken aback. He could tell that through the shock, was veiled pain and discomfort. The sort of discomfort that was inextricably intertwined with the shame of a parent. The shame that their child, the child that they had swaddled and fed and loved, had grown up to be a drug addict.

"She stopped. She had a problem, but she went to rehab. She's clean," Laura stated emphatically.

The lady doth protest too much.

"Are you sure? What did she need the money for?"

"For food and expenses, she said she started her new job next week."

"What was her new job?"

"As a, uh ... cashier at Rockwell's Pharmacy," Laura responded, agitated.

He made a note of the alleged location of employment.

"Does she still attend school?"

"Sometimes."

"Sometimes?"

"She was an honor roll student. Then something changed. She started hanging out with the wrong crowd, or something. She started dressing different, acting different. Staying out late, coming home drunk or stoned. I don't know what's wrong with her. I started getting calls from her school that she hadn't been attending her classes for weeks on end. We held an intervention, she went to rehab. She was fine for a while, then she relapsed. We sent her back to rehab. When she came back, she seemed happy and healthy. Now I don't know where she is! I've tried calling her phone and it's no longer in service. I went to her friend's place where she told me she was staying, and they told me that she left weeks ago. And they didn't have a number for her! All I know is that I am her mother and I need to bring her back home to make sure that she gets the help that she needs! Now are you going to help me?! Or am I just wasting my fucking time?!" Laura yelled, having finally lost her composure.

He remained stone-faced, careful to not let on that she had gotten to him. *Fuck. Fuck. Fuck. Fuck. Fuck. Fuck. Fuck. Fuck. Fuck.*

"Please...help me," she pleaded tearfully.

•   •   •

"So, are you going to help her?" Thomas cheerfully asked.

They were at the pub. They generally met once a week, sometimes more (depending on how rough Thomas's week had been). Thomas sat nursing a gin and tonic, while William was draining his third rye and coke.

"Hundred bucks a day. Plus expenses," he mumbled.

"Can they afford it?"

"The husband's a doctor. An anesthesiologist," he replied grumpily.

"Well, they're not starving," Thomas giddily replied.

"Yeah."

"Why d'you give her such a reasonable rate? They can afford to pay," Thomas asked, knowing the answer.

"I like her. She's tough. Tough but kind."

"Sounds like your mom," Thomas offered.

"Shut the fuck up."

Thomas laughed.

"To be honest, I'm surprised. You've always been adamant that when it comes to family issues, you drew the line at unfaithful spouses. Why the change of heart?" Thomas asked, seeming genuinely curious.

"She's just some spoiled rich kid who ran away from home. She's not accustomed to living life outside the lap of luxury. She won't be hard to find. The pharmacy is a solid lead; I'll find her in no time at all," he shot back.

"Fair point."

"I need a favor," Will said reluctantly after a pause.

"Oh? What sort of favor?" Thomas asked with a wry smile.

The prick was busting his balls. He knew how much Will detested asking others for help. *Fuck. Fuck. Fuck. Fuck.*

"I need you to get that cop buddy of yours to check out the kid and the family. I need to know if any of them have got a record. I need to know if they have any skeletons in their closet."

"Is that all?" Thomas asked mockingly. "You know how much I hate going to him for favors."

"I know. Although, I suppose I could pull a dick move and point out that you were the one who personally vouched for the crazed asshole that shot me and then left me for dead," Will responded with a smile.

"You're right. That would be a dick move."

•   •   •

Rockwell's Pharmacy could optimistically be referred to as a "shit hole." It was located in a rough and dangerous part of the city. Solely on the basis of the exterior, Natalie's parents would definitely not approve of her job choice. He was hesitant to even enter the business as he was certain that he would catch one (if not all) of the Hepatitis'.

If possible, the interior was nastier than the exterior. The ceiling tiles were all visibly stained from a previous water leak. The dust on the shelves was so thick that from a distance it appeared as if they were coated in fur. The floor was riddled with various types of stains, some of which were most certainly blood or rust.

"How may I help you today?" asked a bored teenage boy.

"Yeah, two questions: where do you keep the hand sanitizer? And is there enough to cover my entire body? All of a sudden I feel filthy."

"Huh?" asked the clearly stoned teen.

"Never mind. Is your manager around?"

"Uh, I'm not sure. What seems to be the problem?"

Fuck. Fuck. Fuck. Fuck. Fuck.

This kid was most certainly stoned. If he wasn't, he had a type of mental disability or some shit like that.

"My daughter just got a job here. She's sick with the flu, she sent me to pick up her schedule for next week," he said as calmly and parental-like as possible.

"Oh, okay. Just hold on," the likely stoned teen mumbled.

The kid reached for his walkie talkie. "Hey, Phil, are you still unavailable? There's some dad here that needs to see you."

Fuck. Fuck. Fuck. Fuck. Fuck.

This was taking too long. Will was starting to get agitated. It was imperative that he moved this along. He needed to get back home.

The boy's walkie talkie hissed. "Tell him to leave a name and number and I'll get back to him as soon as possible."

"Can I get your name and number?"

Will took a chance. There were only so many places that this prick could be.

"His office is in the back, right?" he asked, trying to keep his patience.

"Uh...yeah, but he's like, uh, currently unavailable."

"That's all that I needed to know. Thanks."

He brushed past the kid and marched to the back of the store. *Fuck. Fuck. Fuck. Fuck. Fuck. Just keep calm. Just breathe. Just keep calm. Just breathe.* He barged through the "Employee Only" doors. The area was even more filthy than the previous section of the store. Rickety shelves held shabby items (many of which were expired). He weaved through all of the detritus and clatter, making his way further into the bowels of the store.

He found the Manager's Office near the loading dock. However, calling it an "office" was a bit of a stretch. It was closer to a closet. A closet that reeked of weed. He hated the odour of weed. It was worse than cigarette smoke, more putrid than a skunk. It was a malicious scent that set him on edge. *Fuck. Fuck. Fuck. Fuck. Fuck.*

He banged on the door.

"I'm busy!" a muffled voice barked.

Fuck. Fuck. Fuck. Fuck. Fuck. Fuck.

He kicked open the door. The manager, startled, hacked out the smoke from the depths of his lungs. He quickly stood up and raised his hand in the "stop" gesture.

"Hey, man. You can't be back here, it's employees only!"

He quickly encroached on the manager's personal space. Making direct eye contact, Will placed both his hands on the man's shoulders, and pushed him back onto the chair. He grabbed a shitty folding chair that was leaning against the wall and proceeded to sit.

"I need you to listen; I do not like repeating myself. Understand?" he asked menacingly.

"Yeah, man. I understand," the manager forced out.

"Natalie Haynesworth."

"Okay...who?" he asked, seemingly confused.

Fuck. Fuck. Fuck. Fuck. Fuck. Fuck.

He caught the manager's gaze going to the phone on his desk.

"Listen. If you go for your phone, I'm going to feel like we're having a problem. Do we have a problem here?"

"No, man! We're good. We are good," he assured him.

"I need the address and contact information that you have on file for Natalie Haynesworth," he said, desperately trying to remain calm.

"I honestly have no idea who the fuck that is!" the stoned manager yelled.

Fuck. Fuck. Fuck. Fuck. Fuck. Fuck. Fuck.

"Listen to me, you, stoner-fuck! I need you to reach really hard into the drug-addled cavity that is your brain and locate Natalie Haynesworth's contact information," Will growled at him.

"I swear to God, I have no idea who that is! She has not applied for a job here! I have never even heard the name before you got here!"

He knew when people were lying to him. The stoner was telling the truth. *Fuck. Fuck. Fuck. Fuck. Fuck. Fuck.* Natalie had lied to her mother. He had presumed that this had been the case, but he needed to be certain. He hadn't planned on things going off the rails like they had. He had fucked up. He lost control. He needed to get the fuck out of there.

"Do you have security cameras in this shithole?"

"Yeah, but they don't record anything; they're just for show – to deter shoplifters," the frazzled manager nervously spewed out.

"I'm going to leave, and you're never going to see me again. The cops don't need to be called, right?" Will asked as pleasantly as possible.

"No, man. Fuck the police! Just leave," he pleaded.

He was livid with himself; he had to learn to control his temper. He couldn't afford to be fucking up like this. He would either end up dead or in prison. He now found himself at a loss for words.

"I'm sorry. Goodbye."

Fuck. Fuck. Fuck. Fuck. Fuck. Fuck.

Status update on the case; reporting to Laura about the progress (or lack thereof). He decided to call her from the car. The experience of the pharmacy still clung to him; it wasn't just the overpowering aroma of weed or the stupidity of the staff, it was his own threat of violence that shook him.

Usually it takes only a few minutes for the adrenaline to abate within his body. Tonight, he realized that although it has been fifteen minutes since the altercation, the surge had not ceased. He switched the phone to his other hand, when he realized that his left hand won't stop shaking. He clenched his hand into a fist and then slowly allowed his fingers to uncurl. Still, the tremors persisted.

He forced himself to place his hand on his leg, but found himself gripping the fabric of his pants.

Stop.

He moved the hand from his leg to the steering wheel. Allowed himself to grab the wheel and squeeze; he had a death grip on it. Anything to prevent his extremities from shaking.

The phone rang. Will then realized that Laura may be asleep. It was only ten pm, but the hubby and her could be early risers.

"Hello?" answered Laura, groggy.

"Hey, it's Will...did I wake you up? Were you sleeping?"

"No. Just dozing off; I was doing some reading."

"So, the pharmacy that Natalie said she was going to start working at?"

"Yeah?" He could hear the tension building in her voice.

"I talked to the manager, there is no record of her application. Seems like she was lying to you," he said, trying to soften the blow.

"Are you sure it was the right one?"

Truth is beauty, my ass. He felt a pang of pity for her.

"Yeah."

"I see," she responded, trying to remain calm.

"I was certain that the pharmacy would've been enough. Now I need some more information. Do you know the names and numbers of her friends, boyfriends, ex-boyfriends; anyone that can give me something that'll help find her."

"She didn't have any boyfriends. Not that I'm aware of anyway. I think I can find a number for her best friend, Jocelyn. Although I haven't seen the two of them together in a while."

"That'd be great. Text me the number when you find it. Would it be possible for me to come over tomorrow? It'd help if I could see her room; go through some of her stuff. If that's acceptable, of course," he said, trying to not sound like a creep.

There was silence on the other end of the phone. He was worried that he would have to clarify the situation; reassure his client that he wasn't some pervert that was anxious to rifle through her teenage daughter's belongings.

"Yes, if you think that would help," Laura finally responded.

"Thank you. One more thing: is there a time I could arrange to speak to your husband?"

"My husband? I don't know, he works so much. He's on the night shift this week."

"He is aware that you hired me, right?"

The last thing he wanted was additional drama. He had no desire to deal with a pissed-off husband/father who had been kept in the dark.

"Of course. He wanted to be at the meeting, but he had to work," she said, sounding miffed.

"Sorry...Look, talk to your husband and let me know if there's a time that works for him. The sooner, the better," he said, as amicably as possible.

"Will do."

"Also, you should get in touch with the bank. See if you can get any information about withdrawals; which ATMs she uses most frequently, that kind of thing. It may give us an idea of her whereabouts, like the places she visits most often."

"She doesn't have a bank account," she said with a sigh.

"She doesn't have an account?" Will asked incredulously.

"Well she does, but we froze it before she left for rehab the second time. When she got back, we made a deal that if she needed money, she would have to come to us. If she remained clean, attended NA meetings, we would return her privileges. It was our attempt at keeping her on the straight and narrow."

Fuck.

"Is there a time that I can come over tomorrow?" he asked, back on track.

"After lunch? Say, one?"

"That works. Thank you. Night."

"Night."

She sounded so fucking tired. Her farewell had sounded so meek, as if she had to force the syllables out of her mouth. He released his hand from the steering wheel. Keeping his arm extended, he kept his palm flat. The tremors persisted.

• • •

"So, tell me about your mother."

"That's very Freudian of you."

"William, please take this seriously."

"Sorry. She raised me; taught me right from wrong, taught me how to be strong, not to judge someone on the color of their skin, and most emphatically: how to treat women with respect."

"She sounds like quite the woman."

"Tough as nails."

"Are you still close with her?"

"She died."

"I'm sorry."

"She outlived my bastard father, so that's something."

"Do you mind if I ask what happened?"

"Lung cancer. She smoked like a chimney; a pack a day, sometimes more."

"I'm so sorry. Did she suffer?"

"No. She went out on her own terms. She got to die with some measure of dignity. We should all be so lucky."

"Are you saying that she committed suicide?"

"Yeah. They gave her pills for the pain. She took a bottle full of pills and chased it with a bottle of wine."

"Did she tell you what she was planning?"

"No. I suspected."

"Did she say goodbye to you?"

"No. She wasn't one to talk about her feelings. If she had, she would've known that I'd realize that something was wrong."

"That must have been very hard for you, not having any closure."

"She left me a note."

"What did it say?"
"I think our time is up."

• • •

He got home twenty minutes after the phone call with Laura. The return of his tremors made him anxious. He hadn't had an assault on his nerves since he got out of the hospital. Fortunately for him, there was a readily available cure. He simply had to make a quick stop at the liquor store.

One twenty-four pack.

One bottle of Rye.

Take as needed.

He popped open a can of beer as soon as he closed the door behind him. He knew that he had to be careful. Not only was he in danger of becoming a fucking cliché (hard drinking PI), but he still had work to do tonight.

Taking another long pull on his beer, he started his computer. The process of booting the computer allowed him to finish the first beer. He walked back to the fridge and grabbed two more. Sitting back down, he logged onto the computer. Opening his browser, he went to Facebook.

Typing in the name, "Natalie Haynesworth," he sifted through the results. Finding the correct profile, he clicked on it and waited for the page to load. The profile was open to the public (fucking teenagers). Examining the profile picture, he noticed the eerie resemblance to her mother.

Scrolling through her wall, he made a note of the various people that littered the numerous selfies that she had posted. *Fucking teenagers*. Laura wasn't wrong, though. Scrolling through the page, it was blatantly obvious that there was an abrupt shift in both Natalie's appearance and attitude. The older pictures exhibited a shy, happy, and somewhat nerdy teenage girl. Over the course of a few months, she seemed to shift to a moody (and eventually depressed) girl in baggy clothes.

In the "friends'" tab, he managed to find the Jocelyn that Laura had been referring to. Jocelyn's profile was also public. (Surprise, surprise). The two definitely had similar tastes and personalities. Jocelyn's pictures also portrayed a shy, kind, and studious girl. There were photos of Jocelyn and Natalie both in private/social settings, as well as school events. Jocelyn had posted pictures that were captioned, "Chess Tournament," "Debate Club," and "Drama Club."

Hopefully, Jocelyn would be able to tell him what had happened to Natalie. He presumed that it was the usual bullshit: Natalie felt pressured to fit in; to look like the popular girls, to have the handsome popular guys pay attention to her. Somewhere along the way, she began to experiment with liquor and drugs, which then led to a problem with drugs. Cut to today, and she's a teen runaway.

By this point, he had finished the two additional beers. Once again, he lifted his arm up, extending it fully. He stretched his fingers. He kept his arm stretched out; carefully examining his hand. The liquor had done its job; the tremors had passed. *Perfect.*

He knew that he should call it a night. Maybe watch some TV before going to bed. He noticed the bottle of rye on his kitchen counter. *One more couldn't hurt. But, just the one.*

He woke up to his alarm and a splitting headache. He had polished off the majority of the rye. So much for restraint and discipline. Dragging his body out of bed, a feeling of nausea spread throughout his body. Barely making it to the bathroom in time, he managed to empty the contents of his stomach into the toilet bowl.

After the sickness had passed, he flossed, brushed his teeth, and then rinsed his mouth out with Listerine. Once in the kitchen, he grabbed three acetaminophen tablets and rinsed them down with water, slurping greedily from the tap. Turning the coffee pot on, he attempted to recall the previous evening's events.

As the coffee brewed, he unplugged his phone from the wall and checked his outgoing calls. He released a sigh of relief upon verifying that he had made no calls during his unfortunate drunken stupor. As an added precautionary measure, he then checked his text messages, which also proved to be devoid of any drunken missives.

Get your shit together, Will.

While the coffee finished brewing, he changed into his gym attire and began to perform his pre-workout stretches. This was his hangover cure; pills, coffee, and a workout. Marching over to the coffee pot, he filled a cup with both sugar and milk, and then added coffee to the mix. Chugging as fast as possible, he emptied the cup, and then repeated the process. As his body was then somewhat caffeinated, he proceeded with his workout.

He hadn't stopped his exercise regimen after leaving the service. It had become an imperative part of his daily routine. It was a matter of personal pride that he had retained his physique gained in the armed services. It was not a matter of shallow appearance; it had to do with maintaining discipline over the external forces that weighed heavily upon all members of society. It was necessary to remain strong in mind, body, and spirit. He abhorred the possibility of becoming soft – of losing his edge.

He was the proverbial juggler; mastering the art of keeping multiple objects in the air, struggling against the certainty that he would eventually drop one, resulting in a domino effect; everything would come crashing down. He needed to retain the element of control. Mistakes like the pharmacy would ruin him.

Ultimately, he recognized that since regaining consciousness in the hospital, he had not been in control. He had merely maintained the facade of discipline and control. Recent events had proven that he needed to regain whatever it was that he had lost.

Standard operating procedure; establish a routine and do not deviate from it. Familiarity did not breed contempt. In his case, it was a security blanket – a comfort object. It enabled him to face the endlessly jarring experience of the outside world. If he were honest with himself, he would acknowledge that he had not felt comfortable among the masses in years. Had he ever felt normal among other people? He honestly couldn't remember.

He hated crowds. He avoided lines if at all possible. Bars and restaurants were generally avoided (save for the periodic drinks with Thomas). The smells, the sounds, the disgusting behavior.

Stop. Focus.

After sweating out the poison that he had imbibed the night before, he showered. Safe within the cocoon of the shower, he explored the scars that littered his body. He often reflected that these were not simply scars, they were effectively a timeline of his life. Scars that dated back to his childhood; the mar on his left arm (broken from falling off of the jungle gym), the wounds from the war; a jagged scar from below the knee to the calf (shrapnel from an RPG), and a hideous scar on his right pectoral (bullet wound). Finally, his hand rested on the most recent scar, the parting curse of Herman.

Some days it hurt. The pain varied from mildly sore to excruciating. He understood that this was simply phantom pain. At first, he was petrified that he was suffering from an infection that was slowly killing him from the inside. After that initial fear subsided, he was worried that the doctors had fucked up and left something inside his body. He had heard the innumerable horror stories of surgical tools and other implements mistakenly left inside a patient. After meeting with a doctor (who had assured him that he was physically healthy), the doctor was certain that it was all in his mind, and referred him to a psychologist.

$$\bullet \qquad \bullet \qquad \bullet$$

"Why did you join the military?"

"Would you believe me if I said that I honestly don't remember?"

"That depends. Are you being honest?"

"I honestly don't remember. I got out of high school and had no direction; no clue what I was going to do with my life. My mother seemed overjoyed at the prospect that I was serving my country. Realistically, I think she was just relieved that they offered to pay for college. We both knew that she couldn't afford it."

"What were you going to study?"

"Didn't have a clue. I had no plans for college. I'll admit that at that point in my life I was coasting – I was on autopilot. I guess I was just living from day-to-day. Maybe I was depressed. Maybe I was just a teenager. I don't know."

"That's a normal feeling for many teens. We were all searching for our purpose and identity at that age."

"Yeah, I guess."

"What was your military experience like?"

"I spent my nineteenth birthday on a military base; it was basic training. A couple of months later, my unit got sent over to Afghanistan."

"It must've been difficult. I can only imagine; all that I know about it is what has been shown on the news and in documentaries."

"It was hot."

"It was hot? That's all that you've got to say?"

"The sand got everywhere. It ruined the beach for me. Patrolling the desert while wearing one hundred pounds of gear, covered in sweat, and trying not to get shot by an insurgent or blown up by an IED. It was ninety percent unfiltered boredom and ten percent sheer terror."

"How did you meet Thomas?"

"He was an untested recruit; new to war. I had been there for a while. I showed him the ropes. Helped keep him alive. Nothing had happened during patrol for a while, at least a week or two. His first day on patrol, we got ambushed by insurgents. We had an RPG fired at our Humvee. Luckily, we weren't inside it at the time. We were trying to speak with some of the village elders, which can take a while when you're working through an interpreter. Although, I did get shrapnel stuck in my leg."

"You were badly injured?"

"No. Got to keep my leg, which is more than others can say. It didn't go very deep, but it did leave an ugly scar. I barely spent a week in the infirmary."

"Was that the only time that you were wounded?"

"No. I got shot by an insurgent. Luckily it happened to be a scared-shitless teenager, who could hardly shoot for shit. I remember the look of pure fear in his eyes when he saw me."

"I've heard that other veterans feel ill at ease upon returning home; they have had to dehumanize the enemy in order to fight them. It can be a hard attitude to shift. Do you bear any ill will towards them as a people?"

"You mean do I demonize them? Do I call them pejorative terms like 'Camel Jockey,' and 'Rag Head?' No. The war's roots can be traced back all the way to the First World War. Maybe even earlier. Their people have been the victim of various empires that have attempted to colonize and exploit them. It's a cluster fuck over there. I'm sure if situations were reversed, we'd do the same."

"Many returning veterans have a hard time acclimating into civilian life. How have you been handling it?"

"I get by."

•   •   •

Out of the shower, he made himself look somewhat professional. While chugging another coffee, he called Thomas. It only rang a few times before it was answered.

"Yeah?" Thomas grunted, aware that it was Will.

"Heard anything from that cop buddy of yours?" he responded, not missing a beat.

"I haven't heard back yet."

"Pester him! Tell him it's important."

"Are you fucking kidding me?" Thomas cried.

"What's the point of having a friend that's a cop if they're not constantly at your beck and call?" he shot back spitefully.

"I imagine that he's probably busy protecting and serving and that kind of shit!"

"Call him again! Tell him that the missing girl is white. He's bound to do something, then."

The line went dead.

"Well, shit," he said to himself.

•　　　•　　　•

On the way to meet with Laura, he stopped by a carwash. He figured that it would make a good impression if he showed up in a clean car, as opposed to the usual filth-covered monstrosity that was the norm. Also, he would be visiting an expensive and exclusive neighborhood and didn't want to draw the ire of the neighbors.

As he drove, he focused on his breathing. Inhale. Exhale. Focus. Discipline. He listened to the music, trying to remain calm. He was listening to one of his favorite live albums, *Nirvana: Unplugged.* He noted with satisfaction that his hands were devoid of tremors. *Off to a good start.*

He passed through several neighborhoods, each more upscale and expensive than the last. Noting the size and elegance of the Haynesworth residence, he momentarily regretted having quoted such a low price for his services. He parked on the street as he felt that this was the more considerate thing to do. It rankled him slightly, realizing that he actually cared what Laura thought and wanted her to like him. Which was strange for him. Usually, he didn't give a fuck what people thought of him.

He parked and turned the engine off. He took a moment to compose himself. Closing his eyes, he took a series of deep breaths. Inhale. Exhale. Repeat. Realizing that he couldn't delay the inevitable, he abruptly got out of the car, grabbing his suitcase on the way out. The suitcase had the dual advantage of projecting both a professional image, and it allowed him to keep the essential tools of his trade; notepads, pens, pencils, laptop.

He walked up the driveway. He noticed that Laura's neighbor, an older Asian male, was staring at him from his porch as he smoked a cigarette. He knew that especially in neighborhoods like this, residents would take careful note of people that they had never seen before. He was sure that both his appearance and his car (which he had purchased at a police auction) made it abundantly clear that he did not belong here. In an attempt to assuage the neighbor's suspicion, he smiled and nodded in his direction. The neighbor slowly and subtly nodded his head in recognition.

Making it to the front door, he knocked quietly, mindful of her sleeping husband. Through the front window, he could see Laura coming to the door. She quickly and quietly opened the door and motioned for him to enter.

She closed the door softly behind him and motioned for him to follow her into the kitchen.

"You're early," she whispered.

"Yeah, I apologize. I guess I'm pathologically incapable of either being on time or late."

"No, it's fine. I'm the same way. My dad always said that it showed initiative," she offered with a sly smile.

That smile. That fucking smile. It made him realize how truly beautiful Laura was.

"Would you like some coffee?" she offered.

"I can never turn down a cup of coffee," he said, smiling.

"Neither can I," she agreed.

As she went through the motions of preparing coffee, he gathered the courage to make small talk with her.

"How are you holding up?" he offered.

"As well as can be expected, I suppose."

"Yeah. You're doing great. You're a tough one. I'd never want to cross you," he attempted to reassure her.

She offered him a meek smile in return.

"Have you filled your husband in on the progress of the investigation?" he asked cautiously.

"Yes. David knows," she answered with a sigh.

Laura's answer revealed the tension within the marriage. His pessimistic and misanthropic nature forced him to wonder if the tension was simply a result of their missing child, or if it was representative of further underlying issues.

"Sorry." Will wasn't sure what else to say.

Laura looked at him, and then quickly averted her gaze. It had only been for a moment, in that brief glance, he had observed what could only be described as heartache. She placed his coffee on the countertop in front of him.

"Cream and sugar?" she asked.

"Both. Please," he stated, thankful that she had opted to ignore the tension.

After the coffee was doctored, they both began to sip from their cups. Both uncertain of what to do next. She picked up her cup and motioned for him to follow her. They walked outside onto the patio.

It was a mild late-summer afternoon. He briefly allowed himself to indulge in a fantasy. This was his home. She was his wife. They were wasting the day away, basking in each other's company. As painful as it was for him to admit, he could get used to a life like this. He could be happy living a life with a woman like Laura. But that was all it was; a fantasy. And there was no logical purpose in lying to yourself. That's all that fantasy was; a pleasant lie. Reality was harsh and inescapable. That is how he knew that it was real.

They sat in silence for a moment. It wasn't an uncomfortable silence. He knew that she was simply taking a moment to gather her thoughts.

"David and I have been fighting," she stated, looking away.

"I'm sorry. I can imagine that this is a very stressful situation," he offered, attempting to convey sympathy.

"We had been fighting before Natalie went missing," she said, making eye contact with Will.

He couldn't think of anything to offer in response. There was nothing that could be said that would fix the problem. Too many people thought of words as a magic healing balm. Words, he thought, didn't do shit. In his experience, it was better to just let people tell their story.

"We had made a deal with Natalie, after she got back from rehab; stay clean and she could finish her schooling here, with her friends. But, if she started using again, we would send her to detox and then to a boarding school that specializes in educating teens who were at risk, or suffering from addiction," she recounted, looking at her cup as she spoke.

"When she got back from rehab, she seemed happier. She seemed like her old self. I honestly felt like she was done with it all. It couldn't have been more than a month before I started to suspect that she was using again. She started to exhibit the familiar patterns and symptoms, all behaviors of her addiction." Laura began to choke on her sobs.

He was never good at dealing with shit like this. He always froze; terrified of doing or saying the wrong thing. Maybe she sensed his discomfort, because she visibly tried to pull herself together.

"Sorry. I'll get us some more coffee," she said, quickly standing.

"No, that's alright. I'll get it," he countered, grabbing her cup and heading inside.

He filled both of their cups again. He witnessed her modest attempts at regaining her composure through the window. Getting the coffee had purely been a selfish maneuver; he had to get away from the situation. Watching as the tears started to fall down her face had set him on edge. Panic had set in. It echoed the flight or fight response. He took a series of deep breaths, strengthened himself, and headed back onto the patio.

As he stepped onto the patio, Laura quickly rubbed the tears off of her face. He pretended that he hadn't noticed. He handed her the cup of coffee.

"Black, right?" he mumbled.

"Yes, thanks. Sorry about that," she said, forcing a laugh.

"Nothing to be sorry for," he offered.

"Anyways, she had clearly started using again. David and I sat her down one day and reiterated our deal. We fought, of course. It took hours for her to admit that she was using again. She broke down. She begged us not to send her away; she didn't want to leave her friends. I remained firm; she had to go. David is a softie; she has always had him wrapped around her finger. He could never tell her no. David told Natalie that we would talk about it and let her know what we decided.

"That night, David and I argued. He was concerned that she would hate us for the rest of her life, if we sent her to that academy. I understood his anxiety; I was worried about it myself. David, he told me that he had always resented that his parents had sent him to a boarding school. That night, we realized that we didn't have it in us to send her away like that. We agreed to send her to rehab again. But, we told her that this was the last time. That if she started using again, we would send her to that academy. We just hoped that she wouldn't call our bluff. You must think that we're terrible parents," she uttered pitifully.

"You did what you thought was right. No one can fault you for that," he asserted, hoping that it was enough.

"We fucked up; we were clearly wrong," she said, shaking her head.

"Beating yourself up isn't going to fix anything," he countered forcefully.

"We fought early this morning, when he got home from work. The fight started over nothing, like they usually do; I had left garage door open. I snapped at him, he snapped at me, back and forth. It was a gradual buildup, then he just blew up. He told me that it was my fault that she had gone missing; I was always too hard on her."

Laura began to resist her sobs once again. The red, teary eyes signaled the impending cascade of tears falling upon her face. He shouldn't be here. He always limited the amount of interaction with clients. He didn't want to get involved. But he couldn't leave. He was trapped. He was a deer in the headlights.

Will gave the only comfort that was easily perceptible. "He was just tired from work and stressed. People always say hurtful shit that they don't mean. Especially when they love each other."

Laura nodded her head. She continued to gaze intently into the contents of the coffee cup. He had to remove himself from the situation. Admittedly, he didn't want to cause her any additional pain or discomfort, but more importantly, he couldn't deal with these scenarios.

"Thank you for the coffee. I don't want to be rude, but I have another appointment later today, so I should probably look at Natalie's room now," he rushed out. He imitated her posture, looking solely at the contents of his coffee cup.

"Oh, of course. I'm so sorry. I shouldn't be babbling on to you about this, I'm sure that you don't want to be hearing this," she apologized, standing up, clearly embarrassed.

"No, no, not at all. I've enjoyed talking to you. I like talking to you. I just have to get to work," he assured her. A jarring realization: he was telling the truth; he did like talking to her, spending time with her. *Danger, William Miller*.

As he stood up, Herman's curse began to evoke searing pain. He gritted his teeth. He wouldn't allow himself to display his pain to Laura. The scar was attacking him; invading his brain – violating his body. It always hurt in situations like this. Laura, the poor woman, bearing this pain. The pain of a mother whose daughter has left her, a husband who works too much, who either couldn't or wouldn't be there for her. She was alone, in a beautiful, expensive home, which in the current circumstance was more of a prison.

They walked back into the house. Laura collected the cups and placed them in the dishwasher. He pressed his hand on his scar, hoping that the more pressure he placed on it, the faster the pain would depart.

"Natalie's room is in the basement, just down those steps, behind that door," Laura said, pointing at the closed door, down the hall from where he was standing.

"I'm sorry to trouble you, but you wouldn't happen to have anything for aches and pains, would you?" he asked, visibly weakened.

She happily complied. Laura approached him, the pills in one hand and a glass of water in the other. She was clearly in mother mode. Moreover, she was clearly a good mother.

Embarrassed, but thankful, he accepted the offered gifts.

"Thank you."

He then headed to the door, pulled it open, and descended the stairs.

•   •   •

Natalie's room had the appearance of the average stereotypical teenage girl. There were the obligatory stuffed animals on the bed, the pictures of friends making pouty and silly faces, pictures of boys, and posters of artists and bands. However, it was abundantly clear that Natalie had good taste in music.

There was a poster of Kurt Cobain, a poster of Nirvana's second album, *Nevermind*, a poster of The Notorious B.I.G. (the classic, in which he wore a crown), and a poster of The Ramones (the original line up). He had expected her walls to be adorned with posters of Katy Perry, One Direction, or that whiny little bitch, Justin Bieber.

He then progressed to her bed, searching under the mattress for clues. His search turned up empty. He rifled through the pillow cases. Nothing. He moved to the bedside table. Pulled open the drawer. There was a box of Kleenex, a Bible, and a well-read copy of *The Shining* by Stephen King. Underneath that was the book *Try* by Dennis Cooper. Natalie had good taste in literature too. Against his better judgement, he began to feel somewhat connected to her.

He flipped through the pages of the books, looking for anything that may have been hidden among the pages. There was nothing. Other than the pictures and the posters, she left nothing behind, save for the superficial. Nothing remained within the room that provided an in-depth glimpse into her as a person.

He looked over at her TV. She had a PS4 and a sizeable collection of games. Quite a few of which were first-person shooter games. He had many of the same games in his own collection. He moved over to her closet. It looked like she had taken the majority of her clothes with her. The only garments that were left looked like they were reserved for weddings and funerals.

Her drawers were devoid of clothes. At first glance, they appeared to be full of odds and ends, junk and other detritus. Looking closer, he realized that the drawers contained arts and craft supplies. There were pens, pencils, paper, ink, paint and paint brushes, small canvases (which varied from blank, in progress, and finished). He didn't know much about art, but they looked as if the artist knew what they were doing. She did have talent, that was unmistakable.

Lastly, he searched the bathroom. The medicine cabinet was empty, except for a jar of VapoRub (expired). The shower was empty. There was no shampoo or conditioner, and no body wash. All that remained was a bar of soap that had been heavily used. He searched the cabinets, which turned up nothing of evidentiary value; feminine products, lotions and creams, and a small, half empty bottle of perfume. No help at all. A waste of time.

He ascended the stairs back up to the main floor. Laura was still in the kitchen. She had resumed drinking coffee. She immediately made eye contact with him. Closing the door behind him, he trudged into the kitchen.

"Did you find anything?" she asked hopefully.

There was no point in sugar-coating things. "No. Nothing that would help me find her."

Her eyes were once again downcast.

"Look, I know how hard this must be, but don't worry too much. She's a kid from a wealthy family, from a good neighborhood. She has no idea how to make it on her own. Focus on two possibilities: she'll either come back on her own, or I'll find her and bring her back."

She slightly smiled, nodding her head. "Oh, one more thing: I found Jocelyn's number."

She handed him a piece of scrap paper with the number printed on it.

"Just so you know, I already talked to her. I asked if she knew where she was, and she told me that she hadn't the slightest idea where she could've gone."

"Well, she very well may not know anything. On the other hand, you're her mother. She's not going to rat on her friend. At the very least, she may be more willing to give me the names of people who may know where she is," he attempted to assure her.

They bade each other farewell, and he exited the home.

As Will descended the driveway, he noticed out of the corner of his eye that there was a man by the side of the house, in a bathrobe, smoking a cigarette. He had to be David. They made eye contact with one another.

"You must be David. I'm sorry if we woke you up," he stated in his best professional tone.

David exhaled a plume of smoke while stating, "No worries. I couldn't get much sleep, even if I tried." He did look exhausted. There were deep and dark bags under his eyes. However, he still maintained the usual air of a doctor that couldn't be shed, even whilst in a bathrobe. The aura of entitlement and smug superiority remained evident.

"I can only imagine how difficult this is for both of you," he said. This was the standard line that he employed when dealing with emotional people. At the very least, when dealing with clients, it provided the illusion that he cared. (He usually didn't.)

"Do you know why we hired you? I mean, you specifically?" David asked, ignoring his offered sympathy.

"No. No, I do not."

"I remembered you from the story in the paper. Your client shot you, right?" David said, staring off into the distance. It was phrased as a question, although it came across as a statement.

"Yeah. That was me," he replied, not offering any of the gory details.

He had received a flurry of inquiries after his return to work from the hospital. Most of them were just idle curiosity seekers, looking for a cheap thrill. While others were participating in some form of dark tourism; visiting the office of a shooting. He quickly sniffed those out, promptly evicting their asses from his office. Some of these rubberneckers had the gall to ask for selfies with Will, asking him to show them his scar. They had promptly left when he quoted them the price for such a picture: a thousand dollars. It had taken a few months, but the macabre interest in him had finally died down.

"That's why I told Laura that we should hire you," David said plainly.

"Oh?"

"I figure that if a man who got shot by his client, just for doing his job, must in fact, be very good at his job. Not to mention that you went right back to work as an investigator."

"Thanks. I hope to fulfill all of your expectations," Will replied, trying to mask his sarcasm.

"Find her. Please. I don't care what it costs. Just find her," David urged entreatingly, which seemed out of character, especially for a man like him.

"I'll do all that I can."

Once safely back inside the car, he locked the doors, turned on the music, and cranked on the air conditioning. He returned to the deep breathing exercise. Inhale. Exhale. After a minute, he drove away. He didn't want to draw any attention.

As he drove back to the office, he reflected on David's appeal. He realized, somewhat alarmingly, that it vexed him. He had developed an image of David the doctor. He was the usual doctor; entitled, arrogant, and just an all-around douchebag. He hadn't failed to live up to his mental image of him. However, his pathetic plea had served to humanize the asshole, somewhat. He didn't want to feel sorry for the prick, but that plea was unforgettable. His outright dislike for David had been minimally watered down. He hated it when assholes let him down like that.

•　　　•　　　•

"I know that you don't like talking about him, but I would like to explore the relationship with your father."

"What about him? I already told you, I only met him a handful of times growing up."

"Why was that?"

"He didn't want to be involved. As I said, he made it very clear to me that he didn't want to be in my life. Monthly child support payments were all that he felt was required of him."

"Tell me about the time that you spent with him."

"My earliest memory of him is when he took me to a bar to watch a football game."

"He took you to a bar?"

"Yeah. I was five or six. I was in my room. My mom called to me from the living room. I walked in, and there was this big man standing by the front door. He looked like he was uncomfortable. That was obvious to me. It was also clear that my mom wasn't happy that he was there. She told me, 'This is Robert. He's going to take you out for the day.'"

"That was it? She didn't tell you who he was?"

"No. She never openly referred to him as my father. It was something we both knew, but never chose to openly acknowledge."

"Did he tell you who he was?"

"No. The first time I met him, he treated spending time with me like it was a chore, or a favor that he was doing for a friend."

"What happened next?"

"I remember sitting next to him in his truck. There was no conversation. He was driving, intently focused on the road. The radio was on, and he cranked it. Anything to hinder conversation."

"He didn't talk to you at all?"

"No. Not in the car."

"Go on."

"We pulled up to this shithole dive bar. I remember that I was nervous to get out of the truck. The area looked scary. He exited the truck, without even checking to see if I was following him. I remember thinking that it was probably safer with him inside, than waiting in the truck. So, I quickly got out of the truck and followed after him.

"Once inside the bar, I found him planted on one of the stools, staring at the tv on the wall in front of him. He didn't even look at me, when I sat on the stool next to him. I don't know if he owned the bar, or if he was good friends with the owner, but no one gave me shit for being there. I was just a kid, I didn't even know what a bar was. But I didn't like it there. We just sat there, watching football.

"Nothing was said. I was too shy to say anything, and he was focused on his beer and the game. Just before halftime, I heard his gruff voice ask, 'You want a coke?' It took a moment for me to realize that the question was directed at me, as he hadn't even turned to look at me when he asked the question. I didn't answer. I remember feeling really anxious. I just nodded my head. He motioned the bartender over and gave him the order.

"And that was it. I sipped my coke, eating from the assorted bar snacks, and he drank and watched the game. When my cup was empty, he got the bartender to fill it up. Never speaking directly to me. After the game finished, he stood up and paid the tab, then walked out the door. I realized that we were done here and followed after him. He got to the truck and unlocked my door for me. We got back in the truck and began to drive.

"It was eerily similar to the trip there. Nothing was exchanged. He just kept his eyes on the road. So, accustomed at this point to the constant silence, I looked out the passenger side window. He drove me home. We were a couple houses away when I heard him mumble, 'You like football?' I told him that I did. That my favorite team was the Roughriders in the CFL and the Philadelphia Eagles in the NFL. He just grunted and nodded in response. Once again, we sat in awkward silence. Then Robert mumbled, 'Well, see you later.' I got out of the truck and went inside.

"My mom was waiting for me in the kitchen. She immediately asked me what Robert and I did that day. I told her the truth; we went to some smelly place and watched a football game. We went back and forth for a while, she wanted me to describe what this 'smelly place' was. Once she got the gist of where it was that we went, she grew red in the face. She took me to the living room and put on some movie. She told me to watch the movie, she had to make a phone call. She went to the bedroom.

"I remember hearing her yell from her bedroom. I didn't hear the entire argument, but I distinctly remember hearing her shriek, 'You prick! You useless piece of shit! You took him to that shithole bar, to watch a football game?! Is that your idea of spending quality time with your son?!' I got kind of scared, so I turned up the volume. The movie was almost over by the time my mom came back from the bedroom. She sat down next to me on the floor and gave me a hug. Then she got up and made us supper. That's my first memory of my father."

●　　　●　　　●

Upon his return to the office, he noted with mild disdain that there was someone waiting outside his office door. It was one of his tenants. Mary was an old Ukrainian woman, who spoke broken English. Her husband had died, and her children moved her into the apartment building. Mary would routinely visit his office, claiming that someone had been inside her apartment; that she had been robbed.

The thefts were, of course, imagined. He wasn't certain if she was suffering from some form of mild dementia, or if she was lonely and looking for company. He had always found the missing items in some random corner of the apartment.

"Hello, Mary."

"William, someone steal from me," she gasped, with a mixture of fear and outrage.

"Are you sure, Mary?" he asked, somewhat playfully.

"Yes, William!" she exclaimed painfully.

"What is missing?"

"A picture of momma and her rosary," she recounted.

"Did you call the police?"

"No, police. You come and look, please."

This exchange was all routine. It never veered off onto other tangents. Mary would claim that she had been robbed, recall what was taken, which caused him to ask if she had called the police. Mary was averse to involving police. He didn't know if this was because she was distrustful of the police, or because she had hidden the items for attention and didn't want to get into any sort of trouble. He had heard the horror stories of the police in the Ukraine and Russia. That they were corrupt, more criminal than the criminals that they were tasked with policing.

"Okay, Mary. I'll take a look."

He had learned from experience that it was easier to agree with Mary's demands. Any attempts at postponement only served to further agitate her. It was best to go with the flow. He would find the "stolen" items and then get back to the comfort and privacy of his office.

Mary lived three floors beneath his office. The building had an elevator, but Mary was petrified of elevators. This meant that he would have to walk with Mary, who could barely manage the stairs. She would loop her arm through his, and they would descend the stairs together. As they made the descent, she muttered indecipherable words under her breath. He was by no means a linguist, but it sounded like her native tongue.

"How are you holding up, Mary? Is the apartment okay? Nothing broken?"

"It's good, Will," she answered with a smile, patting his hand.

This routine of theirs had been going on for months. It had started mere weeks after her arriving in the building. It wasn't until this moment that he realized that Mary was his favorite tenant. Mary functioned, to a certain extent, as a surrogate mother. Their routine interaction allowed him to retreat into this fantasy. Mary could've been his own mother (had she lived, of course). He knew that fantasy was dangerous, but in this context, he felt that it was harmless.

Having made it to Mary's apartment, she retrieved her keys which hung on a necklace. She always kept the keys hidden underneath her sweater. She opened the door and motioned for Will to enter the apartment.

The apartment was kept remarkably neat. Mary, at such an advanced age, was still able to clean the apartment. Her television was on, tuned in to the history channel. It was some conspiracy theory-driven program about the end of the world. He longed for the days when the history channel actually aired reputable programs about the history of the human civilization. Honestly, who gives a flying fuck about *Ice Road Truckers*?

The apartment was virtually littered with photographs of her family and friends. Photographs were on every available surface in both the living room and her bedroom. The walls were full of framed photographs, most of which were black and white. The pictures were clearly cared for. It was obvious that she dusted the frames on a routine basis.

Mary motioned to a blank space on the wall. "Momma picture's missing," she reiterated.

He knew the picture. He had seen it on one of the previous searches of her apartment. It was a picture of her mother on her wedding day. The picture had stood out to him. Not only did Mary's mother bear a strong resemblance to her daughter, but her mother was beautiful. Mary had kept the rosary draped over the picture frame.

"May I take a look around, Mary?" he asked, as sweetly as possible.

"Yes. Look, look," she affirmed.

For the second time that day, he searched through someone's private space. This search would undoubtedly be fruitful. Through the previous searches in Mary's apartment, he had uncovered her usual hiding spaces.

He searched beneath the cushions of the sofa, underneath her mattress and bed, and the water tank of the toilet. He pawed his way through the cupboards and drawers in the kitchen, as well as the pantry. Nothing. He was beginning to fear that Mary had found a new hiding spot.

Mary stood near him, clutching her fists. Looking towards him, visibly shaken. As he found himself back in the kitchen, he realized that he hadn't searched the fridge. *Dumbass.* He opened the fridge. The frame wasn't inside. Somewhat disheartened, he then progressed to searching the freezer.

The frame and rosary were underneath a pint of ice cream. He lifted the print off of the frame and carefully removed it from the freezer. Grabbing a tea towel off of the oven door, he placed the frame and attached rosary on the cloth. He then passed it to Mary.

"It's very cold, Mary," he offered in explanation.

"In freezer?!" Mary cried, genuinely shocked.

"Yeah, it was underneath the ice cream," he answered calmly.

"Freezer," she repeated, quietly.

"Yeah."

"Ghosts," she said firmly, making eye contact.

"Ghosts?" he asked, stifling a laugh.

"I'm haunted," she stated resolutely.

"No, Mary. No ghosts. Ghosts would be too scared to mess around with you."

Mary looked at him and smiled.

•   •   •

He finally made it back to his office. For his valiant search, Mary had given him a gift of borscht, which she had made the previous afternoon. He held the large Tupperware container, struggling to not spill the contents as he groped for his keys in his pocket.

Having finally managed to maneuver his key into the lock, he then threw open the door and crossed the threshold into his sanctum sanctorum. He placed the container in the fridge and then locked the door. He was (as a habit of the armed services) very security-conscious; he had three separate locks on the front door.

The locks served to solidify his sense of isolation and the security of his personal space. The sense of comfort that his office provided was unparalleled. The comfort was so intense that he had often thought of his office as some sort of womb.

Having placed himself in his office chair, he turned on his computer. He took his phone out of his pocket and entered Jocelyn's number into his phone.

Having saved the number in his contacts, he then shredded the paper into infinite pieces and deposited the scraps into the wastebasket.

Remembering the poster in his Natalie's room, he turned on The Notorious B.I.G.'s debut album, *Ready to Die*. He began to bob his head along to the heavy beat of the music. He didn't feel up to making a phone call. He had had enough contact with people today. He began to compose a text message to Jocelyn. He struggled composing the message. He was worried how Jocelyn, a teenage girl, would respond to such a message from an unknown stranger. He resigned himself to drafting the most straightforward message he could manage.

Me: Hello, Jocelyn. My name is Will, and I'm a private investigator. As you know, Natalie has run away. I was hired by Natalie's mother to find her and bring her home. I would like to talk to you. You may have some information that could help me find her. Please message me ASAP.

He clicked the "send" button. It was out of his hands now. Once again, he found himself resigned to playing the waiting game.

About an hour later, his phone binged. Picking up the phone, he noticed with glee that Jocelyn had messaged him back. He unlocked the phone and read the message.

Jocelyn: Hi. Natalie's mom had mentioned that she hired a PI. I'm busy today with clubs and homework, but I can meet you tomorrow. I work at a café called *Fancy*. I have a break at 7. Does that work?

Me: Yeah. I'll see you then. Thank you so much for your assistance. You're doing the right thing.

He had wanted to lay it on thick for Jocelyn. People like to feel that they're important; this is especially the case when it comes to investigations. Even the humblest person likes to be able to regale their friends and family with details about how they helped an investigator solve a mystery. It was just human nature.

She responded back a few minutes later.

Jocelyn: She's my friend.

That was it. That simple message conveyed to him the stark reality; Jocelyn truly cared. He was at a loss for words. He honestly had no clue what to reply. He resolved to simply bid farewell.

Me: Good night. I'll see you tomorrow.

Jocelyn: Night.

He noted with satisfaction that the composition of her messages illustrated the maturity and serious nature and intent of Jocelyn. There were no acronyms, emoticons, and no lengthy delays. He understood why Natalie and Jocelyn were best friends; they were two of a kind. He hoped that Jocelyn could and would help find Natalie.

·　　·　　·

He dreamt of her that night.

It may have been a dream, but it felt like more of a flashback. It felt so fucking real.

The dream/flashback was a replay of the last time that he had seen his mother alive.

He hadn't thought about it in a very long time. He made sure not to think about it. It was an event that he had vainly attempted to forget, but couldn't, not entirely. It was one of the many memories of his past that constantly threatened the fortifications that he had erected within his mind. These memories were constantly besieging his consciousness. Lurking just beneath the surface. They only struck when he was vulnerable; at his most defenseless.

They were sitting in her apartment, having supper. A family supper. His mother had always insisted on holding a family supper at least once a week. As he grew up, his mother had maintained the attitude of "us versus them." Mother and son against the world. This weekly supper, he thought, was a surviving remnant of that attitude.

The cancer was eating her alive at this point. She didn't look overly ill. He would later reflect that she had maintained her beauty; she didn't look like a cancer patient. She just looked like his mother.

"What did the doctor say?" he asked, concerned.

"She's ordered some more tests, but it's not looking good," she said, using her fork to push her food around the plate.

"Well, did she give you anything for the pain?"

"Yep. Gave me some pills; they make me feel dizzy."

"Do they help?"

"Yeah, but the downside is this damned dizziness," she complained.

He couldn't voice the question that weighed so heavily upon his mind. He was petrified of the answer. He desperately wanted to know if his mother would survive. In his life, she had been the one constant, and his only ally.

"Well, when is your next appointment?" he asked nervously.

"Next Tuesday."

He said nothing. He simply nodded his head. There was nothing that could be said.

His mother looked at him across the table.

"Don't worry, Will. You worry too much," she said, smiling.

"Okay, Mom," he said, rolling his eyes.

"Eat your supper, it's getting cold."

That was all that was said. He knew when his mother had had enough. There would be no more discussion about her illness. He would later recall that he had felt unsettled. It was more than the sickness. He couldn't identify it. He chose to ignore it.

They finished their dinner. As was their custom, she had cooked, so he washed and dried the dishes. They finished the evening by watching her favorite movie, Casablanca. As his mother began to drift off to sleep, he bid his farewell.

"Mom, I'm going to go. Thanks for supper," he said, crouching in front of her chair.

"Okay, Will. I'll see you later."

She hugged him and kissed him on the cheek.

That was the last time that he saw his mother alive.

•　　•　　•

He awoke in a sweat.

The sheets were damp from his perspiration.

He could feel his heart pounding in his chest.

He tore the wet sheets off of his body with disgust. Sliding his feet off of the mattress, he stood up. He made his way to the kitchen. Starting the coffee brewing, he took a cup from the cupboard, filled it to the brim with water, and chugged it back until it was empty.

He put the glass down on the counter.

He closed his eyes and took a series of deep breaths.

He found solace in the fact that having been tormented in his sleep, the ghosts of his past would not haunt him during the day. He doubted that this was in any way a kindness on their part. Rather, it was due to the increased fortifications that he emplaced in his consciousness. If he followed his strict routine, the dead would be kept at bay.

Once the coffee was brewed, he filled his largest mug with coffee, adding cream and sugar. Taking another deep breath, he chugged the entire contents of the cup. He grimaced slightly as he felt the heat from the coffee burn his insides.

He repeated the process twice.

Having received a strong dose of caffeine, he went to his room and changed into his gym attire. He began his workout with a conscious intent that he would work his body harder today. It was inarguably a form of masochism. He was punishing himself. He was lambasting himself for his failures. Brutalizing himself for his weakness. Only when he could no longer physically push himself, did he grant himself a reprieve.

For the second time that morning, he could feel his heart pounding in his chest. He could hear the rhythm of his heart, beating in his eardrums. He felt the nausea overtake him. Barely making it to the bathroom, he vomited into the toilet bowl.

Admittedly, he was pleased.

He had punished his body not only through the workout itself, but he had pushed his body to the point of illness. The act of vomiting had also functioned to purify his body. He had purged his body of weakness.

After flossing and brushing his teeth, he took a shower.

His attention was drawn to the scar; the curse of Herman. It was red and irritated. He gently caressed it. It was sore. He hissed through gritted teeth as his fingers traced the scar. This was new; the phantom pain was a regular occurrence, but this was something else. Once out of the shower, he dried off and gently rubbed a dollop of lotion on the affected area.

Once he had made himself as presentable as possible, he returned to the kitchen and poured himself another cup of coffee. He exhaled exasperatedly.

He wouldn't be meeting Jocelyn until the evening. This provided him with the opportunity to finish his other open case. It was, as usual, a case of infidelity. The client was a woman, which was rare. The majority of his clients, in instances of marital transgressions, were generally male. Whether this was because wives were generally more trusting than their male counterparts, or they were more willing to ignore their spouses' obvious failings, he didn't know.

The client, Ava Schmidt, had been growing suspicious that her husband of seven years, had been unfaithful. Her husband, Aaron, regularly traveled for work. He was a consultant for an international firm. Aaron had begun to frequently "work" late into the evening, which was not like him, Ava said. He would always come home around six. If he was swamped with work, he preferred to do it from home, in his office.

The case was ridiculously easy; some of the easiest money that he had ever made.

He had waited in his car, outside Aaron's office, for hours on end.

He had emptied the thermos of coffee early on in his vigil. He'd had to relieve himself into an empty water bottle. The late-night stakeouts had always reminded him of being on night watch at FOBs (Forward Operating Bases). He remembered the fear that he had always felt while on watch. Petrified that if he dozed off, or let his attention wander, the base would be attacked, and they would be killed, and it would be his fault.

It was this lingering memory of fear that effectively assisted in keeping him awake during the long and tedious hours of surveillance.

He waited for hours.

Will saw the husband exit the offices and approach his car. He kept his eyes glued to his cellphone as he walked. He quickly started his car and peeled away, screeching his tires in the process. *Douche.*

He followed Aaron's car, keeping one car length between them as a precaution.

Aaron began his trip in the business center of the city and was making his way to some of the seedier parts of the city. Will had an inkling where he was heading to. It was a cheap motel. This particular no-tell motel had a reputation as a hangout for prostitutes.

The husband parked in the motel lot.

Will momentarily parked his car on the street, as to avoid arousing the suspicion of the cheating husband. He could see Aaron walk up a flight of stairs onto the second floor. He knocked on a door and was promptly granted entry.

He then pulled his car into the lot, parking in a spot that would provide him with an acceptable vantage point. He could see that the blinds on the motel room were closed. This left him with very few reasonable options. He opted to wait, his camera at the ready, on the passenger seat beside him. He would wait until Aaron left the room, confident that he would then be able to snap a picture of him bidding farewell to a woman that was clearly a prostitute.

Once again, he waited.

The wait was exhausting; borderline intolerable.

It wasn't until two in the morning, that the door had finally opened.

Aaron and the hooker exited the room together. He was wearing some frilly robe that clearly belonged to her. The prostitute was wearing only a skimpy bikini. The duo made their way to the outdoor pool.

The pool was easily visible from Will's parked car.

The woman jumped into the pool. Aaron stood at the edge of the pool, watching her. Words were exchanged, but he couldn't hear exactly what was said. The gist was that she wanted to skinny dip. He observed Aaron smiling nervously. The woman had taken off her bikini and thrown it at Aaron. This had overcome any reticence Aaron may have had at the time.

He disrobed, pulled off his underwear and jumped into the pool.

He began to take a series of pictures, a number of which managed to capture Aaron's readily identifiable face.

It only took a few minutes for the two to begin having sex.

The prospect of having sex in a public pool didn't excite Will. He was too much of a germaphobe for that. And he would definitely not have sex in the pool of a no-tell motel. He did, however, take a series of pictures of the sexual act. He had all that he needed for the client.

They finished and returned to the hotel room. He remained in the parking lot. He didn't want to draw attention to himself, so he waited until Aaron left the motel. He only had to wait about fifteen minutes.

Aaron left the room and descended the steps. He had a contented smile on his face. He wasted no time. He got into his car and started the vehicle. As Aaron's car approached him, he shifted as low as possible in his seat, so he wouldn't be visible. The car then exited the lot.

He gave it a few minutes, just to be safe. He then started his car and headed back to his office. Once he had returned to the office, he connected his camera to his computer. He perused the collection for the most damning photographs, selecting only those which left no doubt about the guilt of the husband.

Once the damning evidence had been collected, he printed them off. He then placed these photos in an envelope. Case closed.

However, things were not that simple. For whatever reason, Ava had been reluctant to come to the office to collect the evidence and close the account. Every attempt at scheduling a meeting had been met with cagey deferrals. The excuses were weak; so flimsy that they were laughable. She had guests, other appointments, or family emergencies. He didn't think that the reluctance to meet was due to a lack of funds; it was clear that she and her husband were quite wealthy; Ava came from a well-off family.

Will didn't like having open cases. He wasn't particularly fond of not being paid for his work, either. This had gone on for weeks. Enough was enough. It was time to settle-up. He emailed her (he still wanted to be discreet) and told her that if she didn't come to his office and pay her bill, he would be forced to pursue legal action. Of course, he had no intention or desire of engaging in a legal battle. He wagered that she wouldn't want her dirty laundry aired in a trial; most rich people don't enjoy being sued.

She had quickly responded to the threat, assuring him that legal action was not necessary. She booked an appointment with him. The meeting was set for ten in the morning. Today. He was now waiting in the office. Waiting. Waiting. It was half past, and she was still not there. *Fuck.*

He tried calling her phone (no longer concerned with being discreet), but there was no answer. Frustrated, he immediately re-dialed her number. This time it went straight to her voicemail. He gritted his teeth. Perhaps she may have called his bluff regarding legal action. There was nothing he could do. Nothing but wait. He was enraged, but resolved to wait fifteen more minutes.

Of course, she didn't show up.

He groaned and lifted himself out of his chair. There was no point in waiting around. He thought that he would head back to the apartment and take a nap before he had to meet Jocelyn. As he approached the door, he saw the feminine silhouette of Ava. Taking a deep, exasperated breath, he opened the door before she could knock.

Ava looked taken aback. Her mouth hung open in shock. She wore large chic sunglasses. Her nose was somewhat red and irritated. She either had a cold, or she had been crying. He was confident that it was the latter.

"Mrs. Schmidt. You're late," he plainly stated.

"I know. I'm sorry. I was having a hard time getting out of bed today," she murmured.

"Come on in," he said, motioning her inside.

He flicked the light switches back on.

They retreated back to his main office, located at the back of the suite. Upon being bequeathed with the building by his father, he quickly went about renovating this large and vacant apartment into an office suite. His private residence was located across the hall.

As they sat across from each other, he was overwhelmed by the sorrow emanating from Ava. He found himself being besieged by pangs of sympathy.

"Would you like a drink, Mrs. Schmidt?" Will asked, as kindly as possible.

"It's not even noon!" she replied, stifling a laugh.

He could tell by her reaction and the beginnings of a smile on her face that she would not be averse to a drink.

"That may be, but I think you and I could both use a drink."

"Well, alright. Just the one," she acquiesced.

He went to the mini kitchen outside the office. Grabbing the rye out of the freezer, he then filled two glasses half full. He then grabbed a bottle of pop from the fridge, adding a moderate splash to each glass.

Returning to the office, he handed Ava the stiff drink.

"Thank you, Mr. Miller," she said, taking the glass.

"Call me Will."

"Then call me Ava. Mrs. Schmidt, makes me feel so old," she laughed slightly.

She didn't look old. Tired. Heartbroken. But not old.

They sat in silence for a few moments. Each simply sipping from their drink. He began to feel the tension build in his stomach. He was never very good at small talk or social interaction in general. Laura being the only exception. He forced his mind not to think about her.

"Ava. I have some pictures for you," he said gently.

As he grabbed the envelope from his desk drawer, he looked up and noticed that Ava was downing the remainder of her drink. He slid the envelope across the desk, trying not to make eye contact with the woman.

"Did he cheat?" she mumbled quietly.

She had phrased the question so quietly and meekly that he had to strain to make out the words. The question preceded a vacuum of silence. He said nothing. He felt that responding to the question in the affirmative would somehow make him morally culpable. He vowed then and there to never take a wife on as a client in a cheating case.

"Please, just look in the envelope," he pleads, feeling like a coward.

"I don't want to look at the pictures. Just tell me; yes or no?" she asked, oddly calm.

He realized that there was no escape. He was trapped. He couldn't bring himself to force her to view the photos. She had been through enough. The situation he now found himself in was, irrevocably and inescapably, an instance of the truth being the only path to freedom.

"Yes. He has been unfaithful," Will found himself answering.

She didn't respond. She merely nodded her head. She reached into her purse and retrieved her chequebook and a pen.

"Is it acceptable if I make it out to cash?" she asked.

"Yes. That's fine," he responded, shocked.

Her pen flourished across the cheque. She tore the cheque out and slid it across the desk. He eyed the amount. She had paid him far too much.

"Ava, this is more than I quoted. This is too much," he protested.

"And here I thought that private investigators were all slimy conmen, set on fleecing people out of their money," she quipped, a fake smile plastered on her face.

"Most of us are. But I cannot accept this. It's too much."

Ava continued to put on a brave face.

"You did a good job, and I feel horrible about keeping you waiting. Please, just accept it."

He would later think that if it had been any other woman, on any other day, he would've simply torn apart the cheque, and demand that they write another one, with the correct amount.

"Thank you," he said, conceding defeat.

Ava had piqued his curiosity. Normally, he would never get involved in a client's personal affairs, but he simply had to know.

"Ava, I don't normally do this, but what are you going to do now?"

"Nothing. I'm not going to do anything," she responded flatly.

"Nothing?!" he asked, not believing his ears.

"No. I thought that he was cheating. I just needed to know the truth. And, now I know."

"And yet you're not going to leave him?" he asked, incredulously.

"No," she replied, firmly.

"But, why?" he asked exasperatedly.

Ava slowly stood up. She pushed out her chair and walked around to his side of the desk. She approached him, not breaking eye contact, her movements careful. Looking him in the eyes, she bent down and passionately kissed him. It was a kiss full of heartache. It was a farewell. Each knew that they would never see the other again.

She abruptly removed her lips from his. She raised herself back up to a standing position. Without looking back, she grabbed her purse off her chair, and walked towards the door. She pulled open the door and stood before it. With her back still facing him, she uttered the most heartbreaking statement that he had ever heard in his adult life:

"Because, I love him. And I just can't help myself."

•　　　•　　　•

Fancy.

The very name of the cafe made him cringe.

It was meant to be ironic.

He arrived early. He couldn't restrain himself; he had to be early. There was no room for error when it came to timeliness. In his experience, it was better to be early; there were simply too many variables to consider.

It was a café that catered to the hipster crowd. As soon as he entered the café, he noticed the clientele and rolled his eyes. He had always loathed hipsters. Their fashion sense, their superior attitude, and most annoyingly, their earnest (faux) indifference, and outrage at anything that didn't conform to their hipster ethos.

There was (of course) a bearded hipster playing acoustic guitar (badly) on stage at the back of the café. He was sitting on a stool, wearing a wool cap. It was summer, so clearly the cap was a fashion statement of some sort. Further fashion statements included: a belt that had a series of padlocks affixed, one white sneaker (left), and one black sneaker (right). He was wearing a (stained) white shirt with *FEMINIST* in bold on the front. Will disliked the hipster on sight.

He made his way to the counter. There were a number of hipsters in front of him. The two directly in front of him were all talking about the Farmer's Market. The. Fucking. Farmer's. Market. He noticed that the hipsters couldn't pass up an opportunity in which they could flaunt their moral superiority. They were discussing the moral imperative of buying organic produce and supporting local farmers. This set his teeth on edge. Their inane dialogue began to threaten his peace of mind.

It felt as if he was awash in a crowd of poseurs, who couldn't utter a single sentence that didn't feature the words: free trade, organic, vegan, tofu, gluten-free, and the farmers market.

It was precisely for situations like this that he was thankful for his earbuds and music.

He scrolled to the artist Immortal Technique, selecting *The 3rd World*.

The heavy beat and rhythm massaged his eardrums; obliterating the repulsive dialogue of the hipster crowd. The music effectively isolated him from the distasteful clientele. This sense of solitude was all that enabled him to remain in this horrendous café.

It took an agonizing amount of time to make it to the front of the queue. As it was his turn to order, he removed the earbuds and silenced the music.

"Hello, what can I get you?" asked the perky barista.

"How much espresso can you legally sell me at one time?" he asked, serious.

"I have honestly never been asked that before," the barista replied, shocked.

"Never mind. I will take the largest coffee that you sell, with five shots of espresso."

The barista's eyes bulged in shock. She tried to play it cool, like she routinely got this order, but he saw through the pitiful attempt at deception.

"Sure. That'll be on the other side," she answered, motioning to the other end of the counter.

He paid and walked to the other half of the counter, as instructed.

A different barista (a skinny male, with a moustache that made him look like a sex offender) provided him with his beverage.

"Hey, is Jocelyn working tonight?" he asked the sex offender look-alike.

"Sorry, man, I can't give out that kind of information," the creepy moustached man replied righteously.

"I understand that. It's a good policy. However, I'm supposed to meet her here. I don't see her anywhere. Admittedly, I'm a bit early," Will responded, unable to stop himself from clenching his fists.

The moustached barista glared at him, as if he were attempting to size him up; discerning Will's hidden lascivious intentions.

"Listen, man. I'm not going to divulge employee info to the public. Especially when the people asking are creepy perverts."

"Are you calling me a creepy pervert?" he asked, through gritted teeth.

The barista smiled indignantly in return.

"That's rich, coming from a guy who looks like he is a registered sex offender," Will said venomously.

The words were out of his mouth before he realized that he had said anything.

He was losing control. *Fuck.*

The situation was in danger of becoming dangerously fucked.

"Okay, man. That's it, I'm calling the cops," Mustachioed Barista said, heading towards the phone which resided on the counter near the swinging doors located under the *Employees Only* sign.

Will began to assess the situation, debating whether he could mediate the circumstances; smooth the man's ruffled feathers. Apologize and hope for the best. He didn't want to have to explain the situation to the police and the crowd's attention had been drawn to the tense situation at the counter.

Before the moustached man could reach the phone, Jocelyn emerged from behind the swinging doors, holding a tray of freshly baked muffins. Both men simultaneously noticed her arrival. Will quickly smiled, nodded, and waved her over.

"Jocelyn, I'm William Miller," he said quickly.

"Jocelyn, go to the back," Mustachioed Barista instructed hurriedly.

"You're William?" Jocelyn asked him, somewhat surprised.

"Yeah."

Jocelyn approached the counter, getting closer to him.

"You know this guy, Jocelyn?" the moustached hipster asked.

"Yeah, kind of. He's the guy I was talking about, the one who's looking for Natalie," she said.

Mustachioed Barista held the phone in his hand, skeptically examining Will on the other side of the counter. Jocelyn noticed the man's visible apprehension. She placed the tray down on the counter, walked over to the agitated guy and placed the phone back down on the charger.

"It's cool," she said authoritatively.

Jocelyn then walked back over to Will. She wiped her hands off on her apron. She looked down at the watch on her wrist, then raised her gaze back to him.

"I said seven, dude. You're early."

"Yeah. I'm early. I apologize. I can wait."

"It's cool. Give me fifteen minutes. You can sit over there," she said, pointing to a table for two by the window.

"Okay."

She grabbed a plate from below the counter and placed a muffin from the tray onto the plate.

"Here. Take a muffin. It's my treat," she said with a smile.

He took the plate from her. The muffin (if it could be called that) didn't look all that appealing to him. Thankfully, he had his coffee, which he could use to wash down the baked good.

"It's gluten-free," she added helpfully.

Fuck.

• • •

He waited patiently at the table. The moustached douche glared at him from his position behind the counter. He tactfully chose to ignore the prick.

The muffin was dry and tasted like baked garbage. He left the remainder of the muffin on the plate, hoping that his distaste for the pastry wouldn't offend Jocelyn. He needed her to be open and honest with him. He wanted to avoid anything that could hinder this exchange.

Jocelyn emerged once again from the back of the café. She approached the table, holding two cups of coffee.

"How's the muffin?" she asked, with a wry smile.

"It's good. Very tasty," Will said, trying to muster sincerity.

Jocelyn burst out laughing. "It's okay. The muffins taste like shit. I was just messing with you."

He felt a smile break out on his face. "You got me there. It is seriously the worst thing that I have ever tasted."

"I know, right? All that gluten-free crap tastes terrible."

"So why are you working at a hipster café that exclusively sells that garbage?"

"Because I need money, and the hipster crowd is willing to spend five dollars on a small coffee, and seven bucks on a muffin," she answered, laughing.

"This muffin costs seven fucking dollars?!" he asked, genuinely outraged.

Jocelyn laughed hard, nodding and smiling.

"I got you another coffee. Everyone is impressed by the amount of espresso. How are you not dead?"

"I need caffeine. It is necessary for me to function normally."

"Don't we all?" she asked.

Once again, he spotted the moustached prick glaring at him from behind the counter.

"Sorry about earlier. I hope I didn't get you in shit with your boss," he apologized, nodding in the moustached hipster's direction.

Jocelyn turned around quickly and shot a nasty look back at him.

"Oh, don't mind him. That's Derek. He's my supervisor and my ex-boyfriend."

"You dated that douchebag?" he asked, wincing. The words had escaped his lips before he was conscious of what he had said.

She laughed. "Yeah, for a bit. We broke up just before he grew that unfortunate moustache."

"Oh. Good for you."

They were engulfed by an awkward silence. Each knew what they had to discuss, but neither were certain how to begin.

"Do you know where Natalie is, Jocelyn?" Will asked, softly.

"No. I wish I knew. But I haven't heard from her in a while."

"When's the last time that you talked to her?"

"A couple of days before she took off, I think."

"Did she say anything to you about taking off?"

"No. We made plans to go see a movie. She never showed up. I tried calling her, but there was no answer. I messaged her, but she never messaged me back."

"Does she have a boyfriend?"

"No. She had a boyfriend, Cameron, but they broke up."

"Before or after she went missing?"

"Before. Like, a week or two."

"Do you think she's with Cameron somewhere?"

"No. No way. There are rumors going around that he's seeing some cheerleader. Natalie and him are over."

"Do you think he'd be willing to talk to me?"

"I could talk to him. Maybe, I could give him your number?"

"That'd be great."

They each took a break, sipping from their coffee.

"Why did she start using?" he asked abruptly, hoping to catch her off guard.

"I don't know. She told me she tried it at a party once, like a long time ago; the beginning of the school year, I think. Pills are everywhere. It's not just the junkies and burnouts that use them. Smart kids use Adderall to help them study, others use opioids to relax. I'm sure that you're aware that there is an opioid epidemic; everyone is using them."

"Have you?"

"I tried them a couple of times. I didn't like the way it made me feel."

"Do you know who she bought her pills from?"

"Nope. She never mentioned anything to me. She didn't really like talking about her issue with drugs. She always got sad whenever the topic came up."

"Why did she stop going to school?"

"I'm sure you remember high school. You don't look that old. It's a rough environment. Especially for girls. Girls can be mean; vicious, even. They started spreading rumors about her: first, it was that she was a pill popping addict, then when she got back from rehab, they had more shit to talk about. Started playing the Amy Winehouse song, *Rehab*, whenever she walked by.

They would say shit like, 'Natalie is such a pill...head.' High school isn't exactly a warm environment."

He did remember what high school was like. He hadn't exactly fit in either. He hated school, the teachers, and the kids, too.

"Do you have any idea where she could be hiding? Did she have any places that she liked to go?"

"No. I told you. I haven't got a clue. Natalie liked to go for walks by the river, she liked going to the bookstore, she liked to paint, she liked to read and play video games. There was never any one spot, you know? She's not like those people who hang out at cafés, she's not a mallrat or anything either."

"Did she ever talk to you about her relationship with her parents?"

"She complained about her mom nagging her, her parents fighting, the pressure to keep her grades up. I guess it's the usual shit that teens complain about."

"Nothing out of the ordinary?"

"Nope. There's nothing."

"So, Natalie never talked about running away? Or just leaving?"

"I told you, no."

"Did she ever mention attending boarding school?"

"No. Why? Her parents are sending her to boarding school?!" Jocelyn asked, shocked.

"No. It was just something that the family had been talking about."

"Oh. Well, she never talked about that," she said, dismissively.

"I'm just confused," Will admitted.

"Why?"

"Well, she's a kid from a good family – a wealthy family, she isn't from the streets; she has no idea how to live that life. She has a pill addiction, but she's never been homeless. I just can't for the life of me figure out who she's living with, how she's getting by. She told her parents that she was getting a job, but that was a lie."

Once again, a silence enveloped the two of them.

He drained the remainder of his coffee.

"Jocelyn, I think you know something. I know that there is something that you aren't telling me. I know you're her friend and you want her to be safe. So, if you know anything, please tell me," he said plainly.

"Hey, I am her friend. I do want her to be safe. I'm sorry, but I don't have anything that can help you."

She had begun to tear up. He didn't want to be an asshole. He didn't want to embarrass her at her workplace. He feared that his cynical and misanthropic nature had gotten the better of him. She was just a kid. Not the usual people that he dealt with.

"I'm sorry. I guess I can be an asshole sometimes," he apologized.

She used her index finger to wipe away the tears that were collecting at the corner of her eyes. She sniffled and took a lengthy sip from her coffee.

"It's cool. Look, I've got to get back to work. But I'll talk to Cameron. Then I'll send you his number."

"Thank you. I greatly appreciate all of your help," he said, rising from his seat.

He offered her his hand, which she shook.

She then gathered up the empty cups and the plate with the half-eaten muffin. She smiled and nodded at him, then headed to the back of the café. He exited the café, nodding at the moustached hipster, known as Derek, on the way out.

Once back in his car, he took a moment to collect his thoughts.

He was nearly certain that Jocelyn knew more than she was telling him. However, he was conflicted, as there was a possibility that his pessimistic conception of humanity was unduly influencing his perception. At this point, he accepted that he had very few concrete leads. At this point, she was his best and only lead. He exhaled exasperatedly, as he realized that this meant.

Sitting in his car.

Waiting.

Waiting.

Waiting.

Waiting.

Waiting.

The café closed at ten. Three hours of fucking waiting. He was starving. He had had nothing to eat other than the half of that nasty gluten-free muffin. It was sitting like a rock in the pit of his stomach.

He crouched down in his seat as he saw Jocelyn exit the café. Derek was standing next to her. He couldn't make out what they were saying from his position, but if he had to guess, Derek was attempting to woo Jocelyn; get back into her good graces. Some men just didn't fucking get it. He was of the staunch opinion that if women were interested, they would let the man know.

The two employees broke apart, Derek heading down the street, and Jocelyn heading to her car. He heard the car beep as she unlocked the car doors. She wasted no time in entering the vehicle. He noticed that the car remained dark for a few moments before she cranked the ignition and began to drive away.

He allowed a few seconds to elapse before he started the vehicle and then began his pursuit. There wasn't much traffic in the area this late at night, but it was dark enough that he wouldn't have to be too concerned about being spotted. Overall, he wasn't too concerned, the target was a teenage girl, she knew nothing about detecting a tail.

If this had been a movie, Jocelyn would have led him to wherever her friend was hiding. Sadly, real life rarely imitated film. It was about a ten-minute drive. He had followed her back to her house. He could see a man and woman, who were clearly her parents, through the living room window. He parked a few houses back and began to wait on the off chance that Jocelyn would sneak out of the house after her parents had gone to sleep.

Originally, he was only going to wait until eleven. His desperation and frustration forced him to continue. Midnight came and went. Nothing. Then another hour elapsed. Still nothing. It didn't look like Jocelyn would be leaving the house tonight. His exhaustion and hunger ultimately convinced him. He ended the watch shortly before two o'clock.

He went home and fell asleep.

He awoke after a disturbed sleep.

He reflected on the question that he had posed to Jocelyn: how does a girl like Natalie just disappear? It didn't make any sense.

He lay in bed, reviewing his options.

He still had not heard back from his friend, Thomas. There had been no new activity on any of Natalie's social media accounts. She had stopped attending school, and she had no known employment. Her phone was disconnected; or she had begun to use a new unknown number. Her best friend claimed that she didn't know where she was, but had promised to try and get Natalie's ex-boyfriend to talk. Will assumed that Natalie was using again. It would be a waste of time approaching dealers for help; they wouldn't rat out their clients (and besides, no one would believe he wasn't a cop) and it was likely that he would wind up getting himself (or someone else) killed.

There were few options.

He could plaster the city with missing person posters, but this required man power and took too long. This would only result in every crazy person offering bullshit tips. Or worse, he would be awash in false sightings; good Samaritans who thought they had seen Natalie. Flyers and posters were truly a last resort; it signified that there was no chance in finding them.

When it came to missing persons and fugitives, the most reliable course of action was following the spouse/boyfriend/girlfriend, or the parents. Eventually, they would approach the aforementioned.

There remained only a single viable option: follow Jocelyn in the meantime and hope that Cameron would have something useful to impart.

• • •

Sleep was elusive.

He hadn't been able to drift into unconsciousness.

He couldn't keep the thoughts from bouncing around in his head.

Natalie, David, Laura, Jocelyn, Cameron. The names, stories, connections with the missing girl, and how in the hell a girl like Natalie could disappear, endlessly repeating on an infinite cycle.

He had arrived home from surveillance in the early morning. He was hoping to nab a few hours of sleep, then wake up and resume his surveillance of Jocelyn. He needed to get sleep. He dreaded having to make it through the day, operating on zero sleep. It was easy enough to doze off during the routine boredom of surveillance, he couldn't imagine having to go through with it exhausted.

By five o'clock, he gave up on the prospect of sleep.

He raised himself out of bed, sighing exasperatedly. He began his morning routine: coffee, workout, and shower. Once out of the shower, he sat in his favorite chair. He could already begin to feel himself dozing off. Shaking his head to free himself from the clutches of sleep, he stood up.

Looking at his watch, he groaned audibly, realizing that there was no time for a power nap. He had to get going. Duty calls. He would need to considerably increase the amount of caffeine he imbibed, if he were to successfully make it through the day unscathed. He brewed another pot of coffee and then emptied its contents into a giant thermos.

He gathered himself, took a deep breath, and headed out the door.

•   •   •

He called Laura to see if she had heard from Natalie. He was somewhat shocked when he experienced a surge of happiness upon hearing her voice.

"I haven't heard anything, Will."

She sounded exhausted. But it was more than exhaustion; it was utter despair.

"I'm not going to lie, I haven't found anything. I'm following Jocelyn in the hopes that she'll lead me to Natalie. Jocelyn told me that she would talk to her ex-boyfriend, Cameron. Maybe he'll have something useful," he recounted.

"I've never heard of Cameron," she commented.

"Jocelyn said that they broke up a week or so before she went missing."

"Really? She never mentioned him. Do you think that he had something to do with her going missing? Or knows why she left?" she asked hurriedly.

"I don't know. I don't want to assume anything."

"Where are you right now?"

"I'm outside Natalie and Jocelyn's school. Maybe she'll skip class and meet Natalie, or at the very least, meet up after school. I don't want to risk losing her."

"Jocelyn won't skip school," Laura said authoritatively.

"Even good kids can cut class."

"No, I mean Jocelyn *won't* skip. Her dad is the vice principal."

"Well, shit," Will muttered. "That'll save me some time."

At noon he received a message from Jocelyn.

Jocelyn: Hey. Talked to Cameron. He says it's cool to talk. He's got soccer practice after school, but he can meet you on the field at 5. Cool?

Me: Yeah. Thanks. Where is the field?

Jocelyn: Next to our school. You can't miss it.

Me: Okay...does he have a number I can reach him at?

Jocelyn: He doesn't feel comfortable giving out his number to a stranger. He says it's easier to just meet in person. I'll tell him to meet you at the bleachers after practice?

Me: Okay. He's serious? He wants to help?

Jocelyn: Yeah. FYI, he told me that he had no idea where she is.

Me: He might still know something. He may not think it's important. Thanks, again.

Jocelyn: No worries.

He fucking hated soccer. He thought it was the most boring sport in the world. It consisted of people chasing a ball across a field. There was no contact; no excitement. The matches could go ninety minutes without a goal being scored. He couldn't understand the appeal.

He parked in the lot behind the soccer field.

As he sat in the car, he desperately hoped that this was not a complete and total waste of his time. He was somewhat unnerved at the prospect of allowing Jocelyn out of his sight. Ultimately, both the desire and prospect of unearthing a new lead from a person so intimately close to Natalie overrode his unease.

It was at this point that he stumbled blindly onto the realization that he was in danger of becoming (if he wasn't already) emotionally invested in the case. He had always been careful to erect and sustain barriers between himself and clients. It was an ability in which he took pride in. His skill at maintaining boundaries with clients was surpassed only by the concrete barriers that were entrenched between himself and all others. He feared that these barricades were crumbling; whether the culprits were Mary, Laura, Natalie, or all of them, he didn't know.

For the sake of self preservation, he needed to finish this.

He took a deep breath and exited the car. The lot was largely empty, save for a few cars. Entering the field, he made a beeline for the bleachers, taking a seat near the top.

Practice appeared to be over. There were a few players on the field, consulting with coaches or training staff. He hoped that Cameron would notice him, this odd man – and realize who he was. He preferred to not have to wander onto the field. This would only result in the other adults taking an unfortunate interest in his presence.

After an interminable few minutes, the athlete speaking to the coach, having finished their conversation, walked to the edge of the field and picked up a bottle of water. As he lifted the bottle to his lips, his eyes were drawn to the man on the bleachers. The player's eyes widened momentarily. He took another sip of his water, bent over and picked up his duffle bag, and began to approach the bleachers.

Cameron ascended the bleachers warily. The other players and coaching staff seemed oblivious to the man and teen on the bleachers. They had simply assembled their gear and then departed the field.

"You're William? The investigator?" he asked, suspiciously.

"Yeah. Cameron?"

"Yeah. Everyone calls me Cam."

Cameron sat down next to him, situating his duffle bag in between them.

"Thanks for taking the time to talk to me, Cam."

"No problem," he answered, looking at the field.

Will decided that he would try to catch him off guard.

"Cameron, do you know where Natalie is?"

The question didn't even startle him; he didn't exhibit any visible signs of distress.

"No. I haven't even heard from her since we broke up," he answered, still looking at the field.

"How long did you two date?"

"Uh, about a month and a half," he mumbled, visibly uncomfortable.

"Who broke up with whom?"

"How is this supposed to help find Natalie?" Cam demanded, irritated.

"Look, I'm not trying to be a prick. Her parents are concerned. She has gone missing. You are aware that she has a drug problem? I just want to bring her home, so she can get help," he explained.

There was a brief moment of silence. Cameron had shifted his focused attention from the field to his shoes. He appeared to be intently studying his feet, as if he were attempting to understand a cosmic secret.

"Cam, I'm not here to get anyone in trouble. If you're worried about your parents finding out about something that will get you in trouble; I'm not a cop. I'm not a teacher. I simply don't give a shit. My only goal is getting Natalie home," Will reiterated, trying to get through to the boy.

Cam silently nodded without diverting his attention away from his shoes. He lurched over and opened his duffle bag. He withdrew a pack of cigarettes. Opening the pack, he pulled out a cigarette, and lit it.

Will steeled himself as he watched the lighter ignite the cigarette. He hated the smell of cigarette smoke. He fucking hated it. But he was eager to get Cameron to talk. He was somewhat surprised that he smoked. Cameron looked like the stereotypical teen athlete; he simply presumed that he wouldn't be a smoker.

"You shouldn't smoke. It'll kill you," he mumbled.

"Yeah, I know. I only have one every once in a while," Cam explained.

He knew that his warning fell on deaf ears. Teenagers were invincible. Nothing could touch them. Bad things only happened to other people. He gave him a moment to enjoy the rush of nicotine. Cameron closed his eyes tightly, exhaling the plume of smoke. Will watched the smoke dissipate, briefly thinking of his mother.

"She broke up with me," Cam finally answered, looking at the ember of his cigarette.

"Did she give you an explanation?"

"No. She sent me a text late at night; I was already asleep."

"What did the text say?"

"Something like, she was sorry, but it just wasn't working out, blah, blah, blah," he explained, jabbing his cigarette in the air, emphasizing his point.

"Was it because of the pills?" he asked plainly.

"I had heard the rumors; that she was a pill popper, that she had been to rehab. But she never *ever* used in front of me. Maybe it was because she knew that I don't fuck around with pills; I'm just not into that scene. When we were together, she didn't ever look fucked up," Cam said, shaking his head.

"So, if you two traveled in different circles, how did you meet each other?"

"We're in the same English class. We had to work on an assignment together."

"Did you ever try to talk to her about the break-up?"

"She stopped coming to school after she sent the message. I did send quite a few messages to her, asking to talk, asking if I had done something wrong, but she never replied. I called a bunch of times, but the calls went straight to voicemail," he said, shaking his head.

"Were you two sexually active?" Will asked abruptly.

Cameron visibly blanched at the invasive question. The question surprised even Will himself. He didn't even consciously realize that the question had been asked until he heard his own voice utter the question. It wasn't until later that he realized the significance of the question.

Cameron fidgeted. He took a long pull off of his water bottle. He glared at him.

"I don't care, man. I'm not going to rat you out to your parents. This conversation stays between you and me. I'm just trying to learn more about Natalie. If you know a person, you are able to gauge their movements, their behaviors. And I need to know, so that I can find her. Okay?"

Once again, Cameron dug into his bag, and grabbed another cigarette. He exhaled deeply, blowing the smoke out towards the field. He didn't want to push too hard on Cameron. He needed the boy to feel comfortable enough to share with him.

"No. We weren't. We fooled around a little bit. Made out under the bleachers, or at the library when no one was around. I honestly didn't care, man. I really cared about her. Everyone thinks that because I'm a jock, that girls are all over me; they're not. I'm shy, man. I'm not good at talking to girls. But, with Natalie, it was easy. It was like a spark. We just, like, connected. She told me that she felt the same way," he said, sighing.

Cameron exhaled heavily. He pulled up his jersey, dabbing the fabric at his eyes. Will decided to change the subject. He allowed a few more moments of silence. Cameron took a few more long drags off of his cigarette.

"Is there a spot that you two frequented? Or any particular place that she liked to go to? Or was there a place that she may have mentioned to you?"

"No. My schedule keeps me pretty busy. I've got practice and games, and homework, and I work for my dad's lawn care company on the weekends. So, we only really got to hang out at school, or at one of our mutual friend's house for a get together, or a party."

He could discern that Cameron was beginning to feel more comfortable talking with him. The somewhat defensive and protective attitude and posture that he had initially exhibited had begun to soften.

"Is she a big partier?"

"No way. When she came back from rehab, I never once saw her take anything! If we were at a party, she would nurse a single beer the entire fucking night," he said emphatically.

"Did she tell you anything about her addiction or rehab?"

"She didn't really like to talk about it. She just basically told me, you know, she had developed a problem with pills, and had to go to rehab. She only agreed to be with me on the strict condition that I didn't use drugs of any kind. I told her, you know, that's not a problem. Like I said, I don't fuck around with pills," he stated vehemently.

"That was it? Nothing about who she got the drugs from or why she started taking them?"

"Uh, no. Not really. She told me that the first pill she ever took was Adderall. She's in AP; her friends in AP had started taking them because they helped them study longer. She took them for exams, but she didn't like the way it made her feel, so she stopped taking them after exams were done," he said, scoping out the area; ensuring that there were no eavesdroppers nearby.

"But she never mentioned anything about taking opiates?"

"Nope. In all honesty, I got the vibe from her that that had been a dark part of her life, that she was, like, done with. She always looked really sad whenever she talked about it," Cam said hoarsely, starting to tear up again.

"So, the topic of pills was off-limits?"

"Yeah. I mean, there was this one time, that kind of rubbed me the wrong way."

"What did she say?" Will asked, his interest peaked.

"It was at a friend's house. They were talking about this wild party that they had been at. There were pills, weed, and booze. I kind of gave my friend a look; like, stop talking about pills, my girlfriend's an addict – what the fuck?! Right? So, later, I was walking her to her house. I apologized for my friend's stupidity, and she said, 'life is so much better on drugs; I miss it so much.' I was fucking speechless."

He allowed another brief moment of silence. So far, Cameron had provided some new insights. However, there was very little that would help him locate her. The boy appeared pensive. Perhaps he was reflecting on his past relationship with Natalie. Will knew that memories, generally speaking, are like a spectre or ghoul; it haunts and pursues those in pain. It feasts on pain. Memory was something best left undisturbed. From what he'd learned so far, Natalie seemed to agree.

"Natalie never talked about running away?"

"Nope. Never."

"Did she mention anything about going to boarding school?"

"Natalie was going to go to boarding school?!" Cam exclaimed, genuinely shocked.

"No. It was just something that she and her parents had been talking about."

Cameron nodded. He looked away, back at the field. He seemed to be digesting this new information.

Based on what Laura, Jocelyn, and Cameron had told him so far: Natalie was quite skilled at compartmentalization. She didn't reveal that she had been threatened with boarding school to her friend or boyfriend, and her parents were unaware of Cameron's existence. Jocelyn and Cameron didn't know who or where she got her drugs from. And, most importantly, she never mentioned that she was thinking of running away. Natalie, it seemed, kept personal information to herself. She shared only the bare minimum.

Natalie is an addict. An addict that was clearly using again. There had to be a source. He couldn't see a girl like Natalie heading to the rough part of the city, buying from a hardcore street dealer. She clearly bought from someone she knew, or someone she went to school with. As Jocelyn mentioned, everyone was using; it was an opioid epidemic. It wouldn't be inconceivable that a teenager from a wealthy family, in a good neighborhood, would sell drugs. The dealer, the wannabe gangster (like they were some sort of badass), would gain popularity and extra money.

"Do you know any kids in school that sell pills?"

Cameron informed him that there were a number of small-time recreational dealers at the school. Most of these were stoners, white Rastafarians; the THC had somehow convinced them that the pigment of their skin had darkened. Due to the increased attention of the police, and the harsh prison sentences for dealing opiates, there was only one kid in the entire school that dealt strictly pills.

Will had noticed the disgust on Cameron's face as he had described this kid. Cameron had made it abundantly clear that not a single person in the school (faculty or student) liked this asshole. Not only was this kid scum, he seemed to have no shame. He embraced the greasy and slimy nature of a dealer of poison.

"What's this kid's name?"

"Alain," Cameron replied, rolling his eyes.

"What does he look like?"

Cameron, once again reaching into his duffle bag, pulled out his phone. He tapped away on his screen for a moment, then passed the phone over to him. It was Alain's Instagram account. Will, to his surprise, recognized Alain. It took a moment for it to click into place. His stomach turned, and his teeth clenched.

Dumb fucking luck. Alain was the kid who worked at the pharmacy. He was certain of it. There were a number of pictures of him posing like he was a badass gangster (of course). He even spotted a picture of him posing in front of a brick wall with a gun (clearly fake) held sideways, aimed at the camera. What. A. Douche. He continued to scroll down and saw a selfie which was clearly taken at the pharmacy. He was holding a price gun, while his other hand was running through his hair. The picture was captioned, "*Sigh, Mondays.*"

He passed the phone back over to Cameron.

"He's quite the...character," Will said, holding back worse insults.

"He's a douchebag. No one likes him. He's fucked in the head. I honestly feel like he's going to grow up to become a serial killer or something," Cam responded, nodding.

As this *Alain* didn't have any friends, he had asked Cameron if he knew he could find him. He did not want to go back to that pharmacy. The fact that the stoner manager had not actually called the cops was a miracle. He didn't want to push his luck. Luckily, everyone knew where Alain hung out; he had made a point of making it well known, so that any and all clients knew where he could be found.

• • • •

Alain hung out at the skatepark. He couldn't actually skateboard, he just liked hanging around the people that did. This fact reeked of desperation. For a kid that had no friends at school (because of his odious profession), he clearly wanted these skater kids to like him. Will had never met this kid, but he could tell that *Alain* most likely offered the kids drugs in return for friendship.

Alain. He hated that name. It was a name that signified two things: the parents were arrogant, obnoxious assholes, and so was their kid.

He watched from his parked car. The park was full of kids skating; doing tricks and wiping out. He couldn't see Alain from his position. He would have to head into the park.

•   •   •

Will had skated, briefly, as a teen. However, as he had begun to progress to tricks, he had witnessed something that caused him to abandon skating entirely. He had begun to grind down handrails. Nothing too dangerous, not at first. He made up his mind to grind down a popular handrail which descended steeply down a series of concrete steps. However, there was a teen in front of him. He and a friend were recording his stunts. Will agreed to wait patiently as they prepared for the trick.

The teen mounted his board and built up speed as he headed towards the railing. Unfortunately, the boy was going too fast, and as he jumped onto the rail, the momentum propelled him rapidly down the rail. He struggled to maintain his equilibrium. Half way through the descent, he lost his balance and fell. He landed on his left foot, the momentum carrying him forward, causing it to snap and jut out at an angle. As he fell, in pain, to the ground, his face cushioned his fall. As the fallen teen rolled over, he exposed the wreckage of his face.

The damaged cartilage of his nose, the missing teeth, and the copious amount of blood engulfing his face, as well as the boy's screams caused Will to reconsider his hobby. Seeing the fallen teen's leg; the pale bone jutting out of his skin, sealed the decision for him. He could envision nothing as senseless as destroying his body for a stupid hobby. He had no desire to pursue skating as a career, and therefore, the decision to quit was simple; he had no regrets.

•   •   •

He made his way into the park. He didn't need to look at the expressions of the skaters to know that he stuck out like a sore thumb. He was an adult. He didn't dress like a skater. He didn't have a board. He was exhausted, and his appearance resonated this sensation. The bags underneath his eyes were so deep that they felt oppressively heavy; as if they weighed upon his head, forcing it to hang limply down. It was a struggle just to keep his head up and remain fully alert. His white shirt was missing a couple buttons and was liberally stained with coffee on the collar.

Despite the obvious glares and curious glances, he continued to slog through the park. Some kids were huddled far off to the side of the park. Based on the aroma emanating from the group, they were clearly smoking weed. Alain, however, was not among them.

He continued on with his task. He kept his head on a swivel; scanning the nooks and crannies of the park. He had nearly finished scanning the entirety of the park. He was beginning to fret that this trip had been in vain, that he would leave empty-handed, and be back right where he started.

As he neared the perimeter of the park, he approached a tall fence. The fence separated the skate park from an adjoining basketball court. He could see that while there was no one actually playing basketball, there were a few teenagers clustered together on the benches. What garnered his attention was the lone figure sitting, legs crossed, on the border of the court.

It was Alain. He was wearing headphones, bobbing his head along to the beat of the music. He was hunched over, sketching into a notepad on his lap, seemingly oblivious to both his surroundings and the people around him.

Will paused outside the court. He was assessing the situation.

He couldn't wait for Alain to leave the court. He was simply too fucking exhausted. He needed sleep. Every part of his body was yearning for rest. He had run out of caffeine hours ago. He could quickly run to a store and pick up coffee, or some of that poison in a can that was euphemistically referred to as "energy drink".

But it had taken too long to dredge up this lead. He didn't want to leave the park and risk losing the kid. And as the pharmacy was out of bounds, his options were severely limited. He took a deep breath, exhaled, and then entered the basketball court.

• • •

"When was the next time you saw your father?"

"I think I was about ten. It had been at least four or five years since the last time I saw him."

"What happened?"

"It was like the first time. I was in my room reading. My mom called me into the kitchen and told me that Robert was coming over to spend the day with me. Robert? She mentioned his name like he was a regular feature in our lives, like I had just seen him the day before, and not years ago."

"How did you react?"

"I didn't want to go. I told her so. The shithole bar was still a vivid memory in my mind. Mom told me not to worry, that we wouldn't be going to that place. I was going to help him do some work at his building. This was the first time it was mentioned that he owned a building, that he had money."

"Were you upset?"

"No. Kind of. It was a complicated situation. I was young, but I could tell that my mom didn't want to talk about who Robert was. The fact that he was my father was something that was left unsaid, but lurked just beneath the surface."

"Did you ever crave a father figure as a child?"

"Not really. It's like they say, you can't miss what you've never had. It wasn't until I started attending school that I even realized that most kids had both a mom and a dad."

"That must have been very confusing for you as a child."

"I remember coming home from kindergarten one day, I was confused. I asked my mom where my dad was; I had heard the other kids at school talking about their mom and dad. Some kids even had a dad pick them up from school."

"What did she say?"

"She looked shocked. Like she had been dreading this day. I don't remember exactly what she said, but she basically made it clear that he wasn't in the picture. Then she served me some ice cream, which was intended to take my mind off of the matter. It must have got to her, though."

"Why do you say that?"

"Well, it was shortly after that incident that Robert showed up and took me to the bar."

"I see. So, what happened next?"

"Robert was supposed to show up after lunch. He was late. I remember that. Mom was pissed. When he finally showed up, he acted like nothing was wrong. I remember that Mom scolded him tactfully, saying something like, 'Oh, good. You're here. I was beginning to worry.' Robert didn't even respond. He hadn't changed that much since the last time that I saw him. He had a few flecks of grey in his hair. He looked at me for a moment and then mumbled, 'C'mon, let's get to work.' That was it. I said goodbye to Mom and followed him outside to his truck.

"He still had the same truck. We traveled in silence. Again. It must have been the first time in my life that I ever experienced déjà vu. He kept his eyes on the road, while I looked outside the passenger side window. It was the epitome of awkward silence. Then, out of nowhere, I hear him mumble, 'You've gotten taller since last time.'

"'You've gotten taller?' That astute assessment was all that he had to offer!? My mom had raised me not to talk back to adults, but I remember thinking, well it has been, like, five years."

"What did you say?"

"I just said something simple, like, yeah. He just nodded his head. He turned up the volume on the radio and then welcomed the silence once again. It felt like hours before the silence was broken. Robert leaned forward and turned the radio down a tad, then settled back in his seat. 'You any good with your hands?' I told him that I had helped my mom build a bookshelf and a night stand. Robert snorted and laughed. 'I guess we'll find out,' he grunted.

"A few minutes later, we arrived at our stop. He pulled into the parking lot of an apartment complex. He opened the glove box and took out a big set of keys. He got out of the truck without saying anything. I followed him out. I followed closely behind him. We approached the entrance, and he pulled out the big set of keys and unlocked the door. I followed him into the building. He didn't even look back to make sure that I was behind him.

"We walked down a few flights of stairs. We got to the basement. Robert approached this metal door marked boiler room. I froze in my tracks. I had just seen that movie, A Nightmare on Elm Street. I had watched it on tv, late at night, after my mom had gone to sleep. I'd been having nightmares for days. The terrifying scenes from the boiler room flashed in my mind. Robert finally stopped and looked back at me. 'C'mon, kid. We got work to do.'

"I took a deep breath, and swallowed hard, like I was choking down my fear. I followed, nervously, behind him. I remember it was loud. I was anxiously looking around, certain that I would spot Freddy Kreuger hiding behind one of the pipes. Robert grabbed a tool belt, and a toolbox, and then breezed passed me, out into the hallway. Thankful that we were abandoning the horrors of the boiler room, I chased after him.

"Once outside, he put on his tool belt, and handed me the toolbox. 'Carry this for me.' It was heavy. Really heavy. I didn't want to complain, as I remembered his mocking remark from the truck. I accepted the challenge, and using both hands, carried the toolbox along with us. Robert took out a small notepad, examining a to-do list.

"'Right. Apartment seventeen; leaking pipe underneath the sink.' I followed him back up the flights of stairs. I remember my arms were shaking from the strain of the toolbox. I was terrified that I would drop it. Then, as if reading my mind, Robert grunted, 'Don't drop that toolbox,' not even looking back at me.

"We finally made it to the apartment. Robert knocked on the door. No one responded to the knock. 'Fuck it,' Robert said, under his breath. He once again retrieved his keys and unlocked the door. The occupants weren't home.

"'Take off your shoes,' he instructed, although he didn't take off his boots. I followed him into the kitchen. He pulled open the cupboard under the sink. There was a pail inside, catching the dripping water from the leaking pipe above. Robert ran his hand underneath the leak. 'Just needs to be tightened,' he grumbled. Robert motioned for me to put the toolbox on the ground. He opened the box and withdrew a large wrench. Looking at me, he said, 'Lefty-loosey, righty-tighty.' Then he handed me the wrench. I crawled under the sink.

"Robert showed me how to put the wrench onto the pipe and turn the valve so that it would create a seal. After a number of turns, the leak finally stopped. I beamed inwardly with pride. I looked back at Robert. 'See? Not so tough, right?' he asked. I nodded in the affirmative. He took a pencil out and scratched a line onto his notepad. 'Alright, grab the toolbox. We're going to apartment three.'

"I picked up the toolbox. My muscles were starting to ache, but I couldn't bring myself to complain. It was a matter of personal pride; I didn't want to look weak in front of him. We made our way to the next apartment. Robert knocked on the door. This time the resident was home and let us in. The resident who spoke broken English, showed us to the bathroom. She indicated that the toilet wouldn't flush.

"Robert simply nodded, took off the lid from the tank and peered inside. 'Chain fell off,' he muttered, in his usual gruff voice. He fiddled around inside the tank for a moment, then satisfied that the chain was reattached, he placed the lid back on the tank. Once again, I picked up the toolbox and we left the apartment. 'You figure that they would've at least checked inside the tank before calling me; common sense, right?' Uncertain of how to respond, I just smiled and forced a laugh.

"The afternoon went on like that. We went to apartments, making small repairs. Very little was said between us. By the time we finished at the last apartment, my arms were throbbing from the weight of the toolbox. Back in the boiler room, the impending physical relief from returning the toolbox outweighed any childish fear of hidden monsters."

"So, the two of you worked, making these repairs and neither of you made an attempt to start a conversation?"

"No. I was nervous around him. I was a very shy child. I was raised to respect adults, so I just simply followed his instructions. I mean, at first, I didn't want to be there. I was essentially just performing a job, waiting until he took me back home. As the day progressed, I'll admit that I started to enjoy it somewhat; we were fixing something that was broken. It filled my childish mind with pride."

"But it wasn't a feeling of pride that a child would typically feel in helping their father?"

"No. I had noticed that Robert and I had similar noses, and our eyes were the same color. But I was a kid. It didn't click; I had no idea that this was indicative of familial relations. Robert, on his part, was treating me as somewhat of a minor nuisance or inconvenience. But he never outright treated me with disdain."

"Weren't you curious as to why your mom sent you away with him?"

"At that point, I figured that he was a friend of my mom's."

"Right. So, what happened next?"

"I remember that at some point, we were pulling weeds. Robert looked at his watch. In his typical gruff manner, he said, 'Time to go.' We went back to his truck. It was another silent ride back to my house. I was tired, so I didn't mind. I could feel myself drifting off to sleep, as I looked out the window, watching the surroundings pass by.

"When we got to my house, he pulled over to the curb. He shifted the car into park. We sat there in our usual silence for a moment. I looked at him, and uncertain of what else to say, I said, 'Bye.' He just nodded his head in affirmation. I got out of the truck, and he pulled away immediately."

"How did your mother react to this particular outing?"

"Not like the last time. I guess she knew that this was what Robert had planned for the day. Maybe she figured that I would pick up some new skills, I don't know. She was waiting in the kitchen for me. As soon as I got inside, she came over to me *and gave me a hug. She looked somewhat sad. I remember that she asked me how the day had gone. She looked depressed, and I didn't want to upset her anymore, so I told her that it had been fun, that we had fixed stuff. Mom just smiled. Then she mistakenly let something slip."*

"What did she say?"

"After I told her that I had had fun, she gave me another hug. As we parted, she said, 'I suppose a boy needs his father.' She had said it so nonchalantly that it hadn't even registered in my mind."

"That was it? She didn't say anything else?"

"That was it. As far as I can remember, that was the only time that she ever referred openly to Robert as my father."

"I see. Did your mother ever talk to you about what happened between them?"

"No. She didn't like talking about it. It was off-limits. Mom didn't like being pushed into talking about personal or private things."

"Like mother, like son."

"Very funny."

•　　•　　•

The gate let out a metallic screech as he pushed through the entrance. Will was momentarily concerned, worried that this would draw attention to himself, but no one seemed to notice. The boys on the court seemed too stoned to care. As for Alain, he was still unaware of his surroundings; listening to music on his headphones, drawing (what he could only imagine was disgustingly shitty art – hormonally charged depictions of women with unrealistic dimensions; large-breasted and tiny-waisted women).

He slowly approached the sitting drug dealer at a slow pace. He didn't want to scare him by approaching too quickly. Walking at a normal pace, he approached Alain, attempting to appear as non-threatening or imposing as possible.

He was standing before Alain. There was no recognition from the teenager. The dealer was more than likely stoned. Sighing, he lightly tapped Alain's shoe with his foot. There was still no reaction from the kid. Exasperated, he prodded him with his foot again.

"Fuck off! I'm drawing, man," Alain mumbled, without looking up from his work.

Will was beginning to seethe. Taking a quick glance around the court, he ascertained that the occupants of the court were oblivious of the activity going on around them. These kids were more than likely all under the influence of something. This assuaged his concerns.

He drew his foot back, winding up, and punted Alain's foot. The kid dropped his drawing pad and fell back onto the cement court.

"What the fuck, man?!"

Alain tried to gather himself. He ripped off his headphones and abruptly raised himself up to a standing position. The rage immediately vanished from his face as he made eye contact with Will. In a split second, Alain's face shifted from anger and outrage, to recognition, to fear.

"You remember me?"

"Yeah, no shit, I remember you," Alain spat, stepping away from him.

"I'm not here to cause trouble. I don't give a fuck how you make your money. I'm just looking for someone. She's probably one of your...clients."

"Yeah, well, I'm not, like, in the habit of giving out that kind of information."

"You're not listening. I'm not a cop. I'm not here to bust you. I honestly couldn't care less about you."

"Yeah, well, that's kind of exactly what a cop would say, right?"

"For fuck's sake! Do you think a cop would've pulled that shit at the pharmacy?!"

"I've heard some cops get up to some dirty shit, man."

He was losing what little reserves of patience he had. He was gritting his teeth. He was resisting the overwhelming urge to begin beating this poseur into compliance. He decided to resort to bribery.

"How about this? How about money for information?" Will asked, baring his teeth in a type of forced smile.

"I'm no snitch, man," Alain said, acting like the tough gangster.

"Look, kid. You've got two options: take my money, give me the information. Or, you can keep acting like some wannabe, badass gangster, which we both know you aren't. If you choose the second option, we'll find out how tough you really are," he said, staring daggers at Alain.

Alain puffed out his chest; trying to call his bluff.

"Kid, I will hurt you. This is not a threat. I'm not trying to scare or intimidate you. I'm simply stating facts. It is in your best interest to take my money and tell me where the girl is."

He held out a handful of twenties. Alain swiped them out of his palm, without acknowledgement or thanks.

"Girl? What girl?" Alain asked, genuinely confused.

"Are you fucking kidding me?! Is your brain that fucked from drugs?! The girl that I came looking for at the pharmacy, Natalie Haynesworth."

"What do you want Natalie for?" he asked, defensively.

"She ran away from home. I'm an investigator. I was hired to find her and bring her back to her parents so she can get some help."

"Natalie went missing?" Alain looked perplexed.

This was becoming stressful. He couldn't determine if Alain was fucking with him; playing dumb, or if he was genuinely shocked to learn that she was missing.

"So, you know her?"

"Yeah. She used to buy from me. She was a, uh, preferred customer."

"Preferred customer? What does that mean?"

"She bought a lot of shit. I gave her deals sometimes."

"Why her?"

"Look, junkies have no customer loyalty; I've got to do whatever I can to keep them coming back," Alain said, shrugging his shoulders.

"You don't feel guilty about that? Natalie is an addict! It's a sickness."

Will was shocked at himself. He didn't know where that outrage came from.

"Hey, man. If I didn't do it, she would just go to somebody else."

The statement reverberated within the core of his being. Will had made similar remarks to those who were outraged at what he did for a living. He told himself that he was nothing like Alain. What he did was not illegal; he was licensed. He didn't deal poison to addicts. He didn't prey on the vulnerable. He reassured himself of these distinguishing factors. But he didn't know if he believed himself.

"When is the last time you saw her?"

"Shit, man, I haven't seen her in a while. She went to rehab; and when she came back, she made it very clear that she wasn't interested in fucking around with pills anymore."

"That changed?"

"Yeah. She showed up at school one day, she looked like shit. She wasn't dope sick. She just looked...rough."

"She wanted to buy?"

"Yeah. At first, I said no. But then she said she would go to somebody else. Look, I know what people think about me, but there are dealers that are much worse than me. I honestly didn't want her dealing with them."

Yes. The drug dealer with a heart of gold.

"Then what happened?"

"It didn't take too long for her to go off the rails again. Her parents sent her back to rehab."

"I know this part, move it along," he said, interrupting him.

"Let me talk, man. Shit."

Will was letting his exhaustion and impatience get to him. He forced his jaw to unclench. He took another set of deep breaths. And then swallowed his pride.

"Sorry. Go ahead."

"So, she got back. Same story; said she was done with all this shit. And, to her credit, she didn't come around."

"I sense a *but* coming," he remarked dryly.

"Yeah, but. She came back a couple weeks after her second stint in rehab. She looked like shit. Again. She gave me a handful of bills and bought the majority of my shit."

"What specifically did she buy?"

"OxyContin."

"How much?"

"A few hundred bucks worth," Alain answered, looking down at his shoes.

He churned inwardly.

What. A. Piece. Of. Shit.

"How did she seem?"

"Huh? What do you mean?"

He once again clenched his teeth.

"I mean, did she seem anxious, depressed, or dope sick? Was she scared?"

"Nah, man. She looked like shit, like she hadn't slept. But she was calm."

"When is the last time that you heard from her?"

"That day. I haven't seen or heard from her since then."

"Is there a way that she can get in touch with you? Like texting, or messaging online?"

"Shit, no. That's rule number one: no phones. Don't you watch tv? Cops can track you with phones, listen to your phone calls, all that kind of shit. My clients gotta deal with me face-to-face," he said, as if he were some brilliant drug lord.

Will handed the kid his card. Alain looked at it distrustfully, making no attempt at accepting the card. He took a step closer to Alain; invading his personal space. He looked him directly in the eye.

"You are going to take this card. You are going to call the number on the card, if and when she gets in touch with you. If she contacts you, and you don't tell me, I will find out. And when I find out, I am going to be very angry. So angry that I will divert all my energy to tracking you down. And, the longer that I have to look for you, the more pissed off I will get. And when I find you, I will break every fucking bone in your useless body. Do we understand one another?"

Alain took the card.

• • •

He was back in his car. Parked.

He was still riding the waves of his spiked adrenaline from his encounter with Alain.

He was pissed that he still hadn't heard back from Thomas.

He called his number.

Straight to voicemail.

He had one more stop to make.

Well, two more stops. He needed coffee first.

• • •

The firm in which Thomas was employed resided near the top of one of the city's tallest skyscrapers. It was comprised of glass and steel. It was the sort of tower which sent a clear and unmistakable message; that it was a building for the elite – a safe place in which to hide the secrets of the rich and fabulous.

He approached the doorman. Luckily, it was the usual doorman. This guy had let him in the building the last time he had visited. The memory of this visit played vividly in his mind. The last time he had been here, Thomas had introduced him to Herman. Herman needed an investigator; Thomas referred Herman to Will, as Thomas had routinely hired him for assistance on his cases.

The doorman nodded at him as he opened the door of the grand entryway. He could tell that he remembered him somewhat, but couldn't exactly recall who he was. He had this effect on people. He didn't stand out to people. At least, he tried not to.

He went to the elevator. Pressing the up button, he looked at the mass of people, both men and women, hurriedly carrying folders and suitcases, their gaze locked intently upon the phones in their hands.

Entering the elevator, he pressed the button for the thirty-third floor. He felt the familiar tingling sensation within his stomach as the elevator ascended, climbing to its destination. There were others behind him (they were going to higher floors) who were all fixated on their phones or tablets. Will rolled his eyes.

As the elevator arrived at his floor, he was overcome with a juvenile impulse. An impulse that he could not resist; not today. As the doors opened, he let out a silent and noxious fart. He quickly departed the area with a broad smile on his face.

He walked down a series of long hallways. The offices on either side were observable as they were screened behind glass. There were embossed labels on the doors. The names of the departments were delicately (and expensively) etched into the glass.

What a bunch of rich assholes, he thought. This is what you get, when you work for a series of rich assholes – you become a rich asshole. You can't resist it. It just rubs off on you. It permeates your very being. It seeps into your pores.

He continued following the route to Thomas's office. He opened the glass partition and approached the secretary. She was rapidly tapping on her keyboard. The tapping ceased as she became aware of Will's presence.

"Hello, how may I help you?" she inquired with a professional smile.

"Hello, my name is William Miller. I'm here to see Thomas," he said, smiling back, trying to make nice.

"Do you have an appointment?" she asked as she scanned the appointment book.

"I do."

She scanned the page with her long-manicured fingernail. A slight frown began to form on her face.

"I'm sorry, sir. I can't seem to find you anywhere in his appointments for today," she said with a faux apologetic face.

"Oh, really? That silly fool. He must've forgotten to pencil me in. Between you and me, I think he has developed a bit of a problem," Will explained, as he mimed the chugging of a glass.

"Oh?" she responded, confused.

"With booze. He's got a problem with booze. He makes plans with his best friend while he's plastered and then just plum forgets."

Her jaw dropped momentarily. She quickly managed to compose herself.

"I see," she quietly responded.

"Yeah, that's actually what I need to see him about. You see, the other night, he got really shitfaced and then tried to drive my car. If that wasn't bad enough, he couldn't see where he was going. He had his underwear on his head. Don't ask, it's a long story. Anyways, he drove it into a light pole. Trashed the front end of my car. He said it was okay if I stopped by to pick up a cheque to pay for the damages."

"I see. It's just that I'm under strict instructions not to let anyone in who doesn't have an appointment."

He positioned himself level with her desk. He leaned over the desk, looking into her eyes. He clasped his hands together, in a begging posture.

"Look, I don't want to embarrass my friend in front of his colleagues. And, most importantly, I don't want him to get into trouble with his boss. I just need to pick up the cheque. It's imperative. You see, I need my car for my job. So it needs to get fixed as quickly as possible."

"Alright. But if you get into trouble with him, you have to tell him that you snuck in," she whispered to him.

"Absolutely. It's a deal."

•   •   •

The secretary ushered him past her desk and motioned for him to continue on down the hall.

"It's the third door on the left," the secretary instructed.

"Oh, he moved offices?" he asked, perplexed.

"Yes. Since he made partner, he got a bigger office; one of the perks. He didn't tell you?" she asked, distracted.

"No. No, he didn't. He failed to mention it," he answered, masking his escalating stress.

He recognized the office. Although, the interior had been redecorated since the last time that he had been here, it was unmistakable. This was Herman's old office. The curse of Herman began to throb. The pain spreading through his body like a cancer.

The details of their initial meeting began to play in his mind. It was vivid. It was an out-of-body experience; but it was more than that. When his memory overtook him like this, he felt like he was some sort of time traveler. He barely managed to drop into a chair before he was completely overtaken by the past.

Thomas had called him to the office.

His cheque was ready.

Thomas had had a client who was going through a messy and contentious divorce. The wife, Emma, was fighting over every single aspect of the divorce. She had filed for dissolution on the grounds of emotional and physical abuse. She had even laid charges of assault against her husband, though the client was adamant that he had never laid a hand on her. Thomas needed Will to find something that would make the wife more amenable.

After some digging into her background (she hadn't covered her tracks; it was pathetic, really), he had found it easily. It turned out that not only had the wife been married (twice) before, she was a gold digger. The first marriage had lasted a little over a year. The second marriage, less than a year.

Each divorce garnered her a large lump sum payment. Both of her ex-husbands, having been coerced, conned, and manipulated into not signing a prenuptial agreement, paid dearly. The first marriage, the wife filed for divorce due to infidelity. However, after speaking to the ex-husband, it became clear that it was a set-up.

This first husband had been celebrating. It was something to do with a business deal. He and his colleagues were at an expensive and exclusive club. He had had a bit too much to drink; he was drunk, but not drunk enough to lose consciousness.

When he woke up the following morning, there was a woman asleep next to him. She was naked.

His wife, who had been out of town visiting friends, just so happened to arrive home; finding her husband in bed – with another woman, who happened to be an escort. Convenient wasn't an adequate enough term to define the situation.

For his wife, it didn't matter that the cheating husband couldn't remember ordering the call girl, or having sex with her. He had kept no secrets from his beautiful (not to mention, much younger) wife. He had told her of his predilection for escorts, and strippers. That part of his life was over, he had assured her.

The husband's excuse; that he didn't or couldn't remember his infidelity, mattered little in the pending divorce. Rather, his excuse made him appear pathetic. Even his own lawyer had privately asked him why he was clinging to this facade. There was no plausible argument to defend his situation. He was the child, caught with his hand in the cookie jar. There was nothing that he could say or do.

He paid.

The second marriage and divorce were eerily similar to the first.

The second time around, the happy couple had held a party at their opulent home. Hubby had a couple of drinks; witnesses testified to that effect (but again not enough to get blackout drunk). It was after the guests had left, Emma (the gold-digging wife) alleged that an argument ensued and the husband punched her in the face. She (of course) had pictures of the bruising on her face.

Of course, the husband didn't remember the argument, and he certainly didn't remember hitting his beloved wife. In fact, he was certain that he hadn't. He had only had a few drinks. He wasn't a cheap drunk. He remembered feeling groggy and lightheaded. He feared someone had drugged him. However, much like the first husband, his past came back to haunt him.

He had admitted to Emma, shortly after they began dating, that he had been married before. He admitted that he had hit his wife during a heated argument. It was the first and last time that he had ever done so. He was remorseful. He attended both couples' therapy and anger management. However, the relationship had run its course. This hadn't led directly to their future divorce, but it certainly hadn't stopped its demise.

He swore to her that he would never, ever do anything like that again. He most certainly would never hurt Emma. He swore his undying love to her. They married four months after they met.

Emma threatened to file for divorce on the grounds of spousal abuse. Emma had her husband over a barrel, and he knew it. If he fought it, the matter would become a matter of public record. He couldn't afford to have his image or his reputation tarnished, and he couldn't afford to lose his job. He had no choice but to concede to her outrageous demands. He signed the divorce papers.

He paid.

• • • • •

Emma was an amateur.

She may have had been able to easily manipulate men, but she was shit at covering her tracks. Emma hadn't bothered to hide behind an alias or an assumed identity. Will easily found records of her previous marriages/divorces. This, in turn, led him to contact her ex-husbands.

Both of the exes wanted revenge. They were both more than willing to offer depositions regarding their relationship with Emma. Their testimony would be damning. They hadn't even needed their testimony. As soon as Thomas mentioned the names of her exes, her face blanched.

She realized that their positions had effectively been reversed; she was the one over a barrel now. She dropped the charges of assault. She granted the client's terms of divorce; she got nothing. In addition, the client was granted a restraining order.

The client was thrilled. More importantly, this effectively brought Thomas to the attention of his bosses. They were happier than the client. In fact, they were so pleased that this win had put Thomas on track to becoming a partner in the firm.

Thomas's success led to guaranteed work for Will in the future. Thomas didn't hesitate to point out, the firm was willing to pay him "the big bucks." Provided that he continued to perform, his fee, Thomas assured him, would continue to balloon.

• • • • •

Rather than mail him his cheque for his help in the Emma matter, Thomas wanted him to come to the firm. Will was annoyed. He had told him to just mail the fucking thing. Thomas insisted that he come to the firm, that he had another job for him. That the job was for one of the founding partners. This was a big deal. Thomas had vouched for Will. He needed to come to a brief meeting. He would consider it a favor.

He reluctantly agreed to Thomas's request.

He made it to the firm.

Thomas was waiting for him by the elevator.

"Thanks for coming, man. I owe you one," Thomas said, as the doors closed.

"What's the rush? More importantly, where is my cheque?"

Thomas reached into his suit jacket and pulled out an envelope. Will grabbed it out of his hands and swiftly put it into his jacket pocket.

"It's a big deal. This'll help both of us, Will."

"Oh?" he asked, bored.

"Yeah, man. It's not a job for the firm. It's a private and personal matter for my boss," he explained, excited.

"And I need to be here because?" he responded, his irritation clearly visible.

"My boss is very security-conscious. He doesn't want to discuss it outside the firm or on the phone. He wants to meet you first."

"What's this prick's name?"

"Herman. If you do a good job, both of our careers are getting a huge boost."

"Herman? Sounds like a pipsqueak."

"He's a big deal. A tough-as-nails lawyer," Thomas insisted.

"With a name like Herman, I guess you'd have to be tough."

"Will, I'm begging you; do not be a smartass. I need this to go well. I want to make partner. I'll owe you, please."

"Fine, fine. Fuck."

Once out of the elevator, Thomas directed him through the hallways to an office. Thomas knocked on the door.

"Come in," a voice shouted through the door.

Will hated Herman on sight.

He looked like the stereotypical rich asshole. He had an aura of entitlement. Despite the fact that Will had come here to help him, Herman looked at him like he was a nuisance. He quickly glanced at Thomas, who was staring at him with pleading eyes – don't say anything.

"Herman, this is William Miller," Thomas said, making the introductions.

"Hello. Nice to meet you," Will said, grinding his teeth.

"Charmed. Sit down, I've got a lot of work to do today," Herman said as he shuffled papers.

Thomas shot him another look.

They sat down in expensive chairs on the opposite side of the desk, facing Herman.

"So, Thomas tells me that you're quite the gifted investigator; that you helped win the case," Herman said, still looking at his paperwork.

"She was an amateur. She was good at manipulating men, which isn't that hard to do when you're a beautiful woman, and most men seem to think with their cock. She didn't know how to cover her tracks."

Thomas shot him another glare. Will shrugged his shoulders in response.

"You make a good point. All women are manipulators and liars, which is why I always counsel my clients to sign a prenup," Herman responded, finally looking directly at him.

It was his turn to look at Thomas. Thomas, however, seemed to miss this glance.

"As I mentioned, Thomas raved about your performance. I think you can help me. I would like to hire you."

"What's the job?"

"Before we get into that, I want to emphasize that what is said in this room stays between us. This is a personal issue, and I do not want or need anyone else in the office to know. If either of you repeat anything, and I mean anything, I will use every legal mechanism at my disposal to ruin your lives. Are we clear?" Herman asked, trying to appear threatening.

"Herman, it's cool. You know you can trust me, and I vouch for Will. He's the epitome of discretion," Thomas explained, before Will could open his mouth and wreak havoc.

Herman looked at both of them and nodded. He picked up a picture of a beautiful woman. It was clearly his wife. Will assumed that it was Herman's wealth and not his personality that snagged such a gorgeous woman. Herman then placed the framed picture facedown on his desk. As if he were protecting her from the difficult subject matter that was about to be discussed.

"I fear that my wife is unfaithful. I need you to follow her, see if my fears are unfounded. If she is cheating on me, I want proof. You understand? Pictures or video. I want that bitch caught in the act, okay?" Herman spat, the veins bulging on his forehead.

"Understood," Will responded, his hands gripping the armrests of his chair.

"Good, here is your retainer. Money is no object. I will pay you a generous fee when the job is completed," Herman said, ripping a cheque from his chequebook and sliding it across the desk.

It was clear from his tone and demeanor that the meeting was over. They both stood and excused themselves. The meeting had taken, at most, five minutes. It was long enough to fill him with loathing for Herman.

"Is your boss okay? He seems kind of fucked in the head," he said, as Thomas walked him to the elevators.

"Yeah, don't worry about it. He's always that way. He's very intense. He's got the reputation of a bull dog in court. It's all just bravado and male posturing; he just likes to seem like a tough guy."

"He's solid?"

"Absolutely, Will. This will be good for both of us. Our careers are on the rise, man."

•   •   •

Awareness of his surroundings began to form as Will regained some form of consciousness. This was how it happened, when his memories came alive. He wouldn't actually lose consciousness, but he wasn't actually present either. It was as if he were existing on a separate and higher plane of consciousness.

"Hey, buddy, you okay?"

He looked at the direction in which the voice came from. It was Thomas. He was kneeling, looking at him, concerned.

"Will, you there?" Thomas repeated.

"Yeah. Sorry. I guess I sort of zoned out," he replied, his mind still muddled.

"How did you get into my office?" Thomas asked.

"I snuck in," he grumbled.

"You need to make an appointment, Will."

"Yeah. I'll remember that for next time," he muttered sarcastically.

"You look like you need to get some sleep, man," Thomas counseled, as he made his way to his side of the desk and sat down.

"I got bigger concerns."

"Oh?" Thomas asked, typing away on his computer.

"Yeah. Like the missing fucking girl, for one."

Thomas quickly looked up.

"Look, I called my friend, and he still hasn't gotten back to me."

"Call him again. Call him now!" He exclaimed, his voice beginning to rise.

"Will, lower your fucking voice," Thomas whispered.

"Call him, please," he said, his voice suddenly calm.

"He's busy. He'll get back to me as soon as he can. Just chill, man," Thomas said, his hands posed in a pleading gesture.

"I can't figure it out," he said, changing the topic, "a girl like her, she just doesn't disappear. She wouldn't know how."

He was coming to the end of his rope. Whether this feeling of despair was brought upon by the haunted location he was in, or just mere frustration, he didn't know. Thomas stood up and came around the desk to sit next to him. He turned to face Will.

"Do you think she might be, you know..." Thomas began.

"I fucking hope not," he growled, "but I can't pick up a trace."

"Will, she's a spoiled little rich girl. It's like you said; she can't make it on her own. She'll come home, sooner or later."

He began to look around the office, once again. He took a deep breath and closed his eyes. He clenched his fists. He couldn't ignore the issue any longer.

"So, you moved into the office of the crazed asshole that tried to kill me?"

"Yeah. Will, I'm sorry, I didn't want you to find out like this."

"You should've fucking told me."

"I was going to. You haven't been to the office in a long time."

"And why is that?"

"Will, c'mon."

"Thomas, I knew! I fucking knew something was off about him! And you fucking told me – you fucking vouched for him!"

"Yeah, I admit it; I fucked up! I made a mistake; it was a bad call."

"A mistake?! That is not an acceptable definition of mistake. He killed his wife, tried to kill me, and then blew his fucking brains out in my fucking office!"

"I know!"

"You know?! Tom, just admit it; you got tunnel vision – you saw an opportunity for advancement and that's all you focused on. You dismissed the signs because it didn't matter to you."

"Will, I made partner. Therefore, I got moved to a partner's office," Thomas explained.

"You had to take this one?"

"It was the only available one."

"You couldn't stay where you were?"

"No. It's about appearance."

"Appearance?"

"C'mon, Will, you're seriously pissed about this? You still work in the place where he tried to kill you. I kind of figured that it wouldn't bother you this much."

"What makes you think it doesn't bother me? I was finding pieces of his fucking brain on my fucking ceiling for weeks! I had to clean that shit up!"

"What was I supposed to do?!"

"I've got to go. Call that friend of yours. I've got to get back to work."

"Will," Thomas began.

He ignored him. He rose out of the chair and swiftly exited the office. He didn't look back. Later that evening, he got a text from him.

Thomas: Will, I'm sorry. I'm a dick. I just called my cop buddy. It cost me, but he's going to do some digging. We cool? Drinks?

He didn't respond to his friend's text message.

•   •   •

"I didn't see my dad again until after graduation. Actually, now that I think of it, I didn't see him until I was about to ship off to basic training."

"Do you know why hadn't he come to see you in nearly a decade?"

"Not a clue. After spending that day doing repairs with him, I honestly felt that I would see him again. For whatever reason, he didn't show up. My mom said nothing, and as I've said already, I knew not to ask or say anything."

"Right. So, was this visit planned?"

"No. He literally just showed up."

"What happened?"

"My mom was at work. Robert showed up. He hadn't changed much. He had a bit more grey in his hair, but other than that he looked the same. I remember that when I opened the door, he just stood there. We looked at each other in silence. It felt like an eternity.

"He finally said something. He asked me, 'is your mom home?' I told him that she had gone to work. He grumbled, 'good,' in response. He didn't ask if he could come in. I hoped that he would. We were just standing there like idiots. I finally cracked and asked if he wanted to come in.

"He nodded and came inside. He made his way to the kitchen table and took a seat. 'Does your mom keep liquor in the house?' he asked. I grabbed a glass and put some whiskey and coke in it for him. 'Good boy,' he said in thanks.

"I grabbed a glass and filled it with water from the tap. I then sat down at the chair on the other side of the table."

"What did he want?"

"Not a clue. I'm nearly one hundred percent certain that my mom had guilted him into coming and visiting me. I'm sure that it wasn't too difficult to guilt the bastard. I mean, I was going off to basic training, and there was a war on. I knew that I was going to war.

"Go on."

"I remember that he drained the glass in one greedy gulp. I made him another one. He finished about half of that before he could bring himself to comment, 'So you're going off to war?' I nodded my head. I told him when I was beginning basic training. Then out of nowhere, he said, 'I was in the army and so was my brother. My father was, too.' This was the most personal information that Robert had ever offered."

"He didn't refer to them as your uncle or grandfather?"

"No. I had suspected it years earlier, but seeing him there, sitting across from me; there was no question in my mind that he was my father. Looked exactly like me."

"What else did he say?"

"He said that his older brother had gone over to Bosnia as part of the peace keeping mission. Said that he 'had a hard time' when he came back. He ended up killing himself. That was it. The rest of the conversation was just idle bullshit. Asked me how I liked school, if I had a girlfriend, et cetera."

"You had nothing to ask him?"

"What do you mean?"

"It was one of the rare occasions that you met with your father. You didn't want to ask him why he was never around? Or what happened between him and your mom?"

"No. I was young and very angry with him. I figured that if he wanted to see me, he could've done something to make that happen. I mean he lived in the same city as us, and I never saw him. I just figured that he didn't want to see me. That he didn't want us."

"I see. What happened next?"

"He had another drink. We had more bullshit conversation; talked about football, baseball, that kind of thing. Then he finished the remainder of his drink, stood up abruptly, and shook my hand. Then he made his way to the door, turned around and said, 'Good luck, kid.'"

"That was it?"

"That was it. Our meeting took less than half an hour."

"When was the next time that you saw him?"

"After I got back from overseas. Before he died."

• • •

He was sitting in his car.

He had just left the law firm.

He did not fault Thomas for his preoccupation with money. The desire for wealth is a symptom of the sick culture that they lived in. He knew that his outrage at Thomas was somewhat hypocritical; he had money; he did own an apartment building. However, what he had never verbalized was that he resisted any and all temptation to use the income that he received from the tenants of his building. He only used the money when he was desperate; bills to pay and no other jobs lined up. To him, the income was tainted. It was a constant reminder of the relationship with his father. He kept his life simple; he did not buy things that he did not need. He preferred to live a spartan existence. He experienced a rush of shame whenever he had to spend the money. He preferred to reinvest the money in the building itself. He could find relief in the fact that he was helping others – people that truly needed it.

He could have made a comfortable living just working as a landlord.

He would never do that.

In Will's eyes this would have been a victory for his father; that his son was living off of the success of his father. He would never give the asshole that satisfaction.

Before getting to the car, he had been enraged; he felt like burning rubber out of the parking lot. Once sitting securely inside the vehicle, this vindictive rage vacated his body. The rage was replaced by exhaustion and an overwhelming sense of failure.

Where are you, Natalie?

He contemplated calling Jocelyn. There was something pressing in the back of his mind; something unknown that was triggering his intuition. He didn't know what sort of card player Jocelyn was, but he decided to bluff. He pulled out the phone from his pocket.

Me: Come clean. I know that you know where Natalie is. Tell me. We need to get her help before she gets hurt.

He hoped that that would be enough.

He placed the phone on the passenger seat. He strapped the seatbelt across his body, but made no attempt to begin driving. Anxiously, he picked up his phone. There was no message. Paranoid, he checked to ensure that the ringer was on. He then placed the phone back on the passenger seat.

Sighing, he picked up the phone again. He pondered the best course of action. *Fuck it*, he thought. He went through his contacts and scrolled to Jocelyn's number. He debated internally for a moment. He watched his finger press the dial button.

It rang interminably.

Jocelyn didn't answer the call. It went to voicemail.

"Jocelyn, it's William, the investigator. You need to call me. I know that you know where she is. Call me back."

He worried that he had committed a grave miscalculation. Had he gone too far?

His neuroses got the better of him. His anxiety spiked, he picked up the phone and once again called Jocelyn. This time, the call went straight to voicemail. Interesting, he thought. Was this a signal of her guilt? Or, was she just a teenage girl who didn't want to be bothered by some obsessed weirdo?

His phone binged.

Excited, he grabbed the phone and anxiously peered at the screen.

It wasn't Jocelyn.

It was a message from Laura.

Laura: Sorry to bother you, but I was just wondering if you'd found anything?

No. He hadn't found a fucking thing. At least nothing concrete.

He formulated an appropriate response to her message. Should he be blunt as possible? Or, should he sugar-coat it? He was able to read between the lines. She was anxious. She had nothing but time on her hands. Time which was undoubtedly spent being horrified by the imaginations seemingly endless supply of terrifying scenarios.

Me: Rounding up some leads. Sorry, in investigations like this, there is always a lot of waiting involved. I know this must be hard. I will let you know when I find something.

Laura: Thank you.

There was a pang of concern in his abdomen. He sighed, and against his better instincts, he messaged her back.

Me: How are you holding up?

Laura: Trying to keep myself occupied. Trying not to assume the worst.

Me: It's important to remain positive. I won't stop until I find her.

Laura: Thank you.

He placed the phone back on the passenger seat. Starting the car, he pulled out of his parking spot and drove away.

• • •

"The next time you saw your father was the last time?"

"Yeah."

"This was when he was dying?"

"Yeah. It was in the hospital."

"What did he say?"

"It wasn't like the movies; it wasn't a dramatic and heart-wrenching experience. It was a conversation frequently interrupted by him either falling asleep or losing consciousness."

"So, he wanted to make amends?"

"Yeah. But he wanted to make amends on his own terms. Even in death, he remained a stubborn prick. In the end, it wasn't about amends, it was his cowardly attempt at penance."

"What happened?"

"Initially, it was the same atmosphere as all of our other visits. I had gotten a call from one of his friends. They told me that he was dying, and he wanted to see me. Naively, I expected him to apologize; to beg for my forgiveness.

"Instead, once I sat in the chair next to his bed, I was greeted with his typical silence. At first, I thought that he was asleep. I leaned forward and noticed that his

eyes were open. We made eye contact and he quickly looked away. He looked like a dog caught pissing on the carpet; as if averting his gaze would spare him shame.

"I was pissed at first. That even when Robert was laying there dying, he couldn't talk to me. It was like he had erected a barrier between the two of us. A fragile barrier. One that would crumble if our silence was broken. However, my rage transformed to resilience. Robert had virtually ignored me for the entirety of my life. There had been no father and son heart-to-heart chats. He said nothing of value to me before I shipped off to war. I was not leaving that hospital room without having a real discussion.

"This in turn led to a conundrum; neither of us wanted to speak first. I think we both felt that this would signal some form of weakness. This was indicative of our interactions in general. We both had something to say, but we were each unable to find the will to speak. Of course, I was the first one to break. The prick."

"What did you say?"

"It was something innocuous, I think. Something like, 'are you in pain?' And of course, he shrugged it off. Said that the drugs that they had him on took care of it. I nodded. Couldn't bring myself to verbally acknowledge that I didn't want him to be in pain. I hated the man, but watching someone waste away in the hospital was unpleasant. Don't get me wrong, his death didn't bother me; this feeling was merely empathy. Not that he deserved my sympathy."

"Why didn't you tell him how you felt? It was an opportunity for some form of closure."

"Closure? I don't believe in it. It's a nice idea; it's good in theory, but in practice? No. Closure was a term invented by psychologists to give their patients false hope. Hope that things can get better. No offense. In my experience, there will always be something left unsaid. My mother springs to mind."

"None taken. So, what happened next?"

"After that exchange, we sort of sat in silence for a while. There was a game on tv. We watched in silence. The Riders ended up winning, so he was in a good mood. I suppose this made him more talkative.

"Out of nowhere, he told me why he had wanted to see me. He told me that I was his immediate family and wanted me to take possession of his apartment complex. He had been encouraged to sell the property by various companies, but he refused as he 'cared about his tenants. They were good people.' He didn't want to sell to some heartless real estate company that didn't care about its tenants. I'm not going to lie; that pissed me off. He cared about his tenants – people who weren't his family, more than his own family. He neglected me and my mom, but not his tenants. Maybe he was greedy (like most landlords) and wanted their money, or maybe he really cared. Either way, it left a fucking bitter taste in my mouth.

"He was telling me that he wanted me to have the building. While he was babbling on about the various tenants and the building, the thoughts were repeating on an endless cycle. I kept asking myself, why weren't you there for me? Why weren't you there for me? It built up pressure inside me until the words erupted from my mouth.

"I asked him point blank, 'Why were you never around?'"

"What did he say?"

"His eyes got kind of wide; you know, like a deer in the headlights. He took a deep sigh. We were once again blanketed in silence. I don't know how long we remained in silence, it seemed like hours but was probably five minutes. His response was classic Robert; uttered while he wasn't looking at me, but at the tv. I had to strain myself to hear it. Robert hoarsely whispered, 'You'll have to ask your mother.'

"I couldn't fucking believe it! 'Ask your mother?' On his deathbed, he had the fucking nerve to feed me another line of bullshit. I was especially enraged because if Robert knew my mother at all, he would know that she wouldn't talk about private matters. He was taking the coward's way out. I guess I shouldn't have expected anything else from him.'

"The matter wasn't resolved at all?"

"No. Robert immediately changed the subject. He wouldn't veer off topic. He was treating the apartment as a matter of life or death, which I suppose for him it was. Robert actually grabbed my wrist in a death-grip. For the first time, he looked me dead in the eye, and said, 'please. I want you take it. I need you to take it. Please.'

"I admit, I was shocked. I had never seen Robert like this before. I was shell-shocked. He wouldn't let go. Immersed in shock and awe, I agreed to his request. Partly so he would let go of me."

"And the other part?"

"I had seen a lot of death in the war. More than my fair share. I was just back from the war. Many of these memories were still fresh. As much as I wanted to, I just couldn't bring myself to refuse a dying man's request. Even if I hated the fuck. Which I did. I do."

"Please, continue."

"Anyway, he told me that he had given instructions to his attorney. He would be coming around with papers for me to sign shortly. The prick knew that I wouldn't say no to him. And that was it. He told me that he was tired and that he needed to get some sleep. So I left."

"That was it?"

"Yeah. He couldn't even bring himself to ask me to come and visit again. He simply muttered, 'you can stop by another time, if you want to.' That comment irritated me. Couldn't believe it. He couldn't even admit that he wanted to see me again. I was enraged by the time I left the hospital. I resolved that I wasn't going to see him again. Fuck him. He had his chance."

"How long after that did he die?"

"A couple of days. I got a call from the hospital. He went in his sleep."

"And you never asked your mother about him? Even after seeing him in the hospital?"

"Not really. I mean, when I gave her the news that Robert had died, she looked shocked. Maybe even saddened. At least a little. I took that opportunity to tell her what he had said. She snapped at me, 'that prick.' She ranted and raved for a bit, about what an asshole he was. She cooled off after a while. I asked her what happened. She sighed (eerily similar to Robert's sigh), and said, 'we were together for a while. We tried to make it work, but it didn't. It's not some epic love story. It's real life. That's all there is to it.'"

"That must've been frustrating."

"At the time, yes. Now? Not so much. It's like I said, my mom raised me by herself. She was a damn good mother. I didn't need anything else. Others have had it worse. It's like my mom said, 'this is real life.' In my experience, life doesn't always have happy endings. You need to take what you can get."

•　•　•

His sleep that evening was fitful.

His dreams were haunted by memories from the war.

He dreamed of the interpreter.

He hadn't thought about him in years.

His memory had always been vicious. It preyed upon him like a cat tormenting a mouse, pouncing unexpectedly, smacking him senseless, unwilling to let him lie in peace. His past became all the more predatory when he was asleep. You are at your most defenseless when you are asleep.

•　　　•　　　•

His name was Ahmad.

He had served as an interpreter for various units. He had proven himself to be both brave and trustworthy. Ahmad was highly sought after for his skills. Unfortunately, this valued assistance to the army also made him a target to the enemy.

Ahmad was aware that he was targeted for death. He didn't need the military intelligence apparatus to confirm it. It was a dangerous job. This didn't bother him, he continued to serve. He wanted to live in a democracy. He wanted his country to be transformed; to be saved.

Ahmad was a devout Muslim. He was well-versed in the teachings of the Koran. He knew that the Islam that was preached by the likes of The Taliban and Al Qaeda, was not the real Islam.

They continued to serve together on operations. They began to interact regularly on a more personal basis. Ahmad told him about his family, what the country was like before the invasion, his plans for the future (when the war was over).

As Ahmad continued to serve as an interpreter, the threats against his life intensified. He sent his family away to live with extended family to ensure their safety. He regularly carried a concealed weapon when not on assignment and routinely checked his car for explosive devices. Ahmad was often told that he had "balls of steel." Will remembered thinking that Ahmad had a death wish, or was too fatalistic. He was dumbfounded that this was a man who was willing to die for an ideal that many in the western hemisphere had forgotten about, or given up on.

Ahmad mentioned to him in private that he had begun to suspect that he was being followed. He had reported his suspicions to his superiors multiple times before he finally was ambushed. Rather than become enraged, Ahmad was proud of his attention and awareness of his surroundings. He felt validated. His intelligence and quick thinking had enabled him to escape from attacks again and again.

Eventually, his luck ran out.

Ahmad disappeared.

It was as if he fell off the face of the earth.

His neighbors had no idea where he was. None of his friends had heard from him. He was a ghost. He was missing for more than a week.

They learned of his fate when a video was uploaded to the internet. Will hadn't wanted to watch it, but felt that he must. He felt that he bore some responsibility for the interpreter's death.

The video showed Ahmad on his knees. He had clearly been beaten or tortured. His face was heavily bruised and swollen. There was dried blood on his face and his shirt. His clothes were stained with dirt and grime. He was grim-faced, but he was clearly hiding his fear from his captors. He would not let them see his fear.

Two masked figures stood next to him. The one on the left was speaking directly to the camera. Will didn't need an interpreter to know what he was saying. It was always the same. Generally speaking, it consisted of ranting about infidels, how Allah is with them, how they will win this holy war and vanquish the invaders, blah, blah, blah.

Ahmad had been helping the enemy; the infidels, the invaders, the godless and decadent west.

Will knew it was coming. He wanted to look away, but couldn't force himself to close his eyes. He saw the masked figure unsheathe the long-curved sword.

They cut off his head.

In the days that followed, nothing really seemed to change. This was war. Things continued on in the familiar routine of the military. He couldn't recall anyone openly mourning for the murdered interpreter. He didn't or couldn't say anything.

The unit got a new interpreter a week later.

He continued to see the gruesome images of Ahmad's death play in his mind on an endlessly repeating cycle, every time he closed his eyes. These haunting images were all the more vivid as he lay in his bunk, trying to sleep. Each time he closed his eyes to drift off to sleep, he saw Ahmad.

Ahmad was one of the first ghosts that relentlessly haunted him. It took weeks, maybe even months, but Ahmad's ghost slowly faded into the periphery.

There were many more ghosts that followed.

They were always there. Waiting.

He awoke to the all too familiar sensation of anxiety and sweat-soaked sheets. Disgusted, he peeled off the sheets and pulled himself out of bed. When he awoke following a nightmare, he felt like a child that had soiled the bed. It was a mixture of shame, embarrassment, and, to a larger extent, revulsion.

He quickly balled up the sheets and threw them into the washing machine. As he started the machine, he fell to a crouch, and allowed himself to lean against the machine. He was attempting to pacify the anxiety traveling through his veins. He could literally hear his heartbeat in his eardrums.

He closed his eyes. He proceeded to fall into his breathing regiment. He continued to take a series of deep breaths. With each breath, he could feel the omnipresent images of the interpreter's execution slowly begin to fade. Of course, the ghosts were never really gone entirely. Rather, they remained at the borders of his consciousness. The barriers that he had constructed were continually assaulted. He feared that they were in grave danger of imminent collapse. He had fallen into the wheel of dysfunction.

The pressure of finding the missing girl was clearly the cause.

It had confronted him with the emotions and human behavior that he had strived so hard to distance himself from. He was not a sociopath or psychopath. It was simply a matter of self-preservation. He once again recognized the necessity of finding Natalie. At this point, it was for purely selfish reasons; he wanted to return to the way things were.

He swallowed hard. Pulled himself up and began with his daily ritual.

After a liberal injection of caffeine, he began his workout.

He pushed himself even harder than usual. It was an effort to diminish or erase the effects of the nightmare. To overcome the shame that he had felt. It was a vain and futile effort to prove his strength, that he wasn't a coward. That he was in control.

People lie to themselves all of the time.

He was no different.

• • •

After working out, he showered. He alternated the temperature from ice cold to scalding hot. After a particularly rough sleep, he enjoyed the juxtaposition of the competing sensations. He enjoyed tinkering with the water; quickly switching from scalding to ice cold, just as his brain began to send his body signals. If done properly, his brain would begin to feel overloaded; it was at war with itself. As with his other routines (rituals?), this served a purpose. It grounded him. Served to remind him of what was both real and immediate.

Turning off the water, he stepped out of the shower.

He dried off.

He attempted to make himself look somewhat presentable.

He made his way back to the kitchen and poured another large cup of coffee. He stared at his phone on the kitchen counter. He still had not heard back from Jocelyn. He doubted that she would. Had he overplayed his hand? Was he wrong?

Although, far from a eureka moment, he found it hard to believe that Natalie would take off without consulting or discussing the matter with her best friend. It made him uncomfortable to admit, but he knew that despite their current spat, if he were in trouble, he would still approach Thomas for help.

He wasn't an expert at women. Knew even less about teenage girls. He could only presume that the ties of friendship were universal, even at such a young age. He was certain that Natalie, a rich girl, couldn't make it on her own without assistance. Even in the throes of addiction, he couldn't see her living on the street.

He ruled Cameron out of the equation. The boy cared about her, that much was obvious. He knew that Cameron wasn't lying. His intuition when it came to reading people was very rarely wrong. As for Alain, his cowardice excluded him from his list of suspects. He was a punk trying to pass himself off as a tough gang banger. When faced with the mere threat of violence, he had shriveled up. In addition, he had no reason to lie. He was a piece of shit drug dealer. One addict was the same as any other.

It all came back to her. Jocelyn.

She hadn't lied to him during the meeting at *Fancy*. Not completely. She may know, or at the very least have suspicions as to where Natalie is, but her answers were for the most part were honest. Honest enough to give him the idea that she was helping him. Lying by omission was still lying. At least technically.

He groaned. It felt as if his mind was still at war with itself.

This fucking case was kicking his ass.

He had never experienced the sort of mental and emotional turmoil that was inherent within this case. Perhaps it was simply a matter of involvement. He didn't allow himself to get this close to clients. Emotional investment was dangerous.

He had a soft spot for Laura. He could recognize that. He was attracted to her. Laura was a beautiful woman, and he was only human after all. These were fleeting passions. He was pragmatic. There could be no future with her. After careful introspection, Will had concluded long ago that he had nothing left of himself to give to another.

Or perhaps more distressingly, it had nothing to do with her. He normally wasn't indecisive. Indecision in the field of battle generally led to a premature death. Maybe his mind was finally coming unhinged. The copious amounts of death, destruction, and carnage that he had witnessed and participated in during the war, followed closely by the climax of his attempted murder and eventual recovery. He wondered if the cumulative effects had finally taken its toll. Had the levies of his mind finally buckled under the pressure?

Once again, he looked at the phone on the counter. It was taunting him. Daring him to pick it up.

Fuck it. He picked it up and dialed her number.

The call, once again, went straight to voicemail.

Fuck.

"Jocelyn, it's Will. I just want you to know that I'm not looking to get you in trouble with your parents, or Natalie's parents. I know you know where she is. I know that you're trying to help and protect your friend. But, she needs help. Help me bring her home so she can get help. Neither of us want her to get hurt. Please, help me."

He ended the call. He hoped that it would be enough.

•   •   •

"Why did you become a private investigator?"

"For the same reason as most people, I guess. I grew up reading Raymond Chandler, Dashiell Hammett, Agatha Christie, and Arthur Conan Doyle. Reading their stories gave me a romantic notion of private investigators. The reality is that the job bears little resemblance to the stories. I don't get to be a hero. I'm not a hero. Maybe there aren't any heroes in this line of work."

"Yes, but that doesn't really answer my question. So, you get home after the war; why did you decide to select that particular career path at that time? You said it yourself, you didn't really have any particular career path in mind."

"My contract was up with the army. I wasn't interested in signing up again; I didn't want to make a career of it. It basically came down to me being exasperated at having to follow orders all of the time. I wanted to be my own boss. Only answer to myself. With Robert's death, he left me the apartment building; I could live solely off of the income from tenants. While I'm by no means wealthy, it's enough for me. I get by. It enabled me to pursue my childish ambition. I got my license and went to work. It was slow going at first. Really slow. It wasn't until Thomas got his job at a behemoth firm that my career started to pick up. Word of mouth does a lot in this business."

"I'm curious; you said that your romantic notions of being an investigator were squashed. It's nothing like the books. Why do you keep working as a PI? Why not try something else?"

"It's a job that permits or enables my certain…behavioral issues."

"Behavioral issues?"

"I don't like being around people. Crowds make me feel…well, crowded, I guess. I like to be alone. I've always felt like I was on the outside looking in; this job requires that. It's a good skill to have. You learn a lot by watching and studying people's behavior."

"I see. And you've never been diagnosed with Post-Traumatic Stress Disorder?"

"No. I honestly don't believe that I have it."

"I understand that. It's just that a few of the characteristics you mentioned are symptoms of PTSD."

"They are unrelated. I've always been like that."

"For how long?"

"For as long as I can remember."

"You've always felt anxious?"

"Sometimes. Look, I can see where this is going. I don't want any pills. I don't need any. I don't have PTSD. Let's move on."

"I'm not trying to upset you."

"You're not."

"It's just that you were referred here because of your complaint that the scar from a gunshot wound continued to hurt. There is nothing medically wrong with the area. You healed remarkably well. It's devoid of infection. It suggests that you are having psychological issues stemming from that trauma."

"I understand that. It's just that I disagree. I've been shot at before."

"But this was different."

"Yeah. I wasn't in a war zone."

"It was in your office. A safe place."

"You can get hurt anywhere."

"That's not the point."

"Oh?"

"For instance, you mentioned that the scar hurts most when you are experiencing stress."

"Yeah. I call it the 'Curse of Herman' or 'Herman's Curse'. I haven't made up my mind yet. Both are so catchy; they roll of the tongue so easily."

"William, please. I'm trying to help you."

"I know. It's just that I don't really believe in therapy. In my experience, talking about your problems, the bad shit that has happened to you, doesn't make you feel better. It's like, it uh...prevents the wound from scabbing over and becoming a scar. The more you talk about it, the more you rip off the scab, until eventually, you're left with a festering wound."

"If that's how you feel, then why are you here? Why do you keep coming back?"

"Now, that is a good question. But, it looks like our time is up."

•   •   •

He was in his office.

The only lead was Jocelyn. She had not gotten back to him. He was in a precarious position. She was a teenager, he couldn't simply show up at her house, or go back to waiting outside her school, or job. A grown man following (stalking?) a teenage girl is not a good look. He feared that if he continued to press, or pursue too hard, he would be in the flimsy position of having to explain himself to an irate parent.

In the face of enraged parents, would they believe him? He doubted it. In this day and age there were simply too many perverted and depraved men. He assumed that all parents of teenage girls found themselves glued to the news coverage of girls being sexually exploited online, or being kidnapped off the street and sold into sexual slavery.

It didn't matter that the likelihood of that happening in their geographical location was virtually zero. They probably had a better chance of winning the lottery or getting struck by lightning. Speaking in generalities, the media preyed on people's fears and insecurities. It didn't matter that the rational part of their brain told them that something so vile couldn't happen here. The part of their brain that was focused on being a parent and protecting their child overrode all other sensibilities.

With few options, he had resigned himself to playing the waiting game, once again. In the meantime, he continued to monitor all of Natalie's social media accounts. Sadly, nothing had been posted. She had both literally and virtually disappeared.

He continued his perusal of her accounts. Hoping that he could find something in her pictures or posts that would lead him to her. The proverbial needle in a haystack. He had heard so many social commentators lament the state of society. We were too invested in our phones, that while we were connected globally through the internet and social media, we were losing our intimate connection with our personal surroundings.

Prior to the search, he had felt the same way. He routinely witnessed the isolation of individuals; heads craned down, looking at their phone, oblivious to everything around them, caught in a detached bubble of narcissism. However, he was beginning to feel that this assessment was bullshit. At least in this case. Most of society really were addicted to their phones. However, it seemed that she was the only teenage girl in the western hemisphere that didn't feel the need to post every thought that crept into her mind, or picture of every meal that she ate.

Finding nothing, he slammed his laptop shut in a mixture of disgust and frustration.

His phone began to ring.

It was Thomas.

He wasn't in the right frame of mind to attempt the awkward maneuver of reconciliation. The situation, he knew, would be difficult to confront. They were at an impasse; neither would be willing to concede. Thomas had always been driven and goal-oriented. He had planned his future while serving overseas. He wasn't the type of man who would let a minor detail like the previous occupant of his office being a crazed killer prevent him from enjoying success.

He selected the "ignore" option.

If his cop friend had finally gotten back to him, he could leave a message. He didn't feel like talking to him. If it were simply a personal matter (a sincere apology for being such a tool), he would deal with it later. After all of this other shit was taken care of. Natalie was the priority.

His phone began to ring again.

Once again, it was Thomas.

He always had been persistent. He once again opted to ignore the call.

The phone binged, signifying a text message.

Excited, he picked up the phone, hoping that it was Jocelyn finally responding to his incessant messages. He should've known better, it was still Thomas.

Thomas: Will, pick up the fucking phone!

He was weary; uncertain if this was merely a case of Thomas's guilt, driving him to connect with him in order to appease his conscience. Before he could determine a course of action, the phone alerted him to another message.

Thomas: 911! It's about the girl! Call me!

He felt his gut tense. The all-too-familiar sensation of despair. Swallowing painfully, he scrolled through his contacts (noting his fucking shaking hand) and called Thomas.

He answered on the first ring. Never a good sign.

"Will, it's about the girl; my guy finally got back to me," Thomas spewed out.

"Okay," he responded, his hand gripping the edge of his desk.

"It's bad news. The cops found her. She's dead, Will. I'm so sorry."

They were at the pub. Thomas insisted that they go out. Initially, he begged off, but Thomas was insistent. Will presumed that he was worried about him; their earlier argument had revealed a crack in the facade of his unyielding exterior.

The police had found Natalie's body in a cabin in the woods.

Although the medical examiner had not yet performed an autopsy, Thomas's contact had guessed (based on his extensive experience) that she had been dead for maybe a day. Based upon the drug paraphernalia among her possessions, the medical examiner surmised that she had died from an accidental drug overdose. It had probably happened shortly after Will's awful interaction with the infernal Alain. His incessant calls to Jocelyn had been in vain - Natalie had probably been dead by the time he started leaving the voicemails.

After years of being haunted by ghosts, he had effectively been chasing a ghost. A literal dead end. He couldn't stop thinking about Laura. This would crush her.

The two were sitting at their usual table at the back of the pub, away from the other louder and drunker patrons. He had the usual: a pint of lager and a whiskey and coke.

"Who owns the cabin?"

"Sorry?" Thomas asked, looking up from his phone.

"The cabin who owns the fucking cabin?!"

"I didn't get a name."

"How the hell did she get into the cabin? Did she break in?"

"No. The owners left a key in one of those fake rock things."

"So, then it's highly likely that she had been there before, and that she knew the owner."

"Yeah. And those rock-key things look ridiculously fake," Thomas added, sipping from his drink.

"Thanks for that astute assessment, Tom. When did they notify the parents?"

"They found the body early this morning. Searched her stuff, found her ID. The parents were notified and made a positive identification."

"Did the father or mother make the identification?"

"Don't know, didn't ask. Why does it matter?"

"This will kill Laura," he mumbled, draining the remainder of his beer.

He envisioned Laura in the morgue, identifying the corpse of her only child. He saw her collapsing to the ground, wracked with sobs, her husband, struggling to support the weight of her body.

"So, you didn't get the name of the owner?"

"No. Why does it matter?"

"I think I know who owned it."

"Will, listen to me; it doesn't matter. You can quit digging. It was an accidental death. She was a drug addict, she relapsed, and then she overdosed. It's shitty, but these things happen. My cop buddy told me that there has been a drastic increase in O.D.'s. It's an opioid epidemic," Thomas responded kindly but firmly.

"Yeah," he answered quietly.

"I feel like there is a big 'but' in that response."

"Something doesn't add up. The more I think about it, the more certain I am that her friend was hiding something from me," he reflected, emptying his other glass.

"What do you mean?"

Will motioned to the bartender for another drink.

"I think her best friend lied to me. I think she knew where Natalie was. I'm willing to bet that the cabin she was found in belongs to her friend's family."

Thomas was poised to reply when the waitress approached the table with his requested drink.

"Anything else?" the waitress asked.

"No, thank you. We're good," Thomas answered abruptly.

He waited until the waitress was a considerable distance away from the table before he responded.

"So, why would she agree to hide her drug-addicted friend?"

"I don't know. That's what I can't figure out. She doesn't strike me as an enabler. It's not like she could've kept her there indefinitely. I mean, what's the end game?"

"She's young, maybe she just felt bad that her friend was in pain," Thomas suggested.

"No. I don't think so. Jocelyn made it quite clear that she wasn't into drugs, she told me as much."

"Huh, whose Jocelyn?" Thomas asked, beginning to slur his words.

"Natalie's best friend! Try to keep up. Are you drunk?" Will asked, shocked.

"Sorry. I've been working all day; haven't had much to eat, and this is my third scotch."

"You always were a cheap drunk."

"Whatever. I've got to get going. I've got to get up early tomorrow morning," he slurred.

"Alright. Have a good night," he responded, smiling at his friend's drunkenness.

Thomas raised himself unsteadily from their table. He was slowly stumbling away from the table, when he paused and turned back around.

"Forget something?" Will asked him.

"Yeah, uh...the cop guy...he checked out the kid's parents; they're both clean – not even a parking ticket. Not that it helps much, now..." Thomas said drunkenly, stopping mid-sentence.

"Thanks, Tom. You're not driving, right?" he asked, concerned.

"Cabbed here. Cabbing home," he said, stumbling away.

Will finished his drink and walked to the bar to settle his bill.

Approaching the bar, he noticed a stylishly dressed trio of women, sipping on expensive martinis. Waiting for service from one of the busy waitresses, he noticed the brunette of the trio eyeing him coquettishly. She looked up from her drink, and they made eye-contact. Smiling, self-consciously, she quickly looked away.

He could hear the brunette's friends giggling and whispering to her, urging her to say something to him. He didn't know whether it was because he was feeling bitter and sick with himself for failing to save Natalie, or whether it was genuine loneliness, but he uncharacteristically made the conscious decision to speak to her.

"Good evening," he said, instantly feeling ridiculous.

The brunette quickly looked up. A slow smile appeared on her face.

"Good evening," she responded in a sultry voice.

Indicating the martini glasses before the group with a nod of his head, he asked, "Celebrating?"

"Oh, no," she said quickly, "more like decompressing. It's been a long week."

"I know exactly what you mean."

"Oh? Is that why you're here tonight?" she asked, seemingly interested.

"Something like that. I was just, uh...debriefing with a friend," he said, feeling even more ridiculous.

"Debriefing? Are you a lawyer?"

"Hell, no. I can't stand lawyers."

Her gaze quickly descended back to her drink.

"Oh, shit. You're a lawyer, aren't you?" he asked, embarrassed.

"Yes, I am," she motioned to her friends, "in fact, we are all lawyers."

"I'm sorry. I'm an idiot. It was a stupid joke. The friend I was with, he is also a lawyer."

"It's okay," she assured him, "that is the general opinion. Nobody likes lawyers. Even when they need them," she smiled.

"I have a hard time believing that anyone could possibly be mean to you," he offered, instantly regretting the cheesy statement.

"I don't know about that. Today, a pissed off client called me a cunt," she said before draining her glass.

"What's his name? I'll kill him," he said.

She looked at him in shock for a moment. He feared that he may have said the wrong thing. He never knew what to say in these types of social environments. He avoided conversation with strangers for this very reason. The tension was relieved as she and her friends burst into laughter.

"I'm sorry that you had a shitty day. Allow me to buy you a drink? Just to show you that not all men are bastards."

"You're not a bastard?" she asked jokingly.

"Oh, no. I am. But I still want to buy you a drink."

She laughed. "Okay," she said, smiling.

The male bartender quickly appeared, taking the order for the ladies, which was typical of the bar environment. Men could stand around all night, waiting for a drink, but a group of beautiful women were always served promptly (provided it was a male bartender, of course).

She motioned for him to sit down on the empty stool next to her.

"I'm Will," he said, introducing himself.

"Teresa," she answered. "And that's Melanie and Jodie," she said, motioning to her friends.

After shaking each of their hands, he sat down on the offered stool. The bartender returned with the ladies' drinks. While he had the man's attention, he ordered a double whisky and coke.

"So, what do you do, Will?" Melanie asked.

He didn't want to answer truthfully. Generally, in the rare occasions when dealing with people in a social setting, he avoided telling people what he did for a living. People always thought it was exciting and glamorous, asking for stories and details. Tonight, especially, he needed to be someone else. To escape the reality. He didn't want to think about the dead girl, or the heartbroken family that she left behind.

"I'm an accountant."

This was always the perfect answer. Accounting, literally one of the most boring professions in the world, ensured that there would be no further questions or inquiries.

"You're an accountant?" asked Teresa, shocked.

"Yeah, I know. I get that a lot," he said forcing a laugh.

"You're seriously an accountant?" asked Jodie, slurring.

"Yes. I know it's not the most exciting profession, but it pays the bills. I'm pretty good at it. My colleagues call me "Captain Crunch," because of all the numbers that I crunch. Which is a joke. A bad one. It's only funny to other accountants."

The ladies laughed.

"So, all three of you work together?" he asked, changing the subject.

"Yep. We are a veritable legal dream team!" Jodie shouted drunkenly.

"I think Jodie has had too much to drink. I'm going to take her home, which will give you two some alone time," Melanie said, helping Jodie off of the stool.

"Nice to meet you two," he said, bidding farewell.

He overheard Melanie whisper "go for it," to Teresa as she helped Jodie drunkenly stumble out of the bar.

"Jodie doesn't usually drink so much," Teresa said, offering an explanation.

"Oh, it's alright. It's okay for people to de-stress once in a while."

"She only had three drinks, she's a real lightweight," Teresa said, laughing.

"Yeah, my friend had to call it a night, too. He never could handle his liquor."

"Thank you for the drink," she said, still smiling.

"It's my pleasure. It's not every day that I get to have a drink with a smart and beautiful woman. Which sounds cheesy. I apologize."

She laughed. "No, it's alright. It was a good line."

"Well, thank you. I try."

Neither of them found any excuse to leave the bar. Nor did they make a move to leave. He remembered what this felt like. A genuine connection. A spark had been lit between the two. He felt like they were existing in the moment, solely for each other. The two of them were in a bubble. They were ignorant of the outside world, ignoring tomorrow, the future, responsibilities, commitments, everything but each other.

They nursed their drinks, neither in a hurry to end the conversation, to retreat back into the world that waited for them. It had been a long time since he had felt like this. When a woman had resuscitated him out of the rut of routine, out of the capitulation of miserable complacency.

They sat at the bar until closing time. Eventually, they had even stopped ordering drinks (much to the chagrin of the bartender). Noticing that the employees were sending none too subtle signals that the two needed to leave as they were wanting to close up, the two stepped off of their stools and made for the exit. He assisted Teresa with her jacket. While not intoxicated, she was stumbling slightly, and her face was slightly flushed.

Once outside, she hooked her arm through his and they proceeded to walk.

"Where are we going?" he asked, laughing.

"To my car," she answered, giggling.

"No, no. You have had far too much to drink. I'll call you a cab," he said, pulling out his phone.

She leaned against him, resting her head against his chest.

"Yeah, you're right. That is a good idea, my good sir," she laughed. "Or, you could drive me home?" she offered somewhat bashfully.

He tore his gaze away from his phone and looked down at her. He had had quite a few, but he wasn't completely sloshed. He supposed it was because he had a high tolerance for alcohol. He figured he would be fine to drive, but he hesitated for a moment. It had been a long time since he had found himself in this position.

When he had got back from overseas, he had frequented bars nightly. He had been chasing three things: intoxication, violence, and sex. Anything to numb his mind to the slow process of re-acclimating back to civilian life. He would find himself heading to various pubs whenever he began to be racked with anxiety or restlessness. He had felt compelled to remain in constant motion; if he remained still, the anxiety would grasp him in its clutches.

Very rarely did he find a woman to take home. He was too reserved and shy to approach a lady. Instead, he resigned himself to drawing the attention of a prospective mate, and hoping that she would approach him. On the rare occasion when a woman would approach him and they engaged in a conversation, he would mention that he had served overseas, and this would normally guarantee a sexual encounter. He had no idea why. Perhaps it was some misguided sense of patriotism on their part.

The pursuit of this trifecta continued for months.

Until he met her.

Lana.

It had been a typical night of drunken antics. He had been thrown out of a bar (couldn't remember the name; far too drunk) for instigating a fight. He had left the premises with the help of the security staff. As the night was still relatively young, he decided to make his way to the next closest pub.

Upon arriving, he detested the place. It was for all intents and purposes, a hipster bar (of course).

"You hipsters multiply like rabbits," he had said, drunkenly.

He then stumbled towards the bar.

He found himself stuck in a seemingly never-ending line of obnoxious hipsters. The man in front of him was wearing his pants so high on his waist that his socks were visible. This questionable fashion statement was complimented by an ill-fitting polo shirt and a fedora. The proverbial icing on the cake; he had a moustache that gave the distinct impression that this man was not welcome within a hundred yards of a school. In fact, the ensemble in its entirety screamed "I am a child molester."

He tapped the hipster-pedophile on the shoulder. The pervert turned around.

"What are you doing here?"

"Sorry?" the hipster asked, confused.

"I think you're in the wrong place. I mean, it's not really your scene is it?"

"What do you mean, bro?" he asked contemptuously, "I come here all of the time, bro."

He hated being called bro. He would rather be called an asshole. Anything better than being associated with the douchebag/fraternity/chauvinistic social structure. "Bro." It made him squirm. It wasn't cool when Hulk Hogan said it, and it isn't cool or hip now. The nomenclature signified the fact that you were a massive tool.

His mind was made up. He was going to fight this man.

"I'm sorry, I just assumed that you would be huddled in your rape van (complete with tinted windows), scoping out the schools in the area, looking for a good hunting spot."

"What the fuck did you say?" the pervert asked, sniveling and on the verge of hyperventilating.

"I apologize, I thought I was being quite clear; you look like a pedophile! Is that what you are?" he asked, encroaching on the guy's personal space.

"Hey, bro, that's not cool to joke about."

"Do I look like I'm joking, Roman Polanski?"

"What?!" the hipster/pedophile aggressively queried.

"Once again, I have made a joke about you being a pedophile. I can see by the confused look on your face that you do not understand the insult. See, Roman Polanski is a director, a very good director. Ever see *Rosemary's Baby*? Amazing. However, he is also a pedophile. Like you. Get it?"

"What the fuck is your problem, bro?"

His hipster friends were beginning to surround him, anxious to come to their brethren's aid. The general look of the crowd made him think of the island of misfit toys. What were these people thinking?

"Well, I would've called you Ben Roethlisberger, but you don't look like you follow sports. And I honestly cannot recall if the woman he attacked was underage."

"Get the fuck away from me, dude."

The hipster's friends came to his aid and ushered the pedophile hipster back into the hive of hipsters, parallel to the bar. His attempt at fisticuffs having been thwarted, he resigned himself to waiting in line.

He heard a gorgeous but muffled giggle directly behind him. He turned around.

That was the first time he saw her.

Her beauty was forever seared into the molds of his brain.

In time, she would be yet another ghoul haunting his life.

If he had known the havoc that this gorgeous harbinger of destruction would wreak upon his life, he would have run in the opposite direction, as if his life depended upon it. At least, this is what he would tell himself in the future. This was yet another lie that he told himself. Her grasp was inescapable.

She was dressed in a black sleek dress.

She always dressed in black, he would learn.

Her arms were covered in tattoos.

Her mascara was thickly applied, giving her a haunted yet beautiful appearance. Her thin neck was adorned with a spiked dog collar, which would have normally caused him to roll his eyes dismissively. On her, it worked.

Her long legs were concealed underneath black pantyhose.

She wore heavy, black combat boots.

The appearance of this gorgeous nymph caused him to sober up, almost immediately.

Her arms were crossed, the tattoos on each arm overlapping creating an odd mash of figures and shapes. The detail that hooked him; she held her nearly empty glass at an angle, between her thumb and index finger. She held onto her glass the same way she had held onto him; vice-like, but with little attention or care.

"Sorry about that," he said, struggling to find the words.

"Don't be. That man is a veritable douche. You're very funny."

Her voice was the essence of sex.

"Are you alright? You're staring," she said, with a playful smile.

"I'm sorry. You're just so fucking beautiful."

The words escaped his mouth. He had been unable to censor himself. He couldn't blame it on the drink. He was intoxicated. However, this was an altogether different form of inebriation.

She smiled once again.

"Buy me a drink."

This wasn't a question. It was a definite statement. She wanted a drink and he would get her one. She had her hooks in him from the beginning. And he blindly obeyed.

• • •

He hadn't been expecting her. Now. Teresa.

She had been a welcome distraction from the detritus and debris that lingered in his mind. The haunting silence that awaited him at his empty apartment was an incubator for the ghost of Natalie and countless others. He knew that they awaited his return. He was not anxious to greet them.

The distraction that she had offered had quickly turned into something else. She offered a glimpse, a possibility at a life that he had given up on long ago. The beginning or the possibility of a beginning was always hopeful. Exciting. Would they fall quickly in love? Was this conversation at the bar merely a one-off? Would the next time be like tonight? Would they get together and have coffee, getting lost in each other? Would they have sex?

Would it be like they were the only two people in the world? How long would the honeymoon phase last? A week? A month at the most? Would the love one day fizzle out? Would they find themselves simply going through the motions? So, they get engaged, married, have a child. Anything to keep the relationship going. They had invested so much time in each other; it would be a waste to begin again. But they would be lying if they didn't find a rare quiet moment when they thought with despair, "how did I get here? How do I get out of this mess?"

He stopped himself.

He really did think too much.

He forced himself to stop.

He was already examining the potential future with this woman that he had just met. He wondered why he was already so certain that this, whatever it was, was doomed to failure. He didn't know if it was due to his profession, or his cynical and pessimistic nature. Maybe both.

However, he knew what he had to do.

"Teresa, I have had a wonderful time tonight. However, I am very good at fucking up these sorts of things. Which is why I am going to pay for a cab to take you home."

He handed her his card.

"I don't do this sort of thing regularly, you know?" Teresa said, the anger quickly beginning to simmer.

"No. I know that. I know. We've both had shitty days, and we have had a lot to drink. I'm just saying, let's not rush it. Like I said, I have perfected the art of ruining these things. I really like you, and I want you to call me," he said with what he hoped was a warm smile.

Teresa sighed. "You're right. Thanks for being such a gentleman."

"Gentleman? No. I'm just too drunk to fuck and I don't want this relationship to start on such a disappointing note. For me, there would be no coming back from that. And you've already had such a shit day, that would be the icing on the cake."

She laughed. Thankfully.

It was at this unfortunate moment that she examined his business card.

"Wait, I'm confused; your card says that you're a private investigator. Why did you tell me that you're an accountant?" she asked, her eyebrows furrowed.

His stomach sank. He hoped that he did not blanch visibly.

"That was a mistake that I would not have made if I had been sober," he offered candidly.

"Which part was the mistake? Giving me the card? Or telling me that you're an accountant?" her anger shifting swiftly from a gentle simmer to an outright boil.

"I didn't mean to upset you, and I don't want to ruin whatever this is or can be. I honestly wasn't expecting to meet someone like you tonight."

"Don't try to bullshit me; I get enough of that shit at work."

"I'm not feeding you a line of bullshit," he remarked earnestly, "Yes, I am an investigator, but I had a really rough day – like out of ten, it could easily be categorized as a fifteen! And based upon personal experience, people have this romanticized notion of the job and always want to ask questions. I didn't – or couldn't bear to talk about it tonight." He let out a long sigh.

"How do I know that you're not lying to me? Full disclosure: I cannot stand liars. I fucking hate them."

"I swear on my mother; the only thing I lied about was my job."

She glared intently at him for an interminable moment.

"Mulligan?" he asked hopefully.

"I hate golf."

"Me too. It just seems fitting in this situation."

"Mulligan," she conceded.

The crisis averted, they stood in silence for a few minutes. Minutes that dragged on.

She opened up her bag and retrieved her business card. Turning him around, using his back as a sturdy surface, she began to scroll on the card. Once she had finished, he slowly turned back around.

Handing him the card, she capped the pen and returned it back to its rightful spot in her bag. He turned over the card to inspect the missive.

"It's my personal number."

"Yes. Yes, it is."

Her cab arrived. She approached the vehicle. Before entering the cab, she turned around and made eye contact with him.

"You know, you may not have gotten laid tonight, but I assure you that you did get lucky tonight," she allowed a slight smile to form.

"Yes. Yes, I did."

·　　　·　　　·

She had wanted a Jameson and coke.

They sat together at the farthest reaches of the pub. He would later reflect (with the benefit of hindsight) that she had chosen an isolated spot in order to ensnare him fully in her trap.

"You don't look like a hipster. What are you doing here?" he asked her, still somewhat drunk.

"I could say the same about you."

"I came here looking for a fight."

"And instead you found me."

Lana always had a gift with words. She had the ability to impart so much while saying very little. It was a characteristic that would come to vex and enrage him in the not too distant future.

He couldn't remember what they had talked about in the ensuing hours that they spent drinking. It was immaterial. He had managed to nurse his drinks. He knew where this was going.

"So, William, where am I spending the night?"

Lana looked at him seductively. Her intense gaze illuminated all that she was going to do to him and just what she wanted him to do to her. Despite the amount that he had been drinking that night, he could already feel himself becoming aroused.

He gulped down the remainder of his drink.

"Let's go," he said abruptly.

They didn't make it very far.

She pulled him into the ladies' room.

She roughly pushed him into the closest available stall.

She crudely removed his pants.

There was no attempt at foreplay.

She mounted him as if she were a predator and he was her meek prey.

What occurred could not be defined as love making; it was completely devoid of passion. Nor could it be referred to as fucking. It was rough, rapid and entirely animalistic. As she climaxed, she bit him where his neck met the shoulder. The more that he moaned, the harder that she bit. Just as he began to fear that she wouldn't let him go, he experienced a mind-shattering orgasm.

He was making so much noise that Lana had to cover his mouth with her hand.

"Holy fuck," she whispered.

"Fuck," he said, exhaling.

They cleaned themselves up.

As they departed the stall, they realized that there were a few ladies standing in front of the series of sinks and mirrors. The women began to applaud, as if they were two performers who had entertained them with a fantastic theatrical performance.

He froze. Lana simply smiled and curtsied. Glowing from the undivided attention of the crowd. This, he would later recognize, was the first of many red flags. Red flags that were missed or ignored.

Some people, he often thought, contained a spark. Some sparks glow brighter than others, while others can only be spotted in the dark. The majority couldn't be recognized amidst the glow of the other innumerable sparks.

Even now, he couldn't consciously recognize which type of spark she had.

If she even had one to begin with.

After their brief tryst, they quickly made their way out of the bar. The crowd milling in the bar seemed to part like the Red Sea as they walked arm in arm to the exit. He remembered thinking that if this were a movie, he would be moving in slow motion and it would be accompanied with The Cardigans, Love Fool.

It was one of the few times in his life (outside of the war) that he felt as if he were experiencing an out-of-body experience. It seemed as if he were a spectator in his own life. He saw himself get into a cab with Lana (which she paid for). He witnessed the cab pull up to an expensive loft which was located in an even more outrageously priced neighborhood. He couldn't afford the loft if he worked three lifetimes.

Judging by her appearance, age, and demeanor, he astutely surmised that she came from money. She lived a life of privilege; a life in which she clearly did not have to work at all. He figured that she was a trust fund baby. Clearly, they were cut from a different cloth.

He worried that he was just a one-night stand.

He could imagine her telling her friends about how she spent the night slumming it.

If it had been any other woman, he wouldn't have cared.

There was just something about her.

She came back from the kitchen, carrying two drinks.

"What are you doing with me?" he asked, bluntly.

Lana smiled.

That fucking smile.

Irresistible.

"Well, I'm not going to buy the cow before trying the milk first."

"Right. And I'm the cow in this analogy?"

"Yes."

"This would mean my milk would be?"

"Shut up."

They tumbled onto her bed.

They didn't leave for days. The two passed the time having sex, sleeping, eating cereal, and watching trash tv. She gently traced her fingers along the scars that lined his body. He provided her with sparse details regarding the war. He painted with broad and generalized strokes as he described his life. It was the sanitized version. The bare essentials. He provided enough heartache to connect with her pain.

In the afterglow of sex, she told him her life story. His suspicions were confirmed.

Poor little rich girl.

Her family came from money.

Old money. A long line of rich old dudes who owned shitloads of property (commercial and residential) who then diversified their wealth by operating a series of hedge funds and other investment firms.

Her mother died when she was a little girl. She was a manic-depressive. She had been fine as long as she remained medicated. Therein lay the problem; she disliked taking her pills.

"My dad found her in the bathtub," she whispered.

He could feel the tears fall from her cheek onto his chest. Lifting his neck, he placed a gentle kiss on her forehead. He pulled up the sheets, covering both of their naked bodies. Patiently waited for her to continue.

Suffice to say that her father checked out after the mother's suicide.

Like many men of his generation, he threw himself into his work. Business trips, company retreats, and for some much-needed down time, trips with his friends from college. Anything to prevent him from focusing on his grief.

He couldn't bear to face his daughter. She was the living remnant of his deceased wife. Lana looked more like her mother as she grew older. He engaged in a relationship with his daughter that was conducted from a safe distance.

She was raised by a series of nannies before ultimately being sent away to exclusive boarding schools. Lana would routinely interact with the children of politicians, various celebrities, and other titans of business.

With puberty, she began to act out. Anything to gain the attention of her distant father. The classic cries for help.

Fighting with other girls (and some boys), drinking and drugs, failing her classes, and as a result, being expelled from a number of the elite schools. All to no avail.

Eventually she resigned herself to finding what joy she could from her seemingly endless supply of wealth and the privileges that it provided. Her father's guilty conscience for being a shit dad ensured it. This, of course, was in addition to her ample trust fund. Shopping, traveling, partying. Life was one big party.

Red flag number two.

Despite her protestations that she no longer cared; that she had made peace with her relationship with her father, he could read between the lines. It was clearly visible; her denials were hollow. She still longed for her father's acknowledgement, his love, his undivided attention. She had moved on to a different method of getting her father's attention.

Lana was clearly into men that her father would not approve of.

He brusquely ignored this. He was smitten. He was foolish. He thought he could gain her love in all its totality.

He fell. He fell hard. She claimed that she felt the same.

Their relationship progressed at a rapid pace.

He got licensed as an investigator. Lana was enthralled. She bought into the excitement and aura that surrounded and permeated the profession. She loved to tag along with him on stakeouts. She would often get bored and resort to tantalizing him with the prospect of sex. With modest protestations, he would fend her off for a while before succumbing to her demands.

She knew that he owned an apartment building. He mentioned it in an offhand way; he had gained it through an inheritance from a distant relative. He had only taken Lana to the building once. He was apprehensive to say the least.

The building was by no means luxury real estate. Nor was it a slum. It simply did not meet the standards of living that she was accustomed to.

He could tell by Lana's reaction that she was shocked at the building. She had probably never been inside an apartment complex before. Her posture was indicative of her discomfort. She was clearly not impressed.

He never took her to the building again.

He stayed at her place for the most part.

Despite his honest efforts at paying their expenses, or at the very least, contributing his fair share, she always refused. She loved spending money. She had no concept of the value of money. It was always there. In his experience, the people who didn't care about money were the ones that had always had it.

He told himself it was his simply a matter of his foolish pride. He loved her, so he swallowed his pride. Still, it was a bone of contention which lay beneath the surface.

He had placed this in the back of his mind. There were more pressing concerns. He had mistakenly exhibited too much of the true damage that resided in his core.

They had been partying with her friends. It was a birthday celebration for one of her various friends/acquaintances/hanger-on's. He had felt a tension building up in his chest. He couldn't fathom the reason for his discomfort.

Maybe it was the shitty club and the shitty music. Perhaps it was the company. Lana's friends were perhaps the most shallow and plastic people that he had ever encountered. He couldn't understand why she associated with these people. At the time, he hadn't realized that she was exactly like them. Obsessed with the material. That which resided upon the surface was all that mattered.

He was trying to retain his composure.

There was a rock in his gut.

His left eye would not stop twitching.

Lana was at the bar, shooting back overpriced feminine drinks.

The tension escalated as one of Lana's more obnoxious and insufferable male friends approached him. Richard. Call me Rich. Fuckface. His preferred nickname was perhaps too on the nose for his liking.

"Enjoying the party, buddy?" Richard slurred.

His expensive cologne overpowered his nostrils, attacking his sinuses. His brain was on fire.

"Not really," he answered honestly.

"C'mon, buddy. You just need to drink a bit more; problem solved."

The bass from the massive speakers was crushing his skull.

"There is not enough liquor in the world that would make the present company bearable, buddy."

Rich leaned in. "What did you say? I didn't catch that."

"I was just saying that that isn't a bad idea."

Rich grabbed two shot glasses from a passing waitress, slamming down a few bills onto her tray. He sloppily passed Will a glass.

"Cheers," Rich said, slamming back the shot.

He followed suit. His situation was becoming so dire, the tension was unbearable. His taste buds did not even register the bitter taste of the liquor.

"So, you're Lana's new squeeze, right?" Rich asked, raising his eyebrows suggestively.

"Yeah. I'm her boyfriend."

He didn't like where this conversation was going. Had Lana actually had sex with this asshole? He couldn't envision a scenario in which she would let a prick like Richard inside of her.

"You're a lucky man, bro. She's a freak," he slurred with a supercilious smile.

He glanced around the bar, scanning for Lana. He needed to break away from this shit heel. His fist was gripped vice-like around his empty shot glass. He visualized how easy it would be to ram the shot glass into Richard's forehead.

"So, what do you do?" Richard asked, changing the subject.

He wasn't going to offer an honest reply. Not to this spoiled brat. He knew what he would do to Richard when he would undoubtedly offer some condescending acknowledgement of his profession. Will was a serf in this asshole's mind.

"I own a restaurant."

"That's fucking awesome! Do I know the place?"

"It hasn't opened yet. We're still finishing construction and hiring the staff."

"Oh. What sort of cuisine will you be offering?"

"That's still open for debate. My partners and I are in a stalemate. It took them forever to concede to my staffing choices. They considered them 'unusual.'"

"What does that mean?"

"Well, any good restaurant needs a draw; something to bring in the masses. For example, are you familiar with that restaurant that is in complete darkness, and the waiters are all blind?"

"Oh, absolutely. I've been there shit loads. The food is okay."

"Right. In a similar vein, my waiters are all going to be dwarves."

"Dwarves? Like from Lord of the Rings?" He asked drunkenly

"No, like you know, little people."

Richard's eyebrows raised in shock.

"Fiscally it makes sense. You know, they're not considered real people, so I don't have to pay them as much. And, as they are so small, we can erect a series of bunk beds in the storage area. They can use that space as their home. We're really worried about them running off, you know. Despite their small stature, the fuckers are surprisingly quick and nimble. You know those small tracking implants they put in pets? I'd looked into the legalities of having those trackers placed inside them, but apparently, it's a human rights violation. Additionally, it is unbelievably difficult to find dwarves with adequate service experience."

Richard began to look uncomfortable.

"The difficulty with the wait staff is nothing in comparison to the kitchen staff."

"Oh, why's that?" Richard asked, casually looking across the crowds of people, trying to identify someone he knew.

"Well, the chef we hired doesn't have hands. Birth defect. Uses his feet for everything. I mean everything. He's a great cook, though. Well, he doesn't want any of the other cooking staff to use their hands. He doesn't want to feel like some sort of circus freak. So, we've been training the other staff members to use their feet in the preparation of food. I can honestly tell you, it is a difficult task to master."

Richard couldn't hide the look of shock on his face.

"Don't worry Richard, I understand your concern, but do not worry, all of the cooking staff will be wearing sanitary booties. Cleanliness is next to godliness, as they say."

"Cool, cool," Richard began to frantically scan the crowd. "What's the place going to be called?"

"Eat a Dick."

"Sorry?" Richard asked, leaning in closer.

"Eat at Dick's. It's the chef's name. He was quite insistent on that."

"Oh, cool. Well, let me know when you open."

Richard having finally identified someone that could save him from this awkward encounter, made a break for it.

"Good luck," he shouted while departing, deftly maneuvering through the crowd.

Despite the absence of the asshole Richard, the tension remained. He needed to get out of there. The sooner, the better. Lana was still cozied up at the bar. He rushed his way through the mass of sweaty people, abruptly edging his way to the bar.

"Hey, baby!" Lana exclaimed upon seeing Will.

She drunkenly and sloppily kissed him on the lips.

"Hey, babe. I need to get out of here. Can we go?"

Her sloshed brain needed to take a few moments to process this information. "Why? What's wrong?"

"I'm not feeling good. Can we go? Please?" he begged.

The tension continued to increase. He sensed a break was imminent.

Lana continued to stare dumbly at him with her glazed eyes.

"We're leaving!"

He grabbed her coat and purse in one hand and grabbed her arm with the other. He dragged her off of the bar stool. She stumbled but his arm steadied her. He could feel the eyes of her friends watching them, shocked.

He didn't care.

He couldn't care.

The exit glowed like a beacon.

A drunken stranger attempted to intercede their exit.

Before the man could even attempt to separate the couple, Will head butted him in one swift movement. He knew from experience that the bouncers would quickly be surrounding him. They couldn't stop.

He picked up the pace, his grip on Lana's arm constricted.

"Ouch, Will. That hurts."

He heard her. But her protestations seemed muffled. The impact of the words did not have an effect upon him. That came later.

Everything seemed to move so slow.

Finally, he was in front of the exit. He ripped open the door and exited the club, pulling Lana who had gone limp, along with him. He could still feel the eyes of the patrons at the bar on him.

By the time he fully regained a conscious awareness of the situation, he was in the back of a cab, sitting next to Lana. She was curled up in a ball, as far away from his as possible. He could hear the faint sound of sniffling.

When an episode like that occurred, he needed to take a few minutes to reassess the event. He possessed a faint recollection of it, but it felt as if it were a distant memory; not something that had occurred mere minutes before.

Sometimes, there is no coming back.

She had witnessed the result of his failure to maintain his balance against the precipice. It was times like this, he often thought, that he had witnessed the abyss that Nietzsche referred to. Yet, he had ignored the fundamental rule: don't look down.

He had stared into the abyss. Again.

This was nothing new.

The danger was that Lana had witnessed the debacle. She had seen him for what he truly was.

Was this the end?

Despite his calm exterior, he was frantically searching his mind for the best way to fix this. He was reticent. He simply could not bring himself to unpack all of his baggage. There was no woman in the world that would stay with a man who was as truly fucked as he was, is, and always will be.

He knew that Lana liked dating a "bad boy." All rich girls with daddy issues did. He understood that this was his draw; Lana liked his edginess. Unbeknownst to Lana, the "edge" that he displayed around her and her friends, was in actuality, a rather dull edge. If he exhibited his true self (warts and all), she would (rightly) run for the hills.

The cab pulled up to her building.

Lana threw a handful of bills at the cabbie, then abruptly exited the vehicle.

"Lover's quarrel?" asked the cabbie, with an obnoxious sneer.

He ignored his initial impulse and did not ram the cabbies face into the steering wheel. Instead, he chose to depart and quickly follow after her. He managed to make it to the door as she had finally located her keys in her purse.

She did not acknowledge him. A bad sign.

However, she did not stop him from following her.

He was physically and mentally preparing himself for the impending fight. He presumed that Lana had been ignoring him for two reasons: firstly, she would have to time to formulate her argument. Secondly, she probably did not want to make a scene; she was afraid of how he would react.

As he closed the door, she was already making her way to the bar. She poured herself a stiff drink. He busied himself, taking off his jacket, and removing his shoes. He looked up from his position on the ground. She was holding her glass, glaring at him.

He raised himself to a standing position. He was ready.

Lana continued to stare and occasionally sip from her drink.

"You look lovely tonight," he offered.

"What in the actual fuck was that about?!"

"I'm sorry."

Lana butted in on his initial apology, "You embarrassed me in front of my friends and hundreds of complete strangers!"

"Honey, be realistic; they had all been drinking and doing drugs. They will continue to do so. It's highly likely that they won't be able to remember what happened."

"So, that makes your hissy fit okay!?" she shouted.

"No. Not at all. I'm just reminding you of your friend's habits. Honestly, how often have they messaged you the morning after a party, asking you what had happened?"

"That's not the point!"

"I know. I'm sorry," he whispered, child-like.

"What came over you? I mean, you really scared me."

He was in checkmate. There was very little he could say or do; other than tell her the truth. This was not one of the moments in which the truth would help him. He would have to give her something. A brief glance, nothing more.

"I'm sorry, Lana," he said, making eye contact and generally trying to provide the appearance of a humbled and broken man.

She immediately adjusted her posture, from defensive; arms crossed, to one of openness; her arms uncrossed, posture relaxed.

"It's...hard for me to talk about."

Lana put her glass down on the bar top and swiftly crossed the room towards him. She took his hand.

"It's okay. You can tell me."

He almost believed her. The truth is, all women tell their female friends everything. Especially about their boyfriend/significant other. He was cognizant of the fact that her closest female friends knew how good he was in bed, the size of his cock, whether he snored or drooled in his sleep, any physical anomalies; all of the gritty details. This was one of the topics that he did not want her friends to scrutinize.

"I...it's something that has stayed with me from the war."

She looked at him with care in her eyes. She had seen the physical scars. She often remarked that she liked them; that they were sexy.

"I don't have PTSD; it's not that...It's kind of like that...It's just every once in a while, if I am under stress, or having a shit day, or feel uncomfortable, I panic and need to leave the situation."

"Oh, baby. You should have told me sooner."

She embraced him. Kissed him gently on the lips.

He knew what was coming.

Make up sex.

Although, in his opinion it hadn't been much of a fight. There had been no lengthy screaming, no throwing of dishes, no hurtful words exchanged. He had been expecting more. It was almost too easy.

The kissing intensified. Soon they were on her bed.

It was, arguably, some of the best sex that they had had, so far.

Afterwards, she leaned over the bed to pick up her phone. Her attachment to that device drove him crazy. She readjusted herself, fluffing her pillow. She was laid back and scrolling through her phone.

"Hey, baby?"

"Yeah?"

"Why does Rich think that you own a restaurant?"

"Who?"

"Rich. You know Richard. He was the guy buying everyone drinks."

"Oh, him. I have no idea. I don't think that I talked to him tonight."

"Are you sure? He's sent me a bunch of messages about how my boyfriend is some kind of psychopathic gourmand."

"He's clearly drunk and on drugs. I didn't talk to him," he protested.

"Babe, were you messing with him?" she asked, lightly prodding him.

"I wasn't. But if I had, I wouldn't understand what the big deal is. I thought that you liked it when I messed with people."

"I do. Just...not with my friends. I don't want you to embarrass me in front of them, okay?"

"I told you, he must be mistaken. I just have one of those faces, I guess."

She dropped the issue. They huddled together, naked. In the dark.

He could feel her to begin to drift off to sleep.

Richard. He had referred to her as a freak. That comment, and the fucking smirk on his face. He couldn't believe that she would have sex with an asshole like that. The thoughts began to operate in a vicious cycle. He kept revisiting the look on Richard's face.

That. Smug. Little. Prick.

He needed to address this.

He should let it go.

It didn't matter. It was in the past.

"Lana?" he asked, quietly.

"Mmmhmm," she answered half asleep.

"That guy, Richard. Were you two...involved?"

There was no reply.

"Lana?"

Silence.

She was asleep. Or at least, pretending to be asleep. Avoiding the issue.

He laid there in the dark. Ruminating.

It should have been a speed bump in their relationship. Maybe it was. Perhaps, with the benefit of hindsight, he was reading into things; attributing significant meanings to people and events where there was none.

Things proceeded. For all intents and purposes, he was living with her. They had each said, "I love you." He meant it. He thought that she had meant it, too. Things just felt off. Like there was a distance growing between them. It was nothing that he could identify clearly.

Shortly after the incident, Lana made an offer. It was her intention to present it as an honest effort at appeasement; to assuage any potential conflict that could arise.

She gently suggested that he not attend the various celebrations and parties held at clubs. Lana had presented it as a loving offer of comfort. He was not comfortable or happy at the soirées, so he didn't have to go.

This suggestion was welcomed with a veiled suspicion.

Another red flag.

He accepted the offer as graciously as he could manage.

He recognized that the offer was disingenuous. Lana had portrayed this offer as selfless; beneficial solely to him. However, it was clear that her suggestion was entirely for her advantage.

He tried to convince himself that there was nothing wrong, that she wasn't messing around behind his back. That he wasn't losing her. Whether it was a result of his neuroses, pessimism, or his misanthropic attitude, but he could not rid himself of this suspicion.

This suspicion tainted their relationship.

He couldn't look at her like he used to.

He found himself at an impasse.

Fearful of raising the issue, as it would undoubtedly result in a larger conflict, or even worse, it would further sow the seeds of the relationships destruction. He began to view himself and Lana as occupying a new and dangerous position; the relationship was built on shifting sands. The structure's collapse, he realized, was imminent.

As voicing his suspicion would hasten their demise, he felt that there was little that he could do. He assumed a passive and calm position. All he could do was watch and wait. At the time, he felt assured that he could save their relationship.

Everyone lies to themselves.

He was no different.

He tried to trust her. He tried to resist the temptation of following her.

He was plagued with haunting images. Lana with Richard.

Lana and Richard.

Lana and a series of men.

He tried to play it cool and nonchalant when Lana returned home from a late night, but he swore that he could smell a masculine scent on her coat. He asked her, with all of the passivity that he could muster, what she had done that night.

She answered without looking at him, busying herself with putting away her jacket.

He grabbed her from behind, holding her delicately. He started to kiss her neck.

"Sorry, baby. I'm really tired. I'm just going to go to bed."

She gently pried his hands off of her, kissing him gently on the cheek.

He watched her walk to the bed, quickly disrobing and sliding under the covers.

The next time that she had a "girls' night," he was ready.

He followed her discreetly, watching from a distance.

The club was a perfect setting for surveillance. The mass amounts of people, crowded in together, made for ideal cover. It also helped that Lana was not the suspicious type. Neither Lana nor her friends would know the first thing about counter-surveillance.

Initially, he felt both pleased and foolish. He was put at ease, realizing that the douchebag, Richard, was not in attendance. He even began to feel foolish and even somewhat ashamed at his distrust of Lana.

He was relieved, despite the shitty music and the irritating bass of the club's speakers.

His mind at ease, he was getting ready to leave the club. That is until that dickhead and his friends showed up. He hoped that it was merely a coincidence that the two groups were both at the same club. There were, of course, only so many clubs in the city.

Richard and his group of trust fund buddies made a beeline to Lana and her friends.

Fuck.

He watched as Richard (who possessed the unmitigated gall) to creep behind Lana and cover her eyes ("guess who?"). What. A. Dick. He felt a tremor shake his body as he witnessed the look of pure joy upon Lana's face. He cringed as Richard and Lana embraced each other in a hug that lasted far too long.

As if on cue, the hateful images began to cycle through his mind.

Richard and Lana.

Lana and Richard.

Lana kissing Richard.

Richard inside of Lana.

Lana on top of Richard.

Richard and Lana, the secret lovers.

Lana. The liar. The heartbreaker.

He was going to kill him.

It took all of his restraint to not approach the bar and beat Richard to a pulp. The only thing that saved Richard from a beatdown was that he knew Lana would completely break things off with him. There would be no coming back from such a vivid display of violence.

He turned around and exited the bar.

Lana got home late.

He was in bed. Staring at the ceiling.

He was wracked with another tremor when he realized that instead of coming to bed, Lana had gone to the bathroom and turned on the shower. Lana never took showers at night. Especially after clubbing. She would just come home and collapse into bed.

Fuck.

Coming home late. Immediately taking a shower. These things added up to an inescapable conclusion: she had been with Richard. Lana was attempting to wash the stench of Richard's noxious cologne off of her body.

Lana spent a fucking eternity in that bathroom.

She finally emerged from the steamy bathroom and quietly walked into the bedroom. Another fucking warning sign; she came to bed in sweatpants and one of his old shirts. Normally Lana slept in her underwear or nude.

"How was your evening?" he asked, staring at the ceiling.

"Fine. Sorry, did I wake you?" she asked quickly.

"No, I couldn't sleep."

"Oh?"

"Yeah. I kept thinking about something; my mind won't shut the fuck up."

She had slipped underneath the covers, and was on her shoulder, facing the opposite direction. There was a moment of silence following his comment.

"Oh? What's that?"

He couldn't help but notice the tension in her voice as she asked this.

"Oh, something from my time overseas. You don't want to hear about it."

"No, you can talk to me."

Lana rolled over onto her other side and placed her hand on his chest. He remained staring at the ceiling.

"Well, this one time, there was an explosion in an apartment building. We were in the area, so we rushed over. It became apparent that a bomb-maker had accidentally blown himself up too early. Oops, right? Somewhere in the building there had to have been some seriously flammable materials; people reported seeing a fireball erupt! The building was partially collapsed and burning. So, we established a secure perimeter, while the others set to putting the fire out. Well, by the time they got the fire out, the people inside; that is, the ones who couldn't make it out – well, they were charred to a fucking crisp. Although there had been numerous times that I had seen the remains of people who'd been bombed, this time was different. They brought out this little body. It was clearly a girl. Her hands clutched at the remnants of this tiny bear, or some sort of stuffed animal. It had melted into her hands. The thing that you don't realize about fires is that the people who are burned alive; the heat literally causes their eyeballs to pop out of their skulls."

"Holy shit," she whispered.

"When I saw it, I was reminded of something that I had read about Operation Desert Storm. American bombers dropped a couple of one-tonne bombs on a bunker. The first bomb created so much rubble that the people inside were trapped. The second bomb went through the roof and exploded. Something like four hundred people were killed. Women and children. Military intelligence is always something of a misnomer. They thought that the bunker was a command center. The bodies of the innocent victims were apparently charred beyond recognition. I remember not being able to actually imagine what charred corpses looked like. I found out that day."

He caught her confused and disturbed glance out of the corner of his eye.

"Yeah. I don't know why I thought about that. Sometimes these memories just come out of nowhere."

"Are you...okay?" she asked haltingly.

"Yeah. I missed you."

He rolled over to face her. He quickly embraced her; began running his hands over the curves of her body. She pulled her hands up and gently pushed him away.

"Sorry, baby. I'm just really tired. And no offense, but the story you just told me doesn't exactly put me in the mood."

Sulking, he rolled back onto his other side.

"Why did you shower?" he asked, surprising himself.

"What do you mean?"

"You never shower at night. Generally, you topple into bed after a night of clubbing."

"Some drunken slob spilled his pint on me. I cleaned it up, but I couldn't get the smell of beer off of me."

"Oh? I'd best throw your clothes in the wash then; don't want them to stain. Besides, I could do with some clean clothes myself."

"Don't bother. I dabbed at it with some club soda at the bar."

"Better safe than sorry, right? I mean, it was an entire pint. There's no way that you can be completely sure that you got it completely clean, especially in the dark atmosphere of a club."

"Just leave it, Will!"

Her enraged voice had shattered the previous tranquillity of their bedroom.

"Lana, is there a particular reason that you do not want me to look at your dress?"

"Don't be ridiculous; I just want to go to bed and not be kept awake with the noise of you puttering around doing laundry."

He let the conversation lapse into silence. He didn't want to get out of bed. He already knew the truth. Once again, his gaze drifted back to the white ceiling. He willed his mind to remain silent.

He heard Lana sigh exasperatedly.

"I'm sorry, Will. I didn't mean to snap at you. I'm just tired."

She leaned over him and kissed him. It wasn't so much a kiss as it was an imitation; it was the attempt at a loving kiss. It was a half-hearted attempt at reconciliation. It was not the way she used to kiss him.

"Goodnight, babe," she whispered into his ear.

He stared at the ceiling. Willing it to collapse upon himself.

"Night."

•   •   •

He never did find that dress.

It wasn't in the laundry hamper, crumpled up in a ball inside the recesses of her closet, or even in the garbage. He tried to ignore it. But the thoughts and suspicion began to circulate on a loop in his mind.

He didn't want to argue with Lana.

He wanted to talk to Richard.

He finagled Richard's number from a friend of Lana's. He repeatedly called the number throughout the day. Richard never picked up. He was obviously screening his calls; not recognizing the number, he wasn't about to answer.

Will resorted to text messaging.

Introducing himself, he then asked if he was available to meet up for coffee. The douche waited for an interminable amount of time before he responded.

Rich: 11 @ Café Luxor.

Fuck. Even his texts were pompous and condescending.

The café was one of many new businesses in the downtown area. It was part of the massive and inescapable force that is gentrification. Buildings and businesses that had been part of the community for decades being pushed out. There were already three Starbucks within a ten-block radius.

Gentrification dictates that a location can never have too many cafés or hipster, gluten-free, farm-to-table, pesticide free, hormone-free restaurants. Not to mention the overpriced bakeries or cupcake factories.

He had formed a mental image of what the interior of the café would look like. This image meshed with reality perfectly. It was a hipster joint. Of course. The café clearly advertised that all coffee served was fair-trade. Morally, this made sense. For whatever reason, all fair-trade coffee tasted like it was filtered through an old shoe.

Ignoring the barista (a young white female, with too many facial piercings and dreadlocks), he made his way over to Richard.

Richard's phone was figuratively glued to his face. Will stood next to the table for a few moments without receiving recognition. His ire being raised early, he roughly pulled out the empty chair from the table.

Richard quickly looked up, obviously startled.

"Oh, hey. Sorry, didn't see you there." Richard offered with a supercilious grin.

"We have a problem."

"Sorry?"

"You heard me."

"What's the deal, bro?"

"Whatever you're doing with Lana, it's going to stop."

"What are you talking about?"

"You're going to stop seeing her."

Richard rolled his eyes and scoffed.

"Are you threatening me?! What are you going to do?"

"I'll cut your dick off and stitch it onto your forehead."

Richard pushed himself up and out from the table. Will quickly followed suit. Richard slowly walked towards him, sizing him up. Richard pressed his nose up against his own and sharply poked him in the chest.

"You are nothing. Do you understand? I could easily squash you. Do you have any idea who I am? Who my father is?"

Richard poked him in the chest one last time. Will slowly looked down at the offending digit. He quickly grabbed the index finger before Richard could pull back. Clenching his fist around the finger, he snapped it back.

There was an audible pop.

Richard immediately began to scream and moan. Letting go of the finger, Richard crouched down into the fetal position.

Hovering over him, Will remarked, "That was a warning. Stay away from her."

It had all happened so fast.

He couldn't comprehend the fact that he had just broken Richard's finger. It was pure reaction. It was not a premeditated attack; he had met him solely to warn him – scare and threaten him if necessary, but not actual violence.

In the future, he would reflect that Richard had provoked him; that he had set a trap for him and he had fallen for it.

In any case, by the time that he had got back to Lana's place, she had already been told of the incident at the café. She was waiting for him. He opened the door to find Lana, sitting on the couch, arms crossed. Staring daggers at him.

"Hey, baby."

"What the fuck were you thinking?!" Lana screamed at him.

"You're going to have to be a little more specific," he said, hoping to buy himself some time.

"Cut the bullshit! Richard called me from the waiting room of the ER."

Fuck.

"What exactly did he say?" he probed carefully.

"That you met him for coffee only to threaten him and then broke his finger."

Lana stood up and walked over to the bar. She poured herself a stiff drink, her back to him.

"It didn't happen exactly like that," he conceded.

"Why did you do it?" Lana asked, sipping from her drink.

"I know something is going on between you two. I only meant to warn him. He provoked me. Let's be honest, I could've fucked him up a lot worse than a broken finger."

"Does that make it okay?" Lana asked imploringly.

"No. However, I notice that you didn't bother denying it."

He forced himself to stare at the wall. The blank and impassive wall. He knew that if he looked at her, or made eye-contact with her, he would fall apart. She didn't respond.

"I think that we both knew that this was not going to last," she offered mildly.

"Oh."

He had thought he had said it as a question but it came off as a statement.

"You need to pack up your stuff and leave."

The atmosphere was tense. Despite the overall fucked nature of the situation, he couldn't help but observe their physical stance. He stood with his back to the door, staring at the wall. Lana stood at the bar, her back to him, looking at him through the mirror on the wall behind the bar. Disconcertingly, he realized that she was wearing the same outfit that she wore the night that they met.

At least that was what he remembered. Memory has a way of not only fading but fragmenting or transforming with the addition of time. The mind attempts to create and maintain order; removing episodes that were too painful, adding other sequences to create cohesiveness.

They didn't say anything else.

He didn't know and couldn't remember how long they each stood, silently brooding, each in their own space. At some point, some command must have clicked in his mind, as he found himself walking into the bedroom and packing his stuff.

There wasn't much.

He packed light. A few changes of clothes, some books and deodorant.

When he emerged from the bedroom, Lana was gone.

The bathroom door was closed. He could see the traces of light under the door.

"Leave your key!" Lana shouted, through the door.

As if on autopilot, he numbly removed the key from the keyring and placed it on the bar top. He took one last look around. Opened the door and left.

•   •   •

After that it gets a bit hazy.

He remembered dropping his stuff off at the apartment, then immediately heading to a bar. He could remember going to the first couple of bars. He was cut off from one and ejected from the other.

Things start to get really blurry.

There was another bar or club. He tried to get in.

The bouncer wouldn't let him enter.

The only thing he remembered after that was being on top of the bouncer. He was pummeling the man's face. The bouncer's face was already swelling, blood was pouring off of his face, onto the concrete.

He blacked out sometime afterwards.

When he came to, he was standing outside Lana's building.

He had sobered up, somewhat. At least enough to feel the pain in his hands. Lifting them for inspection, he noted with dismay and shock, that there was dried blood caked onto his knuckles.

Brief flashes of the altercation with the bouncer shot through his mind.

He stumbled to the entrance.

He struggled drunkenly to press the correct buzzer. Having finally managed the herculean task of pressing his finger on the button, he let his entire weight press against it.

Fade to black.

He came to, not knowing how long he had been in the doorway.

It was still nighttime.

He walked out of the doorway onto the street.

Looking up at her window, he began to shout frantically, "Lana! Let me up!"

In his drunken haze, he couldn't be sure, but he thought he saw movement behind the curtains.

"Lana!"

It was at this point that an older woman yelled out her window, "If you don't piss off, I'm going to call the police!"

Being threatened with police sobered him minimally. He was in no state to be questioned by the police. Drunk and spattered with someone else's blood; the earlier fistfight (he still cannot remember if he caused irreparable bodily harm), he decided to leave the area.

Before making his escape, he looked back at her window.

She was standing there. Looking down at him. Lana's face conveyed both concern and condemnation. They made eye contact. Richard appeared before him in the window. He looked down upon him, with the bare traces of a smirk.

Richard then lovingly whispered something in her ear and pulled her away from the window. The curtains fell back into place. The light behind the curtain was quickly extinguished.

That was the last time that he saw her.

•   •   •

In the following days, he engaged in earnest and critical self-reflection.

His life thus far, was one of pain and dislocation. The fractured life that he shared with his mother, a result of the void left by his father. The inability of his mother to speak about his father's absence. His father's numerous half-assed attempts at being a part of his life. The war. The numbness that greeted his return. The futile and fruitless relationship with Lana.

Did he have a twisted version of the Midas touch?

Everything that he touched died. It was like he was a cancer in other's lives.

He was a jinx.

He was not the first man to radically shift his demeanor following a heartbreak. The assessment of his life caused him to shift all energy and focus toward self-preservation. He erected various mental defenses to prevent collapse. It required hyper-vigilance and necessitated expurgation.

To maintain and preserve his sanity, he limited his interaction with others. Ultimately, this was not that difficult; he had never exhibited any of the traits of an extrovert. He had always preferred to keep to himself. The only friend that he could generally tolerate for long periods of time, was Thomas.

In the passing months, he would fleetingly reflect upon the ease of this personal transformation. He withdrew from society and relationships with neither stress nor difficulty. Instead, it brought immediate gratification. Like slipping into a warm bath. What did this say about him?

Did he seek isolation because he was broken?

Or was he broken because he had always preferred isolation?

•   •   •

He awoke without a hangover.

Thank God for small favors.

While performing his morning routine, he thought back on last night's events. He thought of Teresa. He enjoyed a few moments of bliss before being plunged back into harsh reality.

Natalie.

He pondered the proper etiquette for situations like this. He doubted that Emily Post provided reliable guidelines for these scenarios. Should he call Laura and offer his condolences? Should he attend the funeral service? Send flowers? There were no experts to consult in this type of situation. He had never had a client die during the course of an investigation.

Except for Herman.

As was his habit, the thought caused him to absentmindedly caress the scar.

He was sitting at his desk, having completed his routine (workout, shower, more coffee), when his phone beeped.

Jocelyn: I need to talk to you.

No shit, he thought to himself.

He texted her the address of his office and hurriedly made his way to meet her.

•   •   •

More waiting.

He made another pot of coffee while he waited for Jocelyn to arrive.

Fifteen minutes later, his intercom beeped.

He didn't need to verify the identity of the caller. He purposefully did all that he could to prevent any random visitors or unwanted guests. Following the incident with Herman, his already heightened sense of security was increased considerably; he added more locks and a security camera. No one entered unless he successfully vetted them as a potential threat. He did not arrange deliveries at his business address, and he scheduled potential clients by appointment only.

Jocelyn could be the only person at his door.

He sat in silence.

Within moments he heard the sound of footsteps. He could practically hear the trepidation in her steps. These were not the steps of someone overly confident. No doubt, due to the flurry of messages that he had sent, and their overall tone, he was certain that she was uncertain as to what to expect.

That was the point, of course.

Experience had taught him that you don't start an interrogation without already knowing the answers to the questions. He knew part of the story. Not all of it, but enough to get a general sense of it.

There was a timid knock on the door.

He had left the door unlocked for her.

"Come in," he answered.

Jocelyn opened the door. Jocelyn stood at the entryway; she was pale and bathed in loss, desperation, and mourning. She appeared hollow in the way that only those who have suffered can truly appreciate and understand.

"Jocelyn, take a seat. I'm going to grab us some coffee."

Jocelyn virtually collapsed into the offered seat. She immediately began to shake and sob. She was on the verge of hysterics. He knew the signs and symptoms. In combat, he had seen enough men and women react in this way following an attack.

He rushed towards her and knelt down in front of her.

"Jocelyn, you're about to have a panic attack. I need you to lean forward and grab your knees."

She was numb. There was no recognition; no clue or indication that she had registered his direction.

He gently touched her arm and guided her body.

"What we're going to do now is breathe. *Breathe*, Jocelyn. One deep breath in and one out." He pantomimed the actions while giving directions like a flight attendant.

Slowly, she started to respond.

"Good, Jocelyn. I'm going to get us that coffee. Caffeine and sugar will help."

He made his way to the mini-kitchen and poured out coffee. He placed heaping amounts of sugar in her cup. Sugar helped with shock. The more, the better.

He quickly returned to the office. Once again, he kneeled down in front of her. He offered her the cup. While she had somewhat regained her composure, her hands were still shaking.

"I'll hold it for you," he said.

He slowly put the cup to her lips. He gently poured the coffee into her mouth. He slowly doled out the contents. He would pour some into her mouth, she would swallow and offer a deep sigh. This process continued until the cup was empty.

"Hold out your hands," he softly instructed.

Taking a deep breath, she slowly raised and extended her arms. There were still signs of tremors, but she appeared to be somewhat under control.

"I'm going to get you another cup of coffee. Keep doing those breathing exercises."

She nodded in reply.

After making another trip to the mini-kitchen and returning with another coffee, he knelt down in front of her, prepared to guide the cup to her mouth as before. She slowly took the cup out of his hands.

"Thanks, but I think I'm okay now."

He nodded and retreated back to his side of the desk.

Jocelyn was staring aimlessly at the wall behind him. It did not take him long to recognize the look etched upon her face. *The thousand-yard stare*. It was a facial feature that he had observed many other soldiers exhibit after being routinely subjected to witnessing the horrific. It was a look that implied internal malfunction or damage. It was a look that blatantly implied one unalterable and unshakeable fact: they were traumatized.

He understood that she had something to say. No amount of coaxing was going to speed along the process. This was going to take some time. This meant waiting. Normally this would have frustrated him. Not now, though. It was clear that what she knew was going to make all the difference. He hoped that what knowledge she possessed regarding Natalie and her disappearance would finally bring him peace. He did not believe in closure. This was not that. He simply needed to discern if he had failed her. If he could have done something to deter or alter the outcome.

Jocelyn made eye contact with him. Rather than divert her gaze away, she let her stare remain in place. This gave him the impression that she was waiting for a cue or signal to begin.

"Tell me. Tell me everything," he commanded gently.

"I hid Natalie. I helped her escape."

"Escape?"

He would remember later, that at the time he had felt it was an odd choice of words. That Jocelyn was being a typical teenager; dramatic and hyperbolic. She gave him a look that was impossible to describe. It struck through his rough facade and reverberated through his very core.

Then he learned everything.

•   •   •

"I know this is hard. I just need you to tell me the story, as best as you can. Omit nothing; not a single detail."

Jocelyn looked despondently at the linoleum floor.

"It's her dad," Jocelyn forced out. He knew before she even finished the sentence. Everything clicked into place like a life-sized jigsaw puzzle. "He...hurt her. All of the time."

He let that evaporate into the ether.

"You mean..." he prompted.

"He was molesting her."

She looked like she was going to fall apart. The tears were beginning to form in the corner of her eyes. He quickly looked away. He doubted that he would ever get better at this.

"And why didn't she go to the police?" he proffered, as gently as possible.

Jocelyn looked at him as if he were a fool.

"*Because* it would *kill* her mother."

His childhood experience was inarguably tainted. It was an unusual story; being separated from his father, his mother maintaining a strict code of silence about the cause of the separation, the continued lack of conversation in the father-son relationship culminating in the deathbed property transfer, followed closely by the death of his mother. Regardless, this excuse failed to resonate for him.

"What does that have to do with anything?"

"I don't know! Natalie told me that growing up, her mom would always tell her the love story between her and her father. How they met, dated and fell in love, got married, got pregnant. It was, like, painted as some great love story. I don't know. It seemed fairly normal to me. Her dad is, like, her mom's only great love. Natalie talked about it like it was some sort of epic love story. That's just what she told me! That's what I know!"

It was as if he felt the echo of her enraged voice bounce off of the walls of his office. He looked down at his desk. He counted to ten; give her some time to breathe, before starting again.

It had been going on for years.

"For how long?"

"At least since she was thirteen."

Jocelyn only found out about it recently. A few months, six at the most. She couldn't seem to remember. Not that the precise time line mattered. It was the events that he was preoccupied with.

"What did she say about it? About her father? Tell me everything."

Jocelyn looked at him with pity. She told him the story and damned him.

Natalie had always been a daddy's girl.

Her and her father were always close. She followed him everywhere. When he was not at work, he would spend all of his time with her. Her mother thought it was adorable. Laura loved how Natalie clung to her father. Laura hadn't had a close relationship with her own father and was overjoyed that her daughter wouldn't experience the same.

Things changed when she was twelve or thirteen. Natalie had been hazy with the exact time frame. She recalled that she noticed that her dad began to look at her differently. More intently than before. Often it was with a look that made her feel uncomfortable. Uneasy. In a way, that if he had been a complete stranger, she would have had been afraid. But this was her father. There was nothing to be afraid of.

One night, she woke up and realized that her father was sitting on the corner of her bed. She was shocked to discover that he was wearing only his underwear. He looked at her and whispered that she should go back to sleep. This carried on routinely for weeks. She would wake up in the middle of the night, and he would be there. He never mentioned it in the following morning, and she was uncomfortable and confused. She deluded herself into believing that he was a loving father, watching his only child sleep, perhaps reflecting upon how quickly she was growing up.

Things progressed rapidly.

One night, Natalie woke up expecting to find her father on the corner of her bed. To her relief, he was not. This sense of relief quickly vanished as she noted the figure squatting next to her bed. It was her father.

"Sweetie, you're burning up. I need you to take this medicine," he whispered.

She remembered thinking that she felt fine. She had a bit of a headache, but nothing serious. She demurred at first, but her father insisted. There was a nasty bug going around. He was her father *and* a doctor. He knew what was best for her. She acquiesced. He handed her a pill and a glass of water on her nightstand. After taking her medicine, her father bade her sweet dreams and promptly left her room.

The following details were disjointed – fractured beyond repair. She stirred from sleep, semi-conscious. She felt warm and pleasantly light headed. Like she was floating on a cloud. This comfort rapidly faded as she realized that her father was in bed with her. He was moaning and grunting, rubbing himself over her body. She was scared, but she felt like she couldn't move, as if this were happening to somebody else. She felt disconnected from the event, but it was real all the same.

She vividly remembered her father's breathing and movement rapidly increasing, grunting, cursing quietly under his breath, until his body seized, and he stopped moving. The rest was a blur. She barely recalled him getting out of her bed and leaving her room.

She was sore the next day. Sore in a way that she had never experienced before. She had nothing to compare it to.

Her father acted as if nothing had happened. Nothing was different. His behavior almost convinced her that nothing had happened. Maybe she really was sick. Maybe it was all some sort of sick and inexplicable dream. Before her father left for work, he handed her another pill.

"You look ill, take this. You should stay home from school today."

This time, she took the medicine without hesitation.

"Was it every night?" he asked Jocelyn.

"No. I don't think so. I don't know for sure. I couldn't bring myself to ask."

He nodded. "Did she know what he was dosing her with?"

"It took her a long time to figure out. Her dad kept a series of stashes all over the place."

"Opiates?" he asked.

"Yes," she answered blankly.

"That's how she got hooked?"

"Yes," Jocelyn mindlessly repeated.

"The piece of shit didn't expect her to get hooked. Or he just didn't care. Probably the latter," he thought out loud.

"I noticed a difference in her immediately," Jocelyn muttered.

The tears began to flow freely. Jocelyn was the epitome of true despair. A living portrait of destruction. There was no hyperventilating, no shaking, no shrieks of heartache. This, he knew, was what real pain looked like; oblivious to the tears being shed, frozen in place.

He needed to get this over with. The poor girl had been through enough. If there was any way that he could've avoided having her tell the story, he would've pursued it with prejudice. If he had been in Jocelyn's position, he would've buried this story in the dark recesses of his mind. Lock it in an empty room. Lose the key. Fuck it.

"I know this is hard. But I need you to keep going," he said, knowing that he deserved to be condemned to hell for this.

Jocelyn wiped the tears off of her face with the back of her hand. She continued the story. By the time she finished, he regretted urging her to finish the story.

It didn't take Natalie long to realize what was going on. What her own father was doing to her. She felt dirty. Like it was her fault. Like she was betraying her mother. Feeling like you're a whore, a piece of shit, unworthy of love or redemption. This, of course, is the perfect storm for addiction.

The abuse continued and Natalie needed more pills to numb herself. Her increased demands and pleas for more pills began to frighten her father. He caved in to her demands. Of course.

An addict will do whatever they have to do to get their fix.

Will served with a guy whose brother was a heroin addict. The topic of addiction came up in the mess hall. He said something about addiction that stuck with Will. "Self-respect is the first thing to go for an addict."

Things continued in this vein. Jocelyn didn't know when for sure, but once again, Natalie needed more pills. Her tolerance was extremely high considering her size. Her father resisted her demands. She only had one thing to use as leverage. At least in her drug-sick mind.

"She refused to let him...you know, unless he gave her what she wanted."

His stomach flipped.

He did not know that much about Natalie. Everything that he had discerned about her was from her mother, her friend and her ex-boyfriend. The people that cared about her. He knew in his core that Natalie, the clean Natalie, would never have done something like that.

It was the drugs. It was her father. *He* destroyed her.

Her addiction continued to escalate. It intensified to the point that she could no longer rely solely on her dad. Natalie started looking for pills from other sources. Enter Alain. Of course, money was an issue. This, in turn, led to stealing. First from her mother and father. Then shoplifting. Selling stolen merchandise to pawn shops.

These actions drew the attention of her mother. Thankfully. Fast forward to rehab. Natalie got clean. Initially, she told herself that she could deal with the past. That she could stay clean. This was wishful thinking.

She had to leave the rehab facility at some point.

She was told that in order to stay clean she would need to learn to avoid her triggers. Her main trigger was waiting at home for her. Natalie fooled herself into thinking that she could get her father to stop.

Her first return from rehab.

She told him in private that things were over. That if they continued, she would have to tell mom. This was a bluff. She didn't want to tell anyone. Especially her mom.

"What did he do?"

"He gave her the impression that he understood. But he also left a couple of pills on her nightstand. 'Just in case.'"

The tension that she had to deal with on a daily basis. That would cause any addict to crack. The cycle started over. Again. And again.

"When did she finally tell you?"

"After her second time at rehab. She looked really good, actually. It was like there was actually life in her again. I felt like I had my friend back. She was over at my house for a sleepover. I don't know why, but I felt the urge to ask her *why*, you know? Why she popped pills. I honestly wasn't expecting her answer. I don't know what the fuck I thought she would say, but it wasn't that."

It was during her second attempt at rehab that she had began to formulate a plan. It was the kind of plan that only an emotionally scarred teenager going through withdrawals could postulate.

A plan lacking a practical outcome.

He couldn't fault her for that. In her position, he doubted that he could have done better. She was preoccupied with gaining freedom. He surmised that this was, in actuality, the goal. *Freedom*. From the monster masquerading as a father. From temptation to use. From everything.

He hated himself for it, but he had to know that he was right. He needed to feel the vindication that he had so far been denied. He had to know that he wasn't the reason that Natalie was dead. That there had been nothing that he could have done. He may have been a fuck up. He just needed to know that he was not that much of a fuck up.

"So, you were in on it from the beginning?"

"Yeah. She did have a plan. At first. But her dad was working on her again. She didn't know what else to do. Neither did I. She was ready to run away, hop on a bus, risk living on the street. She didn't give a fuck anymore. She just wanted to get away."

He cut her off. "It was your cabin, right?"

"Yeah. My family hardly ever goes there. My grandpa left it to my dad. My parents hate it out there. I thought she could hide there until we figured out what to do."

"Was Cameron in on it, too?"

"No," she said, shaking her head, "He was genuinely worried about her. She told me not to tell him anything. She didn't want him to know."

"Yeah, about that; why did she break up with him? He seemed pretty torn up about it. He didn't strike me as the typical jock douchebag."

Jocelyn rolled her eyes before answering. "Why do you think?"

"I don't know. That's why I'm asking."

"He's sweet. But, he's still a teenage boy. He wanted what all boys want."

"Oh, right," he said, feeling like a simpleton.

"And with her dad...it turned her off of that."

"Yeah. That makes sense. So, she never told him anything?"

"No. She felt *dirty*. At least that's how she explained it. She didn't want whatever they had to get fucked up by her fucked home life."

He didn't say anything. While he was at a loss for words, Jocelyn appeared to be finding her rhythm. She continued on, indifferent to his discomfort.

"I don't know the full story, but Natalie mentioned something about how the topic of sex came up; he asked if she was a virgin. He was or is. He wasn't pushing or anything; he was just genuinely curious. She didn't know what to say. I think she just changed the subject."

"Did she have any sort of plan?" he asked, abruptly changing the topic.

"She was going to find work and try to emancipate herself."

"At that shithole pharmacy?"

Jocelyn's jaw dropped. "Yeah, how did you know?"

"Doesn't matter. What happened there?"

"Well, it turned out her dealer works there. She went there to hand in her application for a cashier job. Then she saw him. She completely lost her shit, she flipped out. She didn't even hand in the application. She texted me 911. I headed over to the cabin. I found her huddled in a fucking ball. I rocked her to sleep."

"Where did she find the money for drugs?"

"She didn't. She had finally worked up the courage to go and talk to her mom. She was going to tell her everything. When she got to the house, no one was home. She was nervous and stressed. She must have cracked. She went looking in the usual places for her dad's stash. She found some pills and took off.

"She got back to the cabin. I was waiting for her. I could tell by the look in her eyes that something wasn't right. She broke down. Told me the truth. She couldn't do it. It was just too hard to talk about. I was the only one that she told.

"I got her to give me the pills. I flushed them. Then I had to leave. I guess she had more."

Jocelyn collapsed into tears.

He had no idea what to do. He awkwardly raised himself from his seat. He nervously approached her. Hesitantly, he placed his hand on her shoulder. Jocelyn immediately pulled him into a bearhug. He forced himself to swallow his discomfort.

He would hold her for as long as she needed.

Eventually, she reached the point at which no more tears can be shed. The accumulated tension had been released. She released him. Jocelyn took a few more moments to compose herself. She took a heavy pull off of her cup. After she drained the remainder, she released a deep sigh.

"It's my fault. I lied. I should've told you. I should've told somebody."

"No!" he said, surprising himself. "You did not lie. You just didn't tell the whole truth."

"What's the difference?" she asked in earnest.

"In my experience, liars tell lies to help themselves. Even when they lie for other people. It's always about them. You were just trying to help your friend. You did the right thing. I would have done the same."

Jocelyn wiped the remainder of the tears off of her face.

"What do we do now?" she asked, "Do we go to the police?"

There was no proof of the father's incestuous appetites. He may still have drugs around the house. He didn't want him to go to jail for mere possession of pills. That was not justice. He would not get what he deserved. As long as he was not running a pill mill; providing massive amounts of opiates to his patients without cause, then he would more than likely get off with a lengthy probation and community service. Maybe lose his license. Maybe.

"No. There is no proof. It's hearsay. And the victim is deceased."

"So, what do we do?!" she asked raising her voice in defiance.

"We? We aren't going to do anything. I am going to take care of it."

"What do you mean?"

"It's better that you don't know. You need to focus on getting better."

"Getting better?"

He could hear the bitterness rising in her voice.

"Yes. You're just a kid. You can't be involved with what happens next. Trust me. He will get what he deserves. I need you to go back to normal life."

"Normal life? Are you fucking kidding me right now?"

"Yes. Mourn. Be with your family. Hang out with your friends. I know this is hard. Believe me, I know. But you will get used to it. It will eventually fade from your immediate memory. I mean, you will remember it, but one day it won't hurt as much. It will feel like it happened to somebody else.

"I need you to find solace in the fact that that piece of shit is going to get what is coming to him."

She didn't look happy. This was par for the course. She wasn't going to be happy for a very long time. She needed to work at it. It wouldn't be easy. Or she could give up. And end up like him. He doubted that the latter would be a good fit for her.

She sighed like a typical teenage girl. "So, that's it?"

"Actually, I need three more things from you."

"Like, what?"

"I need directions to your cabin along with the keys to said cabin."

"That's only two things," she said in a huff.

"Right. Lastly, I need you to keep your mouth shut about this. You cannot tell anyone. Ever. Are you up to it? I need to know that I can count on you. I can do what is needed. But only if you are able to keep this a secret. I know, I'm asking for a lot."

Jocelyn simply stared at him. He could feel the palpable tension that the proposal left in its wake. In hindsight, he would reflect that there had been little doubt in his mind that she would accept the offer. Indeed, he would have been shocked if she had rejected him with alacrity. It did trouble him (somewhat) that he had thought little of the unenviable position that this left Jocelyn in.

We all have a cross to bear.

We all have to do our part for the greater good.

• • •

It was a relatively short drive to the cabin.

He lacked a rational or even practical purpose for the trip.

There was no real reason to go.

It wasn't as if it were still a great mystery. There was nothing more to investigate. And yet he persisted. Perhaps it was simply a matter of self-abuse. He was a glutton for punishment. He would nominally categorize this trip as a futile attempt at closure, if he actually believed in the concept of closure. It was simply the penultimate episode of the Natalie saga. He needed to witness the environment that Natalie had taken refuge in, during her final days.

As he approached the cabin, he thought, somewhat distastefully, that there were worse places to die in. By no means did the rustic cabin compared to the mansion that she had resided in, but he hoped that she had at least found something akin to comfort.

Jocelyn had found her.

She was in her sleeping bag. Natalie had looked like she was in a deep sleep.

It was her pale face that caused concern.

Her skin immediately reminded her of the characters from old horror movies that she watched as a child. Actors' faces painted white and grey; a deathly pallor. Jocelyn called her name. No response. Raising her voice, she called her name again. Nothing. She freaked out, approached her and began to shake her. Searching for a pulse, she found nothing. She thought she knew how to find a pulse, but couldn't be sure. She placed her ear on Natalie's chest. Nothing.

She. Was. Dead.

Jocelyn had no idea what to do. She couldn't call her parents. This would entail going into great detail about why Natalie was squatting in their family cabin. The horror stories that she had heard about junkies *OD'ing* were racing through her mind, spliced in with scenes from several movies. So she did the only thing that she could think of.

She took off.

She raced into her car and drove away.

After her freak-out passed, and having watched enough cop tv shows (they could trace her cell phone), she located the first pay phone that she could find in the city, and made an anonymous 911 call.

Her parents were understanding. To her surprise, keeping the secret (specifically, her part in Natalie's escape), was easier than she had thought it would be. Her family had routinely taken Natalie to the cabin in the summer, and she knew where they kept the spare key.

It was a sad story.

Shit happens.

Will was sure that Jocelyn's parents were both happy and relieved that the deceased left no mess in the cabin, despite being dead for a while. The cabin would need to be aired out for some time, but other than that, it should be fine. With the passage of time, he was certain that at the very least, her parents would have little difficulty in resuming their rare visits to the cabin. They may even recount the story to their friends.

Everyone loves a good horror story. People, he knew, enjoyed hearing about the dark side of humanity. People just needed to be far enough removed from the situation in order to truly enjoy it. They just relished the mere possibility that it *could* happen to them, while knowing with near certainty that it *wouldn't* happen.

He stepped out of his car.

Taking a deep breath, he headed towards the door.

He slid the key into the hole and turned.

Something strange happened.

He was transported from a cabin in the woods to his mother's apartment.

It was the day that he found her.

They had always been close. This was only natural. It had always been the two of them. However, it was not a Norma and Norman Bates scenario. They were close in the way that only a single mother and her only son could be. They supported and protected one another.

When he was serving overseas, she was the woman he spent his time corresponding with. And, apart from the dalliance with his father, he was the only man in her life. He could not recall any other man entering or exiting the periphery. He remembered as a teenager; he had asked her why she never dated. She had replied with a quip, "Robert put me off of men. Once was enough."

He had had a bad feeling all day.

Everyone has experienced the unsettling sensation. Awash with anxiety and unease. Tense. Unable to identify what the problem is. Like an animal sensing the coming of a storm, he paced through the day, unable to remain settled.

He called his mother after lunch.

Nothing.

The phone rang until he was connected to her voicemail.

In vain, he told himself that everything was fine. She had been sleeping more and more throughout the day, since her diagnosis. She was always so damned tired. And when she was awake, she complained that the medicine made her nauseous.

She was just asleep.

He was just having an off day.

He called her again an hour later.

No answer.

He hung up in exasperation.

No sooner had he ended the call than he had already begun redialing her number. Again, the call went to voicemail. This time he left a short and simple message, asking her to call him back as soon as possible.

He found himself trapped in two states of mind. He knew in his gut that something was wrong. Yet, he could not bring himself to physical action. He was terrified at the prospect of heading to her apartment. He did not want to risk his thoughts and fears becoming realized.

In quantum mechanics, this was referred to as Schrödinger's Cat.

His mother was both alive and dead at this point.

Indecision and anxiety collided. Fuck it, he thought.

He grabbed his keys and frantically ran to his car.

In order to remain calm, he focused on the fundamentals of driving. When this began to fail, he turned on the radio. Cranking the volume to silence the worried voices in the back of his mind.

Using his key, he quietly entered the apartment. He did not want to wake his mother if she was sleeping. Of course she was asleep. Any other possibility was unthinkable. He would find her laying in her bed. Asleep. He would recount his unease and worry to her and she would laugh at this story. Constantly teasing him about how he worried too much.

Slowly turning the doorknob, he peered into his mother's bedroom. She was under the sheets. The television was on. It was some inane game show that routinely played throughout the normal midday work week.

He silently closed the door.

Exhaling, he smiled.

The oppressive weight had immediately dissipated.

He went to the kitchen to get a glass of water. Or better yet, something stronger to take the edge off. He grabbed the whiskey bottle out of the cabinet, then a glass out of the cupboard. It was only as he was pouring the amber contents into the glass that his attention was drawn to the envelope on the table.

It was propped against the centerpiece in the middle of the kitchen table.

It was labeled Will.

Everything fell into place.

He immediately raced to his mother's room, throwing open the bedroom door.

"Mom?" he asked, his anxiety bubbling over.

"Mom!" he yelled.

His mother did not move.

From the doorway, he looked at her chest beneath covers. He detected no signs of the sheets rising, accompanying her breath. Full of apprehension, he slowly entered the room. His feet padding across the carpet.

There was no rush.

Not anymore.

He approached her bedside. Placing a hand on her cheek, he immediately drew it back. He then placed his two fingers on her carotid artery, searching for even the faintest remnants of a beat.

Finding none, he sat on the corner of his mother's bed, staring vacantly at the wall. He was not sure how long he sat there. He was drawn back to reality. The television broadcast began playing some innocuous theme song to yet another game show. The reverie was over.

Standing up, he took one last look at his mother. Exhaling, he promptly exited the bedroom, closing the door behind him. He entered the kitchen and drained his drink. Feeling the burn of the liquor, he pulled out his phone and made the necessary call.

He pocketed the envelope before the paramedics arrived.

He had placed the envelope in a drawer in his desk. He couldn't bring himself to read it for the longest time. It wasn't until after the funeral that he found himself staring at the plain envelope.

Taking a letter opener, he swiftly sliced the envelope open.

Before he could take the letter out, he needed to get supplies. He grabbed a bottle of whiskey from the cupboard. He didn't bother with a glass. He took off the bottle cap and took a long and painful pull from the bottle.

Feeling the warmth of the liquor in his stomach, he slowly unfolded the letter.

As far as suicide letters go, it was fairly routine.

She apologized for taking her life. That was unnecessary. He understood. She was in pain. She did not want him to have to witness her slow and painful demise. She couldn't bring herself to tell him beforehand. She worried that he would talk her out of it.

The letter in one hand, the bottle in the other, he took pulls off the bottle with the passing of each scribbled line. It was not until he got to the second page that he was shaken out of his numbness.

Only with the certainty of death could his mother bring herself to tell the truth about his father. He had spent the majority of his life believing that his father was an asshole. He was an asshole, but now he had a broader perspective.

He thought his father was absent because he did not want to be a father. He didn't expect to learn that his father had, in fact, been a father five times over before Will was even born.

His father was married with five children.

He owned the building that his mother lived in.

He went to her apartment to fix a leaky pipe.

One thing led to another.

His mother claimed that he did not know that his father was married when they began their affair. She wasn't an idiot; it didn't take her long to discover the truth. But she was in love. He fed her the typical bullshit. He was in love with her. He didn't love his wife anymore, the marriage was a sham at that point, he was going to divorce his wife, etc.

That held her over for a while.

By the time that she came to grips with the fact that he had no intention of coming clean to his wife and leaving her, she was already pregnant with Will. It was unexpected. She thought they had been safe.

She confronted his father. He reacted with hostile indignation. Like a typical asshole, he accused her of intentionally getting pregnant. He told her to take care of it; get an abortion. He didn't want another kid.

This was the last straw for his mother.

She was enraged. In hindsight, she admitted that she wished that she had handled the matter differently. She was heartbroken. She called his wife. Told her everything. The wife reacted as any other self-respecting woman would. She filed for divorce. Kicked him out of the house.

As a result of his mother's vengeful act, whatever semblance of a relationship the two had was abruptly severed. It was made quite clear that she had to vacate the apartment. She acquiesced to his demands and moved to a new place.

The relationship grew more contentious as she made it quite clear that not only was she keeping the baby, but she expected that he would, at the very least, contribute to the child's welfare financially. He reacted with more aggression and indignation. Eventually, she had to sue him for child support.

Meanwhile, his father's infidelity had blown up not only his life, but his family as well. His wife divorced him; his children unanimously sided with their mother. He lost his family but inherited an unwanted one.

And those few occasions when he spent time with his father?

Well, his mother alluded that these were episodes following an occasion in which his father had weaseled his way back into her life (meaning her bed). He supposed his mother, despite her better instincts, still loved the bastard. His father, in the afterglow of sex, told her that he wanted to spend time with his child. Clearly, this was a lie. He just wanted to ensure the possibility that he could fuck her again.

To his mother's credit, this only worked a few times before she finally faced the harsh realization that his father was beyond the possibility of change or growth. He was who he was. People don't change. Not really. So, she bit the bullet and cut off all romantic ties with him.

And his inheritance?

Well, when your wife hates you, your children disown you, want nothing to do with you, won't even visit you on your deathbed, hating you with such passionate rage that they will not even take your money, what else could you do? You get desperate. Someone needs to come to your bedside. Nobody wants to die alone.

Only in the clutches of impending death could his father bring himself to reach out to him. His mother didn't elaborate, but he assumed that his father was scared and wanted at least one of his children present. Perhaps it was his guilt, shame, and fear that prevented him from engaging in meaningful conversation, or offering an apology. Or maybe he was just a prick. He lived life being a prick and then died a prick.

He always figured that his father left him the building as a way of making amends without actually having to utter an apology. Maybe, he knew that after all of these years, there was no point in offering an apology. What could you possibly say in that situation? Nothing could be offered that would ameliorate their fractured relationship.

Hollywood has conditioned people to think that attaining long sought-after insight precipitates a powerful climactic change. They expect some dark and dramatic musical accompaniment. If it had been a movie, the bottle would have slipped out of his hand and shattered on the floor. Real life isn't Hollywood. Art imitates life. Not the other way around. It's a lie.

He didn't feel anything. It didn't matter. Not anymore.

•   •   •

The memory faded. He was back in the cabin. Standing in the doorway.

It had only been a few moments, but it had felt like a lifetime.

There were little remnants to indicate that someone had been squatting here. When you are told that a junkie was holed up in a cabin, your mind begins to paint a picture. He expected the home to be trashed. Graffiti on the walls, a powerful and malodorous stench with no discernible origin. There was nothing.

He told himself he was imagining things.

But this place felt like a tomb.

He casually looked around the cabin.

Was he looking for *her*?

He couldn't find her. He wouldn't find her.

There were pictures of Jocelyn's happy family in expensive frames located throughout the cabin. Natalie died surrounded by images of a happy family. It just wasn't her family. Unexpectedly, he felt bile rising in the back of his throat.

He took a seat on the old leather sofa in an attempt to regain his composure.

Retreat into fantasy.

He imagined that he had found her.

In his mind, Natalie was alive. She was shivering on the street. Propped against a dumpster. He picked her up and carried her back to his car. He told her who he was. Assured her that everything would be okay. He would take her back home. Her mother was worried. She wanted her home.

He envisioned driving her back to her mother.

Reuniting the daughter and her mother.

Will and Natalie did not even make it through the door.

Laura rushed out of the front door, racing to the parked car in the driveway.

Natalie hurriedly unbuckled herself and ran to her mother.

They embraced one another.

Natalie was apologizing for everything. For her addiction, for stealing from her, for scaring her by running away. For everything. Laura kissed her cheek, wiped her tears off of her face. Hushed her. Told her that she loved her.

Laura was holding Natalie close to her chest. She looked up at Will, tears in her eyes, and wordlessly whispered, "Thank you." He offered a slight smile and a wave. He then slowly retreated back to his car.

As he lowered himself into his car, he looked back one last time at the reunited mother and daughter. They were glowing. Everything was as it should be. Then the figure of Natalie's father appeared in the doorway.

There is no safety or comfort in fantasy.

•   •   •

He exited the cabin forlornly.

The drive back to the city was short. He was alone with his thoughts. It was a long enough trip for him to attain a new understanding. An epiphany. He and Natalie were inextricably connected.

In a way, they were both victims of family secrets.

He was affected by his father's infidelity and the secrets that he kept from his original family. Once the truth came out, his father lost his *real* family and took his anger and resentment out on him and his mother.

A child conceived in the shroud of secrecy and raised in oblivious ignorance. Neither his father nor his mother told him the truth. In a way, this protected him from pain. He conceded that this was done not solely for his sake, but for his mother as well. His mother couldn't handle the shame and heartache, so she kept the truth to herself.

Natalie, the victim of her father's malicious secret obsession.

How could she possibly tell her mother? Tell anyone?

Revealing the truth, as in his mother's case, would have imploded her family. What would her future have been like? How do you move on from that? How do you have a relationship with your mother? With other men?

They both bore the emotional and mental scars from their childhood.

He retreated from a fractured life and family to the army. To war.

She found comfort in opiates.

The only difference was that he managed to survive.

He survived his parents. Natalie did not.

Natalie got the worst of it.

His pain paled in comparison. He would try to make it up to her.

● ● ●

His phone beeped, notifying him of a message.

Pulling it out of his pocket, while keeping his eyes on the road, he saw that it was from an unknown number. Unlocking the phone, he then opened the message. It was from Teresa. The message read, "I am. So. Hungover."

He laughed.

Me: You lightweight. That's what happens when you fight above your weight class.

Teresa: Hahaha. You're funny. I demand a re-match.

Me: Are you sure that your liver is up to it?

Teresa: Probably not. I have a better idea: I could take you to dinner?

Me: I'd like that.

Teresa: I'm swamped until the weekend. Are you free then?
Me: That should work.
Teresa: Nice. I'll be in touch.

• • •

Once he got back into the city, he stopped for coffee.

With no other alternatives, with nothing in particular that demanded his immediate attention or action, he went to the office. To reflect. To make sense of everything. To plan. He knew what he was going to do, he just didn't know how.

Within minutes of picking up his mail, sorting out the junk mail, and taking a seat behind his desk, his phone began to ring. Irritated, he pulled the phone out of his pocket. He immediately recognized the number. He was shocked at the identity of the caller.

Laura.

Consumed with cowardice and shame, he contemplated sending the call to voicemail. Afraid, because he could not fathom the pain that she was in, and had no conception of what he could possibly say to her, to console her. Shame, stemming from what he was planning to do.

He slid his finger across the screen, accepting the call.

"Hello," he said, inwardly terrified.

"Hi," Laura responded.

She sounded hollowed out. She had been drinking. That much was clear. Laura was mumbling, slurring her words; drunk speech. He searched his mind for something to say, some words of comfort to give her.

"I'm sorry," he offered, "I'm sorry for your loss."

He rolled his eyes. It was all anyone could say in such a situation. They were just words. Nothing could be said to make her pain go away. There was only silence. He wasn't sure if she was still there.

"Thank you," she finally replied, "I'm not catching you in the middle of something am I?"

He could hear the sound of Laura grabbing a tissue and wiping at her face.

"No, not at all."

"I just...didn't know who else to call. I just need a break from everything."

"I understand. Take your time. I'm here."

"Her school is holding a memorial service for Natalie."

He didn't respond. At a loss for words, he resigned himself to being a listener.

"She would have hated that. Natalie didn't like the spotlight. She was shy. Natalie was such a good student. She loathed going to school, but she was good at it.

"She was my baby. But she wasn't my first child. I met David in university. I got pregnant. I was so scared. I didn't know what to do. We had been together for a few years. I was in my final year. He was going into med-school. I told him that I was pregnant. He felt that with him being so swamped with med-school, and as I was still finishing my degree, that it was a bad time for a baby.

"He was right, of course. It would have been a mess. It wasn't part of the plan. I got an abortion. David took care of me afterwards. He was so good to me. You know, it's weird, I haven't thought about this for the longest time."

Her words were progressively becoming more slurred. He became worried that she was not only drinking, but mixing medication with alcohol as well. Having learned about David, he knew that it wasn't beyond the realm of possibility that she could get her hands on some opiates.

"Have you been drinking?" he asked pointedly.

There was a pause on the other end of the line.

"I'm not judging you. I'm just concerned. I just need to know that you are not in any immediate danger."

"Yeah. I just drank too much wine. Just to help with my nerves."

"Just wine? Nothing else?"

"Nope. Just wine."

He let that settle for a moment.

"I'm so sorry. I'm sorry that I couldn't find her."

He was shocked. It felt like someone else had offered this apology on his behalf. For a moment, he worried that someone else was on the phone. He was taken aback when he realized that he had been the one to offer this futile apologetic offering.

"It's not your fault. You did what you could."

Laura consoled him in the way that only a mother could. Shockingly, he felt like he was a small child. He knew that he was on the verge of collapse. If he let his emotions get the better of him, he would break down into tears. This would not be fair to Laura.

He wiped the forming tears out of the corner of his eyes.

"Will, I've got to go. I drank too much. I'm going to sleep it off."

"Okay. Take care. If you need anything, I'm around," he offered quickly.

"Thank you. Bye, Will."

"Bye."

. . .

The conversation with a heartbroken mother did little to dissuade him from his chosen course of action. Rather, it strengthened his resolve. David was a wolf in sheep's clothing. He had effectively killed all hope of happiness for Laura. He had destroyed a child; he had set a course of destruction that Natalie was unable to steer clear of. Upstanding citizen, dutiful doctor, loving father and husband by day. A monster at night.

Natalie was deprived of childhood innocence. She would not reach adulthood. She would never be able to fall in love, have her heart broken, break some poor sap's heart, get married or have children. Never get to travel. Never get to laugh. It was not right that David was still walking around, virtually unscathed. People would look at him with sympathy.

Natalie needed vengeance.

Maybe vengeance was not the right word. She deserved peace. Whatever that meant.

He thought of Laura.

Admittedly, he felt guilty that he would be causing her more pain.

Sometimes, things need to get worse so that they can get better.

To him, it would be better that she would not learn the truth about her husband.

She was good.

She did not need or deserve to be troubled by further heartbreak.

. . .

He was back in the office.

For the first time in a long time, he looked at it.

He had ignored it. Pretended that he didn't notice it.

He had moved it from its previous position.

After being discharged from the hospital, he had returned to his office. Returning to the scene of the crime was not a troublesome issue for him. He had witnessed so much death and suffering.

What set him on edge was the damned gag.

The Red Herring.

He had hung it on the wall behind him, so that the clients could see it. He was saddened that not one of the clients that had visited his office ever got the joke. Following the incident with Herman, he too stopped finding the joke funny.

He felt uncomfortable with the herring behind him. He knew it was ridiculous, but he could not shake the sensation that it was watching him; glaring at him. It was casting a look of blame and contempt. It was an inescapable impression that rocked his equilibrium.

At that time, for whatever reason, he could not bring himself to completely rid himself of the item. Perhaps he was keeping it as a reminder. To punish him. He was reminded of the Raven in the Edgar Allan Poe poem.

Having removed it from the wall, he placed it on his desk, rotating it, so it was not visible from his position behind the desk. He could not bring himself to discard it. He did not like to touch it. Or look at it.

Today, it drew his attention.

No. It *demanded* his attention.

The stupid fucking gag purchase.

The Red Herring.

The object that had fueled the manic and insane wrath of Herman. The object had, in his mind, enraged him to the point of attempted murder and ultimately, suicide. It still plagued Will.

Not the attempted murder.

Herman had lost his mind. Killed his cheating wife. Shot his hired investigator. Then turned the gun on himself. *Why?* Why did he let Will live? Herman saw that he had only wounded him. He had even stood over him before he had anticlimactically killed himself.

Perhaps, Herman had condemned him to bear witness to something truly terrible. Will had made a career of spying on unfaithful spouses or partners, taking pictures; frozen moments in time – permanent records of a lover's treachery. Witnessing an image that cannot be erased from memory.

A fate worse than death?

From the perspective of the tortured mind of Herman, maybe.

Enough.

Will snatched some old newspapers and blanketed the herring. He did not want to touch it. He continued to wrap layer after layer of paper. For a finishing touch, he rustled some tape from a drawer and spent an entire roll on the hastily wrapped object.

Abruptly rising from his chair, he rushed outside and dropped it in the dumpster.

He quickly returned to his office.

Stopping in the bathroom, he vigorously washed his hands.

Having rid himself of the cursed object and performing his ablutions, he went to lay down. The day had gone on far too long. He was clocking out.

•

He should have expected it.

He had damned himself by going to the cabin.

He had brought something back with him.

A ghost.

The ghost he had hoped he would be able to avoid. Or outrun.

Natalie.

Will awoke out of a surprisingly peaceful sleep.

She was there. Sitting on the corner of his bed. Her back was to him. His breath was literally sucked out of his lungs. He would have screamed, if he could have found the air to breathe.

Slowly, she turned around.

There were tears in her eyes. Her mascara was running. She wasn't angry. She was hurt. Helpless. Her mouth began to open, but no sound came out. As Natalie realized her words were not audible, she immediately shifted from tragic to enraged.

Her mouth began to operate furiously. Frantically.

Nothing.

Natalie slid her body fully onto the mattress. She crawled on her hands and knees until she was immediately above his body. He was paralyzed. Too frightened to move. She then pinned his body to the mattress.

She lowered her face until her nose touched his own. It was cold. Yet, he could feel the hot air coming from her nostrils. Natalie looked directly into his eyes. She raised her arm, placed her index finger next to her mouth.

He understood.

She mouthed the words.

Once.

Twice.

The third and final time. Will understood.

She nodded her head solemnly. Her rage was still evident, but it was beginning to abate. She released him and began to crawl back to the edge of the bed. Having composed herself, she stood up and left the room. At the doorway she looked back at him. Once again, she nodded her head. He forced his head to nod back in acknowledgement.

She left.

It was a warning.

In the morning, in the safety of the daylight, he wondered if what he had witnessed was real. It had felt real. He could still feel her presence. On the border; the periphery. She was waiting. Of that he was certain.

She had told him.

He remembered it vividly.

You let me die. You owe me.

• • •

People lie to themselves all the time.

It was only in the warmth and comfort of the shower that he was finally able to be honest with himself. It may have started out as a conciliatory offering to Natalie; a righteous task wilfully undertaken in order to grant her some form of justice. That was still a part of it. But it was not the *only* part.

He had felt, in the back of his mind, that if he were to proactively pursue David, the monster, and kill him, then this would bring peace to Natalie's soul. He was actively pursued by the ghosts of his past. He did not want another ghoul waiting for him.

Was this the real reason that he was willing to subject Laura to more loss? Inarguably, the only aspect of killing David that bothered him was the collateral damage. Morality did not enter it. However, he did not relish what this would do to Laura. He forced these thoughts out of his mind. Some lines of questioning were better left unexamined.

Lately, he had been experiencing the unexpected, unwelcome, and turbulent wave of memories. He did not know why the most innocuous or mundane memories would rush upon him unbidden at random moments throughout the day. There was no rhyme or reason.

Stepping out of the shower, he was reminded of the waitress's t-shirt.

He had been in some greasy spoon. He was following a target. He was sitting in a booth with his back to the wall. He had sat several booths behind the subject so that he would be able to effectively monitor his movements.

At this point, the waitress (he thought her name may have been Regina), approached him with a steaming pot of coffee. Placing the menu down next to him, she expertly began to pour him a cup of coffee.

"Do you need some time to order?"

He was snapped out of his trance.

He looked up at the waitress (Regina?) and stared at her, confused.

"Do you need some time to look at the menu?" she repeated patiently.

"No, I'll just stick with coffee for now. Thank you."

As she pulled the menu off of the table, her shirt caught his attention. It was tight and black. It was the font that he was drawn to. It displayed a bold white font. The shirt read "sciamachy." He immediately dismissed it. He figured it was some shitty hipster alt-rock band.

When he got home that night, he was sipping a stiff drink, trying to decompress from a long day, when the waitress's shirt barged back into his mind. He had never heard of the word before; he had no idea what it meant.

Determined to put the matter to rest, he opened up his laptop and entered the term into the search engine. He was relieved to discover that it was, in fact, not some terrible hipster band. The leading result was a definition of sciamachy which stated, "an act or instance of fighting a shadow or an imaginary enemy."

The definition was an encapsulation of his entire adult life.

He knew that there was no such thing as ghosts.

Yet, he was constantly hounded by these fucking ghouls or spectres from his past. The most troubling fact was that he only saw the spirits or ghosts of those whom he had known and seen die (the exception being Natalie, of course). He did not see the spirits of random people; he did not see demons. He did not hear voices telling him to harm himself or others. He was not a medium; he knew the people who professed to be spiritual mediums were charlatans and shysters.

He possessed a rational mind.

Still. They were there.

Waiting.

Waiting for him to lose focus, or lose control.

Getting rid of David, he knew, was a means of dispersing the ghost of Natalie. It was a decision based largely on selfishness. It was self-preservation. It was survival. He vainly attempted to convince himself that he could not be faulted for these desires. But he knew he was wrong. Still, he persisted.

People lie to themselves.

All the time.

· · ·

He drove to a book store for supplies.

Stepping out of the car, he placed his earbuds in his ears. He needed music that he could ignore. Something to fill the void. Something to help him think. Nothing too distracting. Scrolling down his iPod, he found what he was looking for.

Life after Death began to play.

He always loved books. He loved to read. Anything and everything. Except chick-lit. This distaste was not based on chauvinism. Rather, he felt that the authors of the genre were untalented. It was trash. Every book followed the same pattern or structure. Like Dan Brown. Every book is the same rehashed story. He could not understand the appeal.

As with most trips to secure supplies, he did not wander. Find it, buy it, leave. He detested window shopping. What a waste of time. The only impediment to his mission was that he had no idea where they would keep the item he was looking for. A female employee approached him. He removed one of the earbuds from his ear.

"Are you finding everything okay?" she asked sweetly.

"I'm looking for a diary."

"For yourself?"

"No. For my niece," he lied. "She's sixteen. An artistic type."

"Oh, I see. Does she have any preferences?"

"How do you mean?"

"Well, we have journals that have covers with anime characters, animals, butterflies, that sort of thing."

The employees sweet and high-pitched voice was beginning to grate on his nerves.

"Gross."

The employee forced an awkward laugh.

"No, those won't do. She wouldn't like those. I'm looking for something leather-bound. Black or brown. Something with unlined pages. Know what I mean?"

"I know exactly what you're looking for," she smiled servilely.

She returned a few moments later with two journals; one in each hand. As requested, she possessed one black and one brown leather journal. He perused the brown leather journal, but was not pleased with the look of the pages. He did not know why, but his gut told him that Natalie would not like it. He settled on the black leather journal. It was perfect.

He paid for his purchase and immediately returned to the office.

He spent the remainder of the day scrawling entries onto the pages of the journal. He was good at remembering information that he had heard. He was working off of the information that Jocelyn had imparted to him. He did not worry about the writing. If all went as planned, David would not get close enough to actually read the pages.

●　　　●　　　●　　　●

They buried Natalie a couple of days later.

Will was there, but he did not enter the church.

He did not want to unnecessarily intrude into the private suffering of a broken family. He already did enough of that in his vocation. He could not view her body either. He hadn't seen her ghost since that night, and he did not wish to push his luck. He just wished to pay his respects. Albeit, without entering the building. He watched the family, friends and other mourners enter the church. He was parked in his car across the street.

He saw the grieving parents. David appeared numb to his surroundings. He looked like an automaton. Laura was shattered. She had tears streaming down her face. She had a white handkerchief in her hand which she dabbed at her face, trying not to smear her makeup. David wrapped his arm around the back of Laura. Will was seized with a violent impulse; he had to fight the desire to rip that arm off of David and ram it down his throat.

He saw both Jocelyn and Cameron enter the church.

The walking wounded.

He had seen enough.

He started the car and drove away.

•   •   •

He waited for her at the bar. He was early. As always.

He was on his second Jameson and Coke. He was nursing them; all things in moderation. He was watching the basketball game on the large flat screen television above the bar. Playoff season.

Date night.

The first date. Always nerve-wracking.

He had hoped that by arriving early and throwing back a couple of drinks beforehand would allow him to mentally prepare for the date. The funeral scene had placed him in a funk. He was in a mood. Granted, he was always in a mood. He did not want to bring that toxicity around Teresa.

She came directly from work.

Teresa approached him, attaché case in hand. She was dressed in smart and practical business attire. She looked somewhat frazzled. She had had a long day, he could tell. Will offered her a slight smile.

"Hey, sorry I'm late. A meeting ran late with a client."

"No problem, I've got nowhere else to be."

"I just hate being late."

"Me too. I'm genetically incapable of arriving anywhere on time. I have to be early. But you don't need to apologize."

"Shall we get something to eat?" she asked sweetly.

"You need a drink first. And I need to finish mine. Take a seat, get off of your feet. You've been working all day."

Smiling, she took a seat.

Will got the attention of the bartender, motioning for service. Teresa ordered a Gin and Tonic. An excellent choice. One of his favorites. He noticed that Teresa was watching the game.

"Basketball fan?" he asked hopefully.

"Indeed," she answered, taking a long sip from her drink. "I like sports. Football, hockey, baseball, basketball. I have four older brothers. So sports were unavoidable. I grew to like them."

"Marry me!" he said with a smile.

She laughed.

Finishing the remainder of their drinks, they headed to the restaurant.

"So, my acute skills of detection tell me that your client is difficult," Will offered.

"You have no idea," she said, running her fingers through her hair and sighing dramatically.

"Just an asshole?"

"The biggest," she answered, emptying her wine glass.

"They tend to pay the best," he replied, "pragmatically speaking, that is."

"Very true. They act like self-entitled assholes, but they pay large sums of money for the privilege. As if the money excuses their behavior."

"My sentiments exactly."

"Enough about work. Let's move on to happier subjects; what did you do today?"

He was so entranced by her that he almost told her the truth.

"Oh, not too much. Just finished up some paperwork for a client."

"You and I are in similar fields. We're both called in to clean up messes of our client's own creation," she stated solemnly.

"Yes. Yes, we are. However, I do the *real* dirty work. Yours is the more respectable profession. The majority of private investigators are con men, shysters, or bullshit artists."

"Is that how you see yourself? A con man?" she asked, playfully.

"I make an honest living despite the profession that I find myself in."

Teresa raised her eyebrow; which signaled that she wanted to hear more.

"I get paid to do a job. I will perform my task to the best of my abilities. I admit that I am not a boy scout. In my darker moments, I have charged more than I normally would. However, I only gouged the people (mostly men and assholes) who could afford it. Most of the times that I quoted a higher than average cost, it was so that they would not hire me. Sometimes it worked, sometimes it didn't. However, pragmatically speaking, in comparison with some of my sleazier colleagues, I am a saint."

Teresa smiled. "I appreciate your honesty."

"I hope you overcharged your client," he responded truthfully.

"No comment," she replied.

That fucking smile. It was a trap.

How could anyone not fall for such a smile?

The smile was not just a smile. It was a presentation of the possible. The endless possibilities that the future offered. It was offered willingly, but was not to be accepted haphazardly. The offering was not to be taken lightly; for it could and would crush those who were deemed unworthy of such a gift.

The rest of the dinner passed as if part of a montage; laughter, smiles, and flirting.

The waiter dropped off the cheque. He went to grab it from the plastic tray but was brushed aside by Teresa. He began to protest, but she raised her hand and politely hushed him. Admittedly, he was somewhat old-fashioned. He always had a deep desire to pay for dates. He supposed that this was a result of his absent father; a man that failed to take care of his lady. He watched his mother struggle to support them both. Perhaps his stance was merely an act which definitively separated him from his father. He did not want to be his father's son.

"It's on the asshole client of mine," she elaborated with a playful smile.

"That's very kind of him," Will responded jokingly.

"Oh, he's wonderful," she answered with a bigger smile.

Teresa paid the bill and they left. He followed behind Teresa. On the way out, he could not stifle the urge to grab a handful of mints from the bowl next to the maître d'. She looked back at him with a confused smile.

"Sorry, I love these mints. I can't find them anywhere. This is the only place that offers them."

She laughed and held her hand out. He dropped a handful of mints into her palm.

"So, now what?" Teresa asked with a smile.

That fucking smile.

•　　•　　•

Post-coital glow.

He was not one to kiss and tell. He was, after all, somewhat old-fashioned.

However, this was his first sexual encounter since Lana.

Sex with Lana had always been more fucking than sex. Animalistic and raw. Primal fucking urges, with just a dash of passion. Sex with her had felt like she was trying to absorb his soul; filling the void of her own. Often, it felt like a race; who could finish first in a moment of pure triumph. There was always a warning before Lana came. She would curl her fingers and dig her nails into his chest; removing small chunks of skin with her long nails.

This was different.

It was passion.

Slow.

Teasing.

Playful.

He did not want it to end.

She had slowly and carefully traced her finger along the scars that adorned his body. She did not ask questions. For this, he was thankful. After completing a circuit with her index finger, she repeated the process. Using her tongue. He had thought he had known what ecstasy was. He was wrong.

Teresa fell asleep.

The room smelled of sex and sweat.

He was at peace, holding her while she slept.

But he could not find sleep.

He recognized this for what it was.

A reprieve.

The quiet still of the night before the shelling began.

It was something for him to hold on to like a life preserver. It would give him the strength to continue on; the perseverance to complete his task. He had something to come back to. Someone to save him from himself.

He drifted off with the narcotizing scent of her hair filling his nostrils.

●   ●   ●

He awoke with a start.

A nightmare. He could not recall the details.

The sun was breaking through the edges of the window blinds.

Reflexively, he closed his eyes.

He stretched out his limbs. For the first time in a very long time, he felt like a child. A child that had slept in, late for school and wanted to stay home. He bathed in the sensation. Let it surround him, engulf him.

Bliss.

His left arm reached out for Teresa. She was gone.

There was a piece of paper on her pillow.

He sat up, leaning his back against the headboard.

He let his eyes adjust to the brightness.

He read the note.

"Sorry, I had to leave for work. Tried to wake you up, but you were sound asleep. I suppose I'd be tired if I were you. Lock up when you leave. Message or call me."

He smiled.

After making the bed, he dressed and then left.

Not before making a call to a florist. He ordered a bouquet of flowers for delivery to Teresa's office. He figured, why not? This was what you did in this situation, wasn't it? He did not want to come on too strong, but he also wanted to make it clear that this was not a one-off to him.

He went home.

He had to complete his morning ritual.

•   •   •

"I've been seeing someone."

"That's good news. What does she do?"

"She's a lawyer."

"What's her name?"

"Teresa."

"Teresa. That's a lovely name. So, Teresa; I'm picturing a strong, intelligent and independent woman."

"Without a doubt."

"Are you familiar with the theory that all men end up pursuing women that remind them of their mother?"

"Should have seen that one coming."

"How are things going so far?"

"Good. Great actually."

"I feel that there is a 'but' lurking behind that statement."

"Yes. Yes, there is."

"What seems to be the problem?"

"Well, as I mentioned before, my profession has shown me that the majority of relationships are built upon the foundation of deceit. Even if they're not cheating on their spouse, they hide things from each other. It's unavoidable. Especially at the beginning. Everyone is hiding their negative attributes or characteristics. They portray the idealized version of themselves; what they feel the other person wants to see. It's only after they have been together for long enough that they begin to drop the facade. By that point it's too late. I'm confronted with two options; either cut their losses and leave, or naively and optimistically stay in it, trying to make it work. Neither of these options are actually preferable. I'll always end up losing."

"Please don't take this the wrong way, but I wonder; is this assessment something that your profession has elucidated for you, or is this based upon something else?"

"What do you mean?"

"Well, you started speaking in generalities, but I couldn't fail to notice that you said, "I'm confronted with two options," as well as "I'll always end up losing.""

"Did I? Must have been a mistake."

"Are you familiar with the term 'Freudian slip'?"

"Do you ever tire of being right?"

"Not really."

"I'm fucked up. I know that. But I had made peace with it. I made it work. I had some element of control; my routine. I did not expect to meet someone like her."

"I guess it's a good thing you're here talking about it."

"You just want to keep getting paid."

"Our time is up. But I want to leave you with this; you owe it to yourself to see where this goes. I can tell that you care about her. Don't end it just because you're scared."

"I'll keep that in mind."

"What are you doing with the rest of your day?"

"Working. Surveillance."

•   •   •

It had been nearly a month.

Twenty-eight days, to be exact.

Twenty-eight days since the burial of Natalie.

He had not forgotten the dire warning of the ghoul.

He just had to time it just right. These sorts of things could not be rushed.

He could not afford to be reckless.

Recklessness caused mistakes.

He had been watching.

Watching and waiting.

Observing the grieving couple.

Waiting for the opportune moment.

Grief can either strengthen a bond, or obliterate it entirely.

It seemed that it was the latter.

There were multiple instances in which, while crouched down in his car, he could hear the shouting of David and Laura. It was not audible enough for him to clearly discern the precise wording of the vitriol between the two, but it was clear that there was true hurt and anger involved.

The frequency of these shouting matches increased.

As they increased, David began to leave the house with luggage.

Will's interest piqued; he followed David.

During these times of marital conflict, David would go to a hotel. Usually the same one. He would stay for a day or two at a time, before returning home. Whether these returns were earnest attempts at reconciliation, he could not be sure. Whatever the cause for his return, Laura would always take him back. He witnessed her lovingly holding him in the doorway.

Soon, things escalated quickly.

Shortly after David's return from his seemingly self-imposed temporary exile to a hotel, he saw David quickly exit the home with more luggage than usual. He packed the trunk with a few boxes and suitcases. It was quite clear that he was leaving her. At least temporarily.

He followed him, again.

This time, David was not traveling to a hotel.

Instead, he pulled into a gated community.

Condominiums.

Expensive.

He could not enter through the gates without being buzzed in.

Looking through his binoculars, he could see a younger man helping David bring his luggage into the condo. He surmised that this was a friend that he was staying with until he could find his own place. Will hoped that this was simply a trial separation. He could not have the bastard change the will.

This move caused him to accelerate the plan.

•   •   •

He waited.

He was across the street.

He parked between two other cars, hoping to not draw attention.

He had stayed alert the entire night with the help of two thermoses of coffee. He stayed low in his seat. Not moving unless he had to piss. This is what the empty water bottles were for. He did not tire. He was not wired, either. The plan was in place. All he had to do was wait. Nothing could be left to chance.

He did not avert his gaze from the condominium.

It was not until eight o'clock that he saw David leaving the condo.

This was fortuitous; he had long since run out of coffee.

His patience was nearly at an end as well.

Following David, he reached out to the passenger seat. He ran his fingers along the spine of the journal. He felt comfort, knowing that it was there, in its proper place. At a stoplight, he checked his appearance in the rear-view mirror. Having been awake for the better part of two days, he looked exhausted, unhinged and deranged.

Perfect.

David arrived at a walk-in clinic.

Will parked far off in an available spot. He did not want to risk drawing the attention of David. Not yet, at least. This phase was all about the element of surprise. Surprise is predicated upon timing. Experience had taught him that this was harder than it sounded.

He waited ten minutes before following after David into the clinic.

Despite the early hour, there were already a few people in line at the front desk.

He absolutely loathed being inside clinics and hospitals.

A veritable cesspool.

Ill people with contagious illnesses.

Airborne germs and bacteria.

It made his skin crawl.

Finally, he made his way to the front of the line.

Approaching the old woman sitting at the computer, he fished for his business card and the envelope in his jacket pocket. He placed them on the counter and slid them across to the woman. She looked confusedly at the envelope.

"Could you take those to Dr. David Haynesworth?" he asked quietly.

"What is this regarding?" she asked, obviously annoyed.

"Sorry, that's a confidential matter. He'll know who I am. I worked for him. Tell him that he needs to talk to me. It's in his best interest."

She looked at him strangely, but followed his instructions.

A few minutes later, the old woman returned.

"Please, follow me," she instructed, clearly miffed.

Will followed her.

He was led to an empty consultation room.

"The doctor will be here momentarily," she stated, closing the door as she left.

He sat down in the chair next to the examination table.

He waited.

Fifteen minutes elapsed.

The prick was trying to show him who was in charge by making him wait.

He smiled at this facile attempt.

Fifteen more minutes passed.

Finally, David entered through the door.

To his credit, the man did possess a skilled and practiced poker face. His profession required him to remain plain-faced as patients would complain of aches and pains in awkward areas. Moreover, he had to remain calm when he had to deliver bad news.

David sat down on the stool.

"Do you want to tell me what this garbage is about?" David asked indignantly.

"Well, I think the note speaks for itself."

He would give no quarter.

Nor would he retreat.

"This is libelous! What, are you trying to do? Get more money?!"

"I don't want your money. Here is a cheque; it is a full refund."

He placed the cheque on the desk in front of David.

"A refund?"

"Yes. I did not find her. I'm not about to take money from a grieving family."

"No, you did *not* find her, did you?" he said, irate.

"No. No, I did not."

David had more than likely spent the entirety of his life masking the monster that lurked beneath the surface. He'd had lots of practice. Confronted, in private, the mask that he had carefully constructed began to slip.

"Quite the investigator, aren't you?" he mocked angrily.

"I did not find her. You're right. But I did not kill her either. That is something that is entirely your fault."

A slight smile crossed David's lips.

"My daughter had a drug problem; she was an addict. She relapsed and died. My family would like to mourn her in peace."

It was Will's turn to smile.

"So, you can take this inflammatory letter and shove it up your ass. No one is going to believe you. You have no proof."

David began to rise from the stool.

"Well, there is the diary. And I cannot in good conscience not deliver it to the police."

David quickly sat back down.

"What diary? What the hell are you talking about?!"

"Natalie. She kept a diary. Suffice to say that there is a lot in it about you. None of it complimentary."

"Bullshit. You are just a pathetic fucking con man looking to extort me. You're lucky that I don't call the fucking police!" David hissed.

"Call the police."

David looked at him with the cold stare of a predator.

A cat waiting to pounce on a mouse.

Will slowly pulled out the journal from his jacket pocket. David tried to keep stone-faced, but his eyes clearly displayed fear. At least for a moment. Then he attempted to regain his weakened composure.

Will slowly read the bookmarked page.

He did not need to even look at the page. He had the grim details etched into his memory. Instead, he was watching David's face for any sign of anger, despair, outrage, anything that indicated that he possessed a conscience.

Nothing.

He finished reading the entry.

"Call the police. I'd love to talk to them."

At a stalemate, they stared at each other.

"That is all hearsay. She was clearly not well. I have never laid a hand on her. I'm her father. For all I know, that entire thing is just a fabrication."

"Cut the shit," Will interjected. "We both know that it's real. More importantly, we both know that you don't want this coming to light."

David crossed his arms and snorted.

"So, this is blackmail?"

"No. Not exactly. I just need answers. And you are going to provide them."

"Answers?"

"Yes. Answers. Information. Then and only then, will we deal with the subject of money."

"And why should I continue talking to you?"

"You know the answer to that. If you do not follow my instructions, I will tell everyone; the police, your colleagues, the health board, the papers, your family, friends, *everyone*. I am willing to risk my reputation because I simply don't give a fuck. Are you? Is your life, your past, so clean that you are willing to deal with an investigation from the police or journalists? I'm sure there is something dark, something you keep hidden. The drug stash at your house, for one. At the very least, you will lose your license and your reputation. Which is the one thing that you care about."

He noticed that David had immediately lost the supercilious smirk on his face.

"I'm listening."

•   •   •

He had imparted the set of detailed instructions to David.

They were to be followed to the letter.

Any variation or failure to conform would result in the nullification of their deal.

David was directed to reserve a room at a certain motel at a specific time the following evening.

He was not to contact anyone during this time.

He was to bring no luggage with him.

He should bring nothing but a pen (blue) and a pad of paper (yellow).

Once had had checked into the room, he was to wait there for him.

He was forbidden from leaving the room.

Before he left David's office, he snatched the card, letter and envelope out of David's hand. (The card, envelope and letter, he would later shred in his office, then burn the remains in an ashtray. He was nothing if not cautious).

•   •   •

Will was more than willing to let David believe that this was about extortion.

A man like David would not be capable of understanding any other possible motive that was not solely for personal gain. Of course, Will was aware of the possibility that David would be planning on attacking or killing him at the meeting.

Always be prepared.

He was exhausted and desperately needed sleep.

This was not an option.

He had work to do.

Laura left once a week to go visit Natalie's grave.

Same day. Same time.

Like clockwork.

He parked down the street from the house; in an area that she was certain not to pass by. He saw Laura close the front door and approach her car. She spent a moment searching for her keys in her purse. Finally, she fished them out and entered the vehicle. Within moments, she had exited the driveway and driven away.

He waited five minutes.

He did not want to risk her coming back to retrieve some forgotten item.

Trying to be as inconspicuous as possible, he exited his car and calmly but quickly walked up the street, and approached the front door. Using his body to block any possible view of the door, he quickly began to pick the lock.

Lock-picking was not the quick and easy process that was depicted in film. It is a laborious and time-consuming process. In the service, during raids, they would either shoot the lock off with a blast or some form of explosive.

He knew that the quickest and easiest method of gaining access was taking a chisel and hammering in the lock. This was too loud and too messy. He did not want to leave any physical trace of his presence.

Minutes later, having managed to unlock the deadbolt, he took a cautious look around the area. No one was outside. He did not see any rubbernecking neighbor watching him through a window.

The house was equipped with an alarm system.

This neither deterred nor worried him.

He knew the code. At least, he hoped his intuition proved correct.

As the feminine robotic voice announced the warning that he had sixty seconds to disarm the alarm, he quickly proceeded to the keypad on the wall directly in front of him. Taking a deep breath, steadying his nerves, he entered the four-digit code.

The green light shone after he hit enter.

"Disarmed," the robotic voice announced.

Natalie's birthdate.

"Thank fuck," he whispered to himself.

Having disarmed the alarm, he quickly returned to the front door and locked it.

He knew from his past surveillance of Laura that he had at least an hour before Laura would return home. However, he did not want to risk the possibility of her returning early. He only wanted to spend ten minutes in the house. Fifteen minutes maximum.

He hurriedly began the process of searching for any possible hiding spots.

He was searching for David's stash.

If Jocelyn's description was accurate, it sounded like he regularly used several different hiding spots, each with various amounts of pills. He had thought that it was more than likely that such a preoccupied man would undoubtedly have forgotten some pills in some location. He was certain that David was not an addict; he may have used pills, but he was clearly not dependent upon them. Whereas, an addict would never have left any pills. An addict would have torn the place apart searching for pills based upon even the most remote of possibilities that there were, in fact, drugs in the residence.

He did not know if David was some sort of sleazy drug dealer on the side, or if he finagled narcotics solely to tranquilize Natalie. He did not care. That was not his concern.

He searched the house as thoroughly as possible, without making a mess in the process. He did not want to trash the place. That would not only scare Laura, but it could possibly make things difficult for him.

The imposed time limit was nearly up.

He began to feel utterly stupid; this was a waste of time – clearly not worth the risk.

There was one place that he had not dared check.

Natalie's room.

He hadn't found anything when he was looking through her room earlier, but Natalie had visited the house after he had been there. Moreover, he had only been searching for clues as to her possible whereabouts, not for drugs.

He quickly entered Natalie's room.

Examining his watch, he noted with annoyance that he was well over the fifteen-minute timeline. Shaking his head, he approached her drawers, and pulled them out swiftly. He looked inside the wooden chest; nothing. He checked for false bottoms in the drawers, rifled through her closet, everything.

Nothing.

He was on his knees, placing the drawers back in their rightful place. As he placed the last drawer back, he craned his neck, hoping to lessen the built-up tension. His attention was drawn to the tiles on the ceiling. Feeling like an even bigger moron, he began to gently poke his finger into the tiles.

He progressed row by row, tapping each tile.

The tiles all appeared to be firmly in place. Like they had sat ensconced in place; unmoved. Untampered. If someone had hidden something in the roof, the additional weight on the tile would be prevalent.

Nothing.

Fuck.

Irate, he approached the closet once again. He looked at the shelf above her clothes. There was one more set of tiles in her closet. Examining his watch again, he swore under his breath. He rapidly approached her desk, grabbed the chair, and placed it in the closet.

One by one, he frantically tapped each tile.

Finally, he found what he was looking for.

It was resting upon the last tile on the far left.

Having popped the tile aggressively, he was rewarded with a small, muffled rattle. At this point he was frantic; he had to get out of the house, but he did not want to leave empty handed. Frenzied, it took a moment for him to consciously recognize the rattle of pills.

Carefully, he slowly pushed the tile up and out. He felt the weight on the tile. He slowly moved the tile to the left, as far as possible, then tilted the tile to the right. He felt the object start to slide. It approached the edge of the tile; he saw it. It was a black balled up sock. Holding the tile with his left hand, he quickly snatched the sock off of the tile.

He placed the sock in his jacket pocket.

Carefully, he placed the tile back in its proper place.

He did not bother looking at his watch.

He knew that he was running low on time.

He quickly placed the chair back at the desk, turned off the light, and raced back to the alarm pad. His nerves wracked; his hand shook as he entered in the code. The feminine robotic voice alerted him that he had sixty seconds until the system armed.

He rushed to the front door.

Peering through the peephole, seeing no one, he felt satisfied that the area was clear.

He exited the home without bothering with the lock. He presumed that Laura would figure that she had forgotten to lock the door on her way out. The alternative possibility was simply too troublesome to fathom.

Wiping the sweat off of his brow, he tried to calmly walk back to his car. Fighting the urge to look behind him; he was certain that he would see Laura's car approaching him. In a matter of minutes, he reached his car, unlocked the door and collapsed inside.

Having no time to waste, he started the car, pulled a U-turn and drove away in the opposite direction. He cranked the air-conditioning. Exhaling deeply, he checked his rear-view mirror.

All clear.

He let out a long and satisfying sigh. Feeling the cool air brush against his hot skin, he allowed himself to relax. As the adrenaline began to subside, he was once again awash with desperate exhaustion. He needed sleep.

He would fill up on coffee.

He could not risk sleeping; he may sleep through the night.

Home.

Coffee.

Waiting.

• • •

His phone began to ring.

It was Teresa.

"Hello," he answered with a smile.

"Hey, you. I have to go to a friend's party tonight. Interested?"

"Depends, is it open-bar?"

"Well, it's at her house; I assume she wouldn't be charging people for booze."

"She is a lawyer; you know how much they love to screw people."

She laughed.

"I'd like to, but I'm actually working. I'm on surveillance as we speak."

"Cool, like a stakeout?" she asked excitedly.

"Yeah, it's a stakeout."

"That sounds exciting."

"Not really. I'm parked waiting for the target to actually go somewhere. Been waiting for hours. To make matters worse, I have to piss like a racehorse and I've run out of empty bottles."

Teresa burst out laughing.

"You know," she began gleefully, "I hear if a man regularly holds it in for too long, it can result in impotence."

"Seriously?"

"Yep. It's common knowledge."

"Well, shit. I guess I have to go take care of that."

She laughed, louder this time.

He grinned, imagining the smile on her face.

"I've got to go, but I'll call or message you as soon as I get off of work. It probably won't be until early tomorrow."

"Okay, talk soon."

Hanging up, he immediately turned off the phone.

He stood up, exited his office and went to the bathroom.

He opened the medicine cabinet and grabbed the bottle of pills. Closing the cabinet, he examined his reflection in the mirror. He felt like he was about to head into battle. He was going to meet David. This had to end, one way or the other.

It was almost time to go.

Having left his phone on the top of his desk, he made his way to the exit. He paused briefly, ensuring that he had everything that he needed. Satisfied, he opened the door and left the office. He told himself that his eyes were playing tricks on him; that it was his imagination. This was a fool's errand. He knew what he saw. Natalie, sitting in his chair. Watching him. Waiting for him to finish the job. To pay his debt.

You owe me.

He was disturbed at his own eerie calm. He was not exhibiting any of the obvious signs of nervousness; his pulse was not heightened, his hands were not shaking, he was not sweating. He was solid.

He kept his mind on the task at hand.

He arrived at the condominium.

He was pleased to see that David was following his instructions. He saw that as David was entering his car, he held a yellow pad of paper at his side. Crouching down in his seat, he waited for David's car to pass him by. He waited three seconds and then proceeded to follow him.

Will ensured that he maintained two car lengths behind David. He did not want to lose him, but he did not want to tip David off either. For his part, David did not display any signs of stress or nervousness. He did not swerve, speed, or drive below the speed limit.

He refused to let his mind wander.

Focus.

He busied himself with the minutiae of driving. Keeping an eye on the speedometer, adjusting the air-conditioning, and keeping an eye on the car ahead of him. He told himself that it would all be over soon.

David pulled off to the motel.

Will drove past the motel, knowing that there was a parking lot ahead that he could turn around in. Having reached the empty lot, he abruptly turned around and drove to the motel. Entering the lot of the motel, he could make out the figure of David in the front office. Will parked in the farthest spot away from the office, without eliminating his line of sight.

He watched as David exited the office, heading right, he then quickly marched to the reserved room. David slid the white key card into the black slot on the door. He smoothly pulled the card out and pushed open the door. Once inside, David immediately closed the door.

Will sat waiting in his car.

He had to be certain that David was not planning anything.

He was leaving nothing to chance.

After thirty minutes had passed, he exited the car, and made his way to the room.

•   •   •

He knocked on the door.

He heard the rustling of movement from inside.

David opened the door with a look of both boredom and contempt on his face.

"May I come in?"

David mockingly stepped aside, extending his arm in a show of welcome and hospitality.

"How much is this going to cost me?" David asked abruptly.

David, the doctor. A walking God complex. Fucking doctors. They were in a profession in which they were in charge. No one questioned their judgement. They were the alpha and omega. They were used to giving the orders and having them followed.

"Shut the fuck up," Will calmly stated.

He saw the ire begin to raise in David's face.

Before he could respond, Will spun him around and pinned him against the wall.

"Spread your legs."

"What are you doing?" he asked, outraged.

"Shut the fuck up and spread your legs."

David reluctantly complied.

Will quickly frisked him. Moving from his legs to the back, to the arms. Finally, he ran his fingers underneath his shirt collar. Finding nothing, Will placed his hand on David's right shoulder and pushed down, until David was sitting on the bed.

"Where is your phone?" he asked, firmly but calmly.

"Why? What do you want with my phone?" David asked, trying to reassert control through his defiance.

"Give. Me. The. Fucking. Phone," Will responded, in a calm monotone.

David, clearly shaken, reached for his jacket on the other side of the bed.

"Don't," Will ordered, "I'll get it. Do not move."

Will quickly snapped up the jacket. He felt for it through the fabric. Finding it, he pressed the power button, turning it off. Satisfied, he then took the phone to the bathroom, leaving it on the bathroom sink. Exiting the bathroom, he closed the door behind him.

Will pulled up the chair, positioning it so that he was blocking David from exiting the room. He stared at David in silence. Clearly unnerved, David began to fidget; running his hands down his pants, then running his hand through his hair.

Will remained silent.

Watching.

"What do you want?" David demanded. A clear change in his tone.

David was trying to mask the fact that he was nervous.

Will leaned forward and reached for the scabbard at his back. He placed the combat knife on his right leg. He waited a moment. David's eyes narrowed at the sight of the weapon. Will remained silent. David's eyes fixated on the weapon.

Finally, David could take it no more.

"What is that? You don't need it. I'm cooperating."

"This is a Karambit. It is one of the tools that I used in the war."

"Will, I already said that I am cooperating. I will do whatever you say."

David was trying to lessen the potential for conflict. Calling him by name was a nice touch. It's what they taught in conflict de-escalation. Regularly stating the person's name was a method of building a connection.

"This combat knife is to a soldier what a scalpel is to a doctor," he continued, ignoring David. "With one crucial and obvious difference, of course. What difference is that, David?"

"I don't know, Will. Please, can we please just talk about why we're here?"

"The difference, David, is that a doctor uses a scalpel to create an opening in a patient's body, so that they heal them. Fix them. This knife was created for the sole purpose of ending life."

David had become pale. Will noticed the faint trickle of sweat beginning to fall down his forehead. Will reverted to silence once again. He was like an animal stalking his prey. Watching David squirm, he realized, filled him with intense sadistic pleasure.

Reaching into his jacket pocket, he closed his hand around the bottle of pills, pulled his hand out of his pocket and swiftly threw the bottle at David. The bottle hit David's chest, bounced off and landed in his lap.

"I think that belongs to you," Will explained.

David did not look at Will. He stared dejectedly at the bottle in his lap.

"I found that in Natalie's room. Did you actually hide pills in your daughter's room?"

"Of course not!" he snapped, raising his voice, "She must have found them somewhere else."

"David, you say that like it is acceptable and normal for a doctor and a father to possess multiple stashes of drugs around the home."

David simply glared at him in response. Will felt as if he were a parent, confronting a petulant child that had been caught with his hand in the cookie jar. His hand closed tightly around the handle of the knife.

"Not to mention, what you did to her."

David glared at Will.

The real David.

The David that he had to work to conceal from the world.

"You raped your daughter, David. According to the diary, you did it a lot."

"She's my daughter, and it's none of your fucking concern," David growled in response.

"This is not a debate, David. I am presenting you with two unalterable options."

David stared at him, becoming red in the face.

"How much do you want?" he asked viciously.

"This is not a matter of money. You have two options. I am not going to lie to you. You are not going to leave this room alive. But, as I said, you have a choice."

David abruptly stood up and shouted, "Help!"

Will immediately pounced on him, pinning him to the bed. He quickly placed on hand on his mouth, while his other hand placed the blade at his throat. Will carefully and slowly placed the sharp tip against the skin.

David's eyes began to bulge. After a moment of struggling, David raised both of his arms above his head, signalling surrender. Will slowly drew back the blade. His other hand still muffling his mouth.

"Are you going to be quiet? Because I am warning you: if you try that again, I will be forced to cut out your tongue. And then we will continue. Do not test me."

David nodded his head obediently.

Will slowly eased his weight off of David. He then slowly and deliberately made his way back to the chair, never taking his eyes off of him. He resumed his former position.

"As I was saying, you have two options."

David was visibly beginning to shake.

"Option one," he continued, in spite of the man's obvious despair, "You take the pen and paper, and you write a generic suicide note. Then, you take all of those pills. Every. Single. Last. One. Rest assured, there are enough in that bottle to kill an adult.

"And just so you are aware; I am only offering you this option out of respect for your wife. This is an option that *you* do not deserve. You will be remembered as a tragic figure; a father who lost his daughter to addiction and could not carry on. You will be remembered as a good father and husband."

Tears began to fall down David's face.

"Option two. To be honest, I hope you choose this option. Option two *is* what *you* deserve. In option two, I torture you to death. I will take this knife and sever your spine. Then, I will begin removing your toes and fingers. Then I will move on to your face. Lastly, I will cut off your cock, and shove it down your throat. You will asphyxiate on your own member.

"I will call the police. I will confess to everything. *Everything.* I will tell them why I killed you; punishment for incest. You may not have killed your daughter, but you are the reason that she is dead. In such a horrific case of murder, there will be an in-depth investigation. There will not be a single dark corner of your life which will escape investigation. It will not just be police, either. It will be journalists, as well. Such a gruesome story is guaranteed to draw both national and international attention.

"It does not matter if they cannot prove it. Your name will be tarnished. Your wife will know what you really are. Your reputation will be ruined. Everyone will hear the truth. Your colleagues, your friends, your family, everyone will know the real you. I do not believe that you honestly want that. In fact, I'm sure that that is all you care about. The superficial and surface appearance. Because there is nothing else to you. I have seen the real you. I know that you have worked hard to hide it."

Pathetic tears were cascading down his face.

"I couldn't control it; I couldn't help myself," he blubbered.

"You misunderstand who I am, David. I am not here to learn why you did it. I do not give a fuck. I am here to make sure that you pay for it. That's it. I do not want to waste my time listening to your bullshit excuses."

David wiped the tears off of his face.

"You are Catholic, right?" Will asked gently.

David nodded his head.

"Think of it as penance. You have done terrible things. You need to pay for it."

David stared at him pathetically. He was broken.

He recognized that there was no way out.

"And, luckily for you, no one gets to see what you really are. You want that, don't you?"

David numbly nodded his head.

It struck him as odd, that at the moment of death, an adult reverts to the behavior of a child. David reminded him of his father on his own death bed. Knowing with absolute certainty what David would do, he felt his animosity toward him abating.

There was still the part of him that wanted to inflict pain on him.

He knew that it was a large part.

It was the greatest part.

Will recognized that that was who he was.

He could control it.

"Have you made your decision?"

David nodded.

"Can I have some water?"

David stood up. Will followed closely behind him to the bathroom. Will reached around him and grabbed the phone. David did not react. He grabbed the plastic cup, peeled the plastic wrapper off of the cup, and filled it with water.

They made their way back to the bed. David morosely sat down on the bed.

Will resumed his position on the chair.

"I'm scared," David whispered.

"I know. I'll stay here with you. Until the end. You will not be alone."

David popped the lid off of the container.

He examined the contents for a moment, before spilling the entire contents into his palm. He dropped a few into his mouth and chased them down with a sip of water from the cup. He repeated this process until the glass and the container were both empty.

Will stepped towards him.

"Open your mouth."

David dutifully complied.

Satisfied, Will sat back down in the chair.

Will passed the pen and pad to David.

David held them. Stared at the pad.

"I don't know what to write," he admitted.

"Just say that you're sorry. You wished that you were stronger. But you cannot continue on."

David merely nodded in reply.

He scribbled a few lines onto the pad.

David placed the cap back on the pen and handed both pen and paper over to Will. After examining the paper, he carefully placed them on the desk.

"Lay down," Will instructed.

David stretched out on the bed.

"I'm scared," David repeated.

"I know. I promise, you won't be alone."

It was his vocation.

He had to bear witness.

•　　•　　•

It was late.

He checked for a pulse.

Nothing.

He pushed in his chair and headed to the bathroom. He grabbed a towel and wiped the doorknob of the bathroom door, the chair and the doorknob. He knew that this was not necessary. He just needed to be sure.

He peered through the peephole, ensuring that there was no one outside; it would ruin everything if he bumped into another guest. Seeing nothing, using the towel, he quietly but quickly opened the door a crack, just wide enough for him to get out. He slipped through the available space, gently closing the door.

He circled around the motel, thereby avoiding the front office.

Arriving at the car, he gingerly stepped into the driver's seat. Quietly closing the door, he placed the keys in the ignition. Scanning the area again, he saw no movement. He turned the key in the ignition. The noise of the engine seemed so loud to him, after being immersed in such silence.

Wasting no time, he drove out of the lot.

• • •

He was back at the office.

She was not there.

He changed out of his clothes.

He placed them in a black garbage bag.

He opened his desk drawer, removing the clothes that he had left there for this very purpose. Fully clothed, he headed to the mini kitchen, retrieving the bottle of whiskey. He poured himself a drink. No mix.

Returning to his chair, he grabbed his phone.

Turning the device on, he was alerted to a missed message.

It was from Teresa.

It was a picture of her at her friend's party.

It was captioned "Wish you were here."

The message was hours old.

He was struck with the overwhelming desire to be with her.

This impulse stood in stark contrast with the all-encompassing numbness that he had been experiencing since his departure from the motel room. There was no malicious joy from the ultimate act of vengeance. No sense of pride from a job well done. He had thought that he would, at the very least, feel some form of vindication. Nor was he saddened at the prospect that it was over. He felt nothing.

Emptiness.

He felt empty; bereft of meaningful substance.

It was a heavy weight to bear.

He had played the part of God.

A vengeful and violent God.

And here he sat, beneath the sword of Damocles.

He quickly grabbed the phone.

He called her.

It rang numerous times before it was finally answered.

"Hello," she greeted, sleepily.

"Hey, it's me. Can I come over?" he asked frantically.

"Will?" she asked startled.

"I apologize for the late hour, but I really need to see you."

"It's too late for a booty-call."

He chuckled.

"It's not a booty-call. I just need to be with you," he replied truthfully.

"Okay. Come on over."

•   •   •

He threw the garbage bag in a pre-selected dumpster. Far enough away from both his business/residence and the motel. He did not want to risk it. He thought he had covered all of his tracks, but there are no guarantees.

Then, he hurriedly made his way to Teresa.

He buzzed the apartment numerous times.

He was anxious.

She buzzed him in.

He raced up the stairs to her apartment.

He knocked, numerous times in quick succession.

She opened the door, in her robe.

Before she could say anything, he pulled her close in a tight embrace.

"Are you okay?" she asked tenderly.

"Yeah, I'm good. Just been a long couple of days at work. Can I sleep here?"

She kissed his forehead and grabbing him by the hand, led him to the bedroom.

He quickly took off his clothes and slid under the sheets.

"I have to be up for work in a few hours," she remarked with a sigh.

"Sorry."

"You're lucky that you're cute," she responded, teasingly.

As she slid under the sheets, he immediately shifted his body closer to her. Kissing her softly on the lips, he slid his head down to her lap. He rested his head there. Teresa began to run her fingers softly through his hair.

He closed his eyes tightly.

He thought of his childhood.

He remembered cuddling with his mother, following a nightmare, or during an epic storm. He recalled the warmth. The scent. The safety. The myriad of sensations was nearly indescribable. He supposed that it felt like love.

As these memories fleeted through his mind, he felt himself fading, falling into sleep.

NOW

There is nothing as frigid, inhospitable, or unforgiving as winter on the prairies.

It was as if Mother Nature, enraged at the effects of the yearly abuse, was vengefully trying to kill her inhabitants.

Will loves it.

It is his favorite season.

. . .

His anxiety surrounding David had slowly dissipated. It became clear that there would be no investigation. He saw the small piece on David's suicide on the local news. The tragedy; a father, husband and well-respected doctor, was found dead at a motel. He took his life following the accidental overdose of his only child.

There was no blood or gore.

His death merited a mere forty-five second clip.

The anchor then moved on to discussing the national opiate epidemic.

The papers had followed suit; echoing the sentiments of the piece on television.

It could not have happened to a nicer guy.

That was not the end.

He had been watching her.

Keeping an eye on her.

She was strong. He knew that. And she did not disappoint him.

She grieved.

But her grief did not consume her.

She was using her pain to push her. He observed that she was attending university. She had sold the family home and moved into a modest duplex. She was working a part-time job and volunteering at a homeless shelter.

Laura seemed to be doing better.

But he had to be certain.

He is shoveling, clearing the sidewalk. He pulls off his gloves to check his watch. He has somewhere to be. He places the shovel back in the shed, changes his clothes, and heads to his car.

He parks in the residential area surrounding the campus.

Ensuring that he isn't in a tow-away zone, Will locks his car and strolls to the campus. He watches. Students hurriedly march to and from campus as they fight the cold invading their bodies.

He approaches the bench that he was so familiar with and waits.

Laura was a creature of habit, like him.

He checks his watch. She would be here any moment.

He sees her.

Amidst the mass of the student body. Class had just let out. He sees her talking to her fellow students. She appears at ease. Comfortable. Despite the difference in age, her companions seem to appreciate her company.

He quickly stands up and walks towards the crowd.

Laura separates from the group of students that she had been talking to. Bidding them farewell, she turns in his direction and began walking. Laura is checking her phone. He speeds up. While she is scanning her phone, he quickly closes the distance between them. Timing the collision, he bumps into her with his right shoulder.

"Oh, I'm so sorry," he says quickly.

Physically jarred, Laura drops her bag. She immediately bends over to retrieve it.

"No, it's my fault. I'm so sorry, I should've been watching where I was going."

As she looks up, he sees the recognition begin to dawn on Laura's face.

"Will?" she asks, astonished.

He stares at her for a moment, playing dumb.

"Oh, Laura. What a small world, I cannot believe I bumped into you," he says, feigning surprise.

"What are you doing here?" Laura asks.

"I come here sometimes. I love to walk around the campus. It's so beautiful. Especially during winter."

"Yes, it is a gorgeous campus."

"What about you?" Will asks as he gestures to her bag, crammed with books.

"Oh, I'm a student," Laura replies, beaming.

"Really? That's fantastic. What are you taking?"

"Psychology. I'm getting my Masters."

"That's amazing. That's one of my regrets; not going to university," he replies.

"Well, you're never too old to learn," she bats back with a smile.

"Are you busy right now? Would you like to get a cup of coffee?"

"Sure, I've got some free time."

• • •

Laura leads him to the off-campus coffee shop, marketed towards university students.

He forces himself to ignore the hipsters.

Laura orders a hot chocolate. He sticks with coffee.

After making small talk for as long as he was comfortable with, he amps himself up to ask the questions that had preoccupied his mind since the night at the motel. He has no idea how to bring something up like that naturally. He decides to just go for it.

"I just wanted to say again, that I am so sorry for your loss. I wish I had found her in time."

Laura stares intently at her cup.

"It's really not your fault. She was an addict. There was nothing that you could do. I've had time to think about it, and despite what the autopsy claims, I feel that she wanted to die. Her addiction consumed her. It made life impossible. She couldn't bear the pain anymore. Why else would she go to an empty cabin? She knew no one would be there."

He stares at Laura empathetically and absorbs her every word.

"I feel that I failed you. That's why I returned the money. I could not in good conscience accept it."

"Yes, David told me. That was unnecessary. But I appreciate the gesture. You're a good man."

He remembers the night at the motel.

"I heard about David too. I'm sorry," he says truthfully, "I wanted to reach out to you, but I didn't know what to say."

Laura nods her head. He sees the tears that are threatening to fall.

She quickly and discreetly wipes the tears off of her face.

"I wasn't entirely surprised that it happened."

"Oh?" he asks while he tries to mask the concern in his voice.

"He had been acting differently for a while. Even before Natalie went missing. And when she was found," Laura stumbles for a moment. "When she was found, he completely changed. It was like he was a different person. People react to grief differently."

He places his hand over hers.

"I am so sorry."

It was the closest he could get to apologizing for the role that he played in her husband's death. He couldn't tell her the truth. That would destroy her. Along with himself, of course. He had to apologize. Perhaps it did not matter that she wasn't fully aware of what he was apologizing for. It just had to be said.

She pats his hand affectionately.

"Thank you," she sincerely replies.

"I don't mean to pry, but I have to be sure; you're doing okay?"

Laura lets a slight smile form on her face.

"Some days are harder than others. But I owe it to David and Natalie to keep going. That's actually why I went back to school. I'm going to work in the field of addiction. I'm going to help people like my daughter."

Will nods in agreement.

"I think that's a wonderful thing to do."

"Enough about me, what about you? Are you still working as a private investigator?"

"Officially, yes. I am still a licensed investigator. But I have been taking a break. Just for a while."

"Don't let what happened eat at you. If that's what you love doing, you have to keep doing it. I'll say it again; it wasn't your fault."

Will simply bobs his head in reply.

"You're a young man, you got a girlfriend or a boyfriend?" Laura asks playfully.

"I have a girlfriend."

"Good. What does she do?"

"She's a lawyer."

"That's good. I can tell by the smile on your face that things must be going well," she teases.

"Yeah, I don't know why she is with me; she must have bad taste in men."

Laura laughs.

"Don't be too hard on yourself. You're a catch."

It is Will's turn to laugh.

His questions were answered. He allows himself to relax. They spend the next hour talking about random subjects, shooting the shit. After he had been through several cups of coffee, Laura looks at her phone.

"Oh, shit. I'm late. I've got an evening class," she says, standing up.

"Oh, no problem."

As she is grabbing her bag and puts her jacket on, he goes to the counter to pay the bill. He returns to the table and dons his own coat. They hurriedly leave the coffee shop. Will walks along with her.

They walk in silence for a while.

Laura would survive.

Will is certain.

He would not see her again.

He would permanently serve as a painful reminder of the hurt that had imploded her family. There would be no way of dislocating himself from the trauma. He could not cause her any more pain.

They reach the campus.

"Well, it was nice to see you again," Laura says, smiling.

"You too. Have a good class," he bids her farewell, extending his hand.

Laura shakes his hand and begins to walk away.

He watches her.

Laura abruptly stops in her tracks. She quickly turns around.

"Will, remember what I said; don't let it eat at you."

Will is speechless.

"So get back to work!" Laura calls to him with a wide smile on her face.

He stands, rooted in place.

He continues to watch her walk away until she disappears from sight.

He turns around and walks back to the car.

It starts to snow.

The sun is starting to set. Darkness is quickly beginning to erupt. He approaches the car door, unlocks it and steps inside. Closing the door, he places the key in the ignition and cranks the engine to life.

He turns the heat on and waits for the engine to warm up.

His attention is drawn to the rear-view mirror.

He sees her.

She is back.

Natalie.

His stomach in knots, he immediately shifts his body in his seat to look in the back of the car. The seat is empty. There is no one there. He slowly turns back around. He stretches the seatbelt across his body. Once again, he glances in the rear-view mirror. He is certain that he will see her again.

Nothing.

He is alone.

Shifting out of park, he pulls out his parking spot and drives away.

Sciamachy.

AFTERWORD FROM THE EDITOR:

Your Lover's Secrets
By Anna Cram

She told her mother every bedtime:
"Please don't turn off the light
I know, I know, it's fairly bright
But the monsters, they come out at night
Please, Mommy, don't let me wake with fright."

Her mother said, "don't worry dear
Monsters, they just aren't ever real
No matter how much fear you feel
You're nine years now, you're old enough,
Old enough to try and deal."

But every night it was the same,
Her daughter would awake with shame
And tears in her too-round blue eyes
At her mother she'd place the blame:

"Why did you sneak into my room
And turn off my bedroom light?
I told you, there are monsters
In this house that roam at night!"

Her mother would try to smile
And say with gentleness beguile:
"There is nothing here but you and me
And your father, that makes three."

Her daughter's face looked as cold and bare
As the sloe-eyed moon that had not a care
To what the father did at night
When he crept in to turn off the light

You don't know who you sleep beside
Until you find out what they try to hide
Monsters, they do come out at night
Or sometimes they are in plain sight

Learn your lover's secrets if you must
But don't cry to me if it's a bust
I warned you here, my dearest friend,
You don't know anyone until the end.

THE END.

NOTE FROM THE AUTHOR

Word-of-mouth is crucial for any author to succeed. If you enjoyed *The Red Herring*, please leave a review online—anywhere you are able. Even if it's just a sentence or two. It would make all the difference and would be very much appreciated.

Thanks!
R.G.

ABOUT THE AUTHOR

R.G. Link lives in Saskatoon, Saskatchewan in a house overlooking the river. His favourite past-times are walking his crusty dog, Bukowski, along the Meewasin Trail and playing with his beloved niece and nephew on the weekends. This is his first novel. He is currently hard at work on his second book.

Thank you so much for reading one of our **Crime Fiction** novels.

If you enjoyed our book, please check out our recommended for your next great read!

Bailey's Law by Meg Lelvis

"An intelligent, immersive police procedural that will leave you pining for another Jack Bailey novel." –*BEST THRILLERS*